"Ship's company, attention!"

Instant silence reigned, broken only by the echo of a thousand heels clicking together. Riker slowly inspected the troops nearest to him and came to a stop half a dozen feet away from the line of officers.

He came to attention and offered an old-style salute. He hoped he had performed the ritual greeting correctly. It was over two hundred years old, and he had never actually seen one living soldier salute another.

"Commander William Riker, Federation ship *Enterprise,* sir."

The man stepped forward, and Riker felt as if he actually recognized him. The family resemblance was strong.

"Captain Lysander Murat, Federation ship *U.S.S. Verdun.* Welcome aboard, sir."

At his words a loud cheer erupted. Riker listened as hundreds of voices chanted "The Day of Deliverance!" He watched as soldier after soldier withdrew bayonet from belt and held it aloft. The sight was chilling. . . .

STAR TREK
THE NEXT GENERATION®

THE FORGOTTEN
WAR

WILLIAM R. FORSTCHEN

POCKET BOOKS
New York London Toronto Sydney Tokyo Singapore

An *Original* Publication of POCKET BOOKS

POCKET BOOKS, a division of Simon & Schuster Inc.
1230 Avenue of the Americas, New York, NY 10020

STAR TREK is a Registered Trademark of Paramount Pictures.

A VIACOM COMPANY

This book is published by Pocket Books, a division of Simon & Schuster Inc., under exclusive license from Paramount Pictures.

ISBN: 0-671-01159-6

First Pocket Books printing September 1999

10 9 8 7 6 5 4 3 2 1

POCKET and colophon are registered trademarks of Simon & Schuster Inc.

Printed in the U.S.A.

THE FORGOTTEN WAR

Chapter One

CAPTAIN JEAN-LUC PICARD entered the transporter room, tossing a brief backward glance toward his first officer, who had paused a moment in the corridor with a look of curious confusion. "Number One? Have you forgotten the way?"

"Of course not, sir." Riker grinned slightly, an ineffectual attempt to hide from the astute captain the touch of nervousness that now clouded his brow. Picard had been in a strange, almost mischievous, mood earlier that morning. He had asked Riker to accompany him to the transporter room to greet their guests. "I believe you know one member of the team," he had said, smiling enigmatically. And that was the only information the captain would provide about Riker's alleged acquaintance.

The conversation took a more serious turn as the two men left the bridge and made their way to the transporter room. Picard's tension was obvious as he checked, for the third time that day, that all was prepared for the Tarn delegate about to beam onto the *Enterprise*. And for the third time that day, Riker reassured his captain. Now if only he could calm himself down.

"Good morning, Counselor," Picard said in his smooth rich voice. Riker almost did a double take. He was so distracted he hadn't even registered Deanna's presence.

"Captain." She nodded in the direction of Picard. "Good morning, Will. . . . Is everything all right?"

"Of course," Riker responded absently, without listening.

"Will?" Deanna questioned with a note of slight concern edging her voice. "Something troubling you?"

He tried to turn on his most charming smile. "No, nothing."

Lying to Deanna was definitely a no-win situation; he could see that she had already figured something out.

"Excuse me, Captain," the engineering ensign interrupted apologetically. Riker looked over at him with almost a feeling of gratitude. "The team is ready upon your orders."

"Very well, Mr. Eddies. Beam them aboard."

2

A few moments elapsed, yielding no sign of the boarding party.

"Mr. Eddies? At your convenience, please?"

"I'm sorry, Captain. There seems to be some kind of disturbance. Sensors read that the team did not transport across."

"That is apparent, Ensign. The question is, where are they?"

"Well, sir, they're still on the *Tsushima*. It's that problem we've been having with one of the targeting scanners."

"Mr. Eddies, you reported that as repaired earlier today," Picard replied with the slightest tone of admonishment in his voice.

"I'm sorry, sir. We ran the tests, recalibrated the unit, and it looked like it was fine." As the nervous ensign spoke he quickly scanned the system board, waiting for the diagnostic software to evaluate the situation.

"Same unit failed again," he finally replied. "It'll only take a minute, sir."

The ensign made the necessary adjustments.

"She's on-line now, sir. It's safe to transport."

"How many more replacement units do we have for that system?" Will asked while the ensign ran a final safety check.

"Just one, sir."

Riker looked over at Picard.

"Just one? We'll have to keep our fingers crossed," Picard announced. "And Mr. Eddies . . ." he continued.

"Yes, sir?" Riker noticed that the poor kid had turned beet red.

"I'm making it your personal responsibility to ensure that we don't run short again."

"Yes, sir," whispered the ensign.

A wave of sympathy washed over Riker. However remiss Eddies might have been in his duties, it was plain bad luck to mess up in front of the captain on the day they were receiving a Tarn delegate.

The ensign attempted the transport a second time. A moment passed before the vague forms of three individuals appeared on the platform and then materialized.

"Very good, Mr. Eddies. Run a full check on why those systems were giving us trouble earlier."

Then, turning to the party, Picard smiled. "Welcome to the *Enterprise*. I apologize for the inconvenience. Lieutenant Garrett, we're certainly glad to see you, and Dr. Eardman, it is a pleasure to have you on board. I've read some of your works."

Picard stepped to one side, making it a point not to speak to the third individual; this was now a question of military protocol. Riker stepped up to his captain's side, faced the Tarn, and came to attention, ignoring the doctor though all his personal desires screamed at him to look over at her.

The Tarn stood several inches taller than Will's six-foot-two frame, his reptilian gaze absolutely devoid of any show of warmth or emotion. The lizardlike Tarn triggered in Riker the instinctive fear of a creature that looked like a cold-blooded hunter from a primordial age. He forced his fear aside, letting his training take over. Stepping up close to the Tarn, he exhaled noisily. The Tarn, surprised by the gesture, exhaled back at Riker. For the Tarn, the gesture was the human equivalent of shaking hands, a greeting gesture that was used at one time to reveal that the one who stood before you had the same scent as others of your hunting circle.

"Commander Harna Karish, I greet you into our circle as if you are of our blood," Will said, struggling with the guttural pronunciation of the Tarn words.

"I accept the greeting as if I am returning to those of my blood," Karish replied.

Picard, who had been silently observing the scene, was surprised that Karish had spoken in Federation Standard. It was, for a Tarn, a major concession to diplomatic protocol.

The Tarn stood before the group, his cold eyes shifting back and forth. His bearing was stiff, accentuating his height. Clothed in the dress uniform of a Tarn warrior, a scarlet coat ribbed with silver and a navy blue sash extending from one shoulder down the length of his back and attached to the opposite hip, he made an impressive and rather intimidating show of restrained strength. Etched into his reptilian forehead was a pewter-colored tattoo of five small stars in a circle.

Riker made a gesture to Harna's forehead, and to the tattoo, which revealed his clan.

"Of the Kala circle, the royal line. We are honored. I am of the circle Riker, of old America, of Earth, and my circle is unblemished."

Riker now turned and introduced Captain Picard. The diplomatic protocol of it was all rather interesting. If Karish had arrived as an actual representative of the Tarn government, it would have been Picard who greeted him first. Though Karish was of a noble circle on his homeworld, his actual role aboard the *Enterprise* was merely as an exchange officer, "for the purpose of observation," as the memo from Starfleet had explained. Karish held a rank that could be considered equal to Riker's in his own fleet; therefore, it was appropriate that Riker make the first greeting. For Picard to do so would have resulted in a loss of face.

A flicker of a gaze from Picard showed that the captain was impressed by Riker's skillful handling. Picard, following Riker's lead, went through the breathing ritual, this time with Harna breathing first, but with head lowered, a subtle but significant signal that he acknowledged Picard's superior position aboard ship.

"Welcome aboard," Picard announced, but refraining from the ritual of shaking hands, since such an act was seen as an aggressive move by a Tarn too close to a foe.

"Thank you, Captain. As a representative of the

Tarn, I wish to express my thanks for your invitation. Admiral Jord sends his regards. He is more gracious in his praise of the Federation than most. We shall see if his opinion deserves the merit it receives in our First Circle."

"As we will endeavor to validate the praises that accompany you, Mr. Karish. I think you will find your time aboard the *Enterprise* to be a profitable experience," Picard said, motioning for the Tarn to follow him out of the transporter room.

He turned and looked back at Will and Dr. Janice Eardman, the ship's new historian.

"Dr. Eardman, I'm glad you've joined us. I hope you can accompany me for dinner tonight."

Eardman smiled.

"Thank you, sir."

"I take it you know our first officer?"

The woman Picard addressed looked straight at Riker. She nodded an acknowledgment in his direction, yet said nothing.

"Fine. Commander, would you mind escorting Dr. Eardman to her quarters and providing a tour of the ship while I offer Commander Karish escort to his quarters?"

Riker could not help but let a flash of discomfort show. Picard had guessed correctly; this was certainly a familiar face. Deanna, meanwhile, was looking straight at Riker, as if sensing something as well.

"Certainly, Captain." The door slid shut as

Deanna, accompanied by Lieutenant Garrett, as well as the captain and the Tarn, stepped out into the main corridor.

Riker's gaze followed them from the room before finally turning to look at Eardman.

"Hello, Janice. It's been some time since the Academy. It's nice to see you again."

He addressed a woman in her early thirties, slender and rather tall. She wore a regulation, one-piece uniform fitted with a low-cut neckline and flattering lines. Her hair, a mass of tawny curls, was pulled neatly away from her face and caught in a silver pin at the base of her neck. Her honey-colored eyes flashed as she smiled slightly, an awkward blend of embarrassment and excitement.

"It's good to see you as well, Will."

"Your goal has been accomplished, I assume?" Even as he said the words Will inwardly kicked himself for being so blunt.

"Depending on the goals, yes, they've been accomplished, the same as yours. I assume you've accomplished yours also, haven't you, Will?"

The two stared at each other, memories creeping up on the conversation like an afternoon shadow. There had once been a moment between them, a wonderful summer assignment together in their third year at the Academy. It could have been far more, but that possibility had disappeared as it became clear that each assumed that the other would willingly follow wherever the other's career path led. Both of them had been drawn, and both of them had almost succumbed. Both of them had left angry, though who had left whom was still, after all these years, an inner topic of debate for the two.

She was given the chance to spend a three-year assignment on Tarett IV, a distant colony that offered intensive archeological excavation and historical archives as yet undocumented. Will remembered the excitement in her face when she had told him of her opportunity. She had then casually mentioned that there was an open slot for an ensign aboard the orbital base above Tarett IV. Orbital base indeed, he thought bitterly, just one step above a shoreside assignment. It was starships that called to him. He didn't want to get stuck pushing padds in some backwater and he had told her bluntly of his views regarding that idea. And that had ended it.

Nine years had given Will plenty of time to reflect on the incident. He had felt bitterness toward her for a little while. Yet he no longer nursed a grudge. His initial sight of Janice had momentarily brought a bit of the anger near the surface, triggering his pointed comment a moment before; however, he had realized long before that it wasn't really anger that he felt toward this woman, simply the sadness of being left.

There was an awkward moment, and then she

smiled, the smile that could so easily melt him, a smile he had wished he had seen one more time before she had walked out the door.

"I like your ship, Will," she said softly.

"Your ship too now, Doctor."

"Lieutenant," she reminded him. "On ship professorial titles don't apply."

He knew that; still, it was a way of paying a compliment. To rank as a professor of history at the Academy before she was thirty had indeed been a major accomplishment.

"Yes, my ship for the moment," she replied. "Starfleet likes their instructors to have a stint of shipboard duty every once in a while, sort of a sabbatical."

He wanted to ask if she had deliberately selected the *Enterprise* knowing he was on board, but knew better than to try and fish for praise.

"Come on, Janice, let me show you around."

Calling her by her first name, especially delivered with his most winning smile, finally broke the ice a bit more and she smiled in return.

Janice handed him a bag and followed him out of the transporter room. The two chatted along the way of superficial nonessentials: the location of the holodeck, the ship's historical records, an overview of the *Enterprise*'s last mission. Each spoke casually to camouflage the unanswered questions, the potential clashing of wills, the long-forgotten hurt.

Riker, nearing the entrance to Janice's assigned quarters, suddenly grinned. "Are you still as crazy about strawberries and chocolate mixed with Venduvian sauce?"

Janice couldn't help a smirk, a lovely blend of embarrassed delight. "I'm afraid so."

"Well, I'll have to fix you some. Maybe tomorrow?"

"You're going to fix me some?"

"Sure."

"And will this be fit for consumption?"

"Of course. I've had plenty of time since . . . well, I've perfected my culinary arts, let us say. We even have a few real strawberries stashed away in the galley, nothing synthetic."

Turning a corner he slowed, nodded toward a door. "Ah, here are your quarters. Spartan but efficient."

He struggled not to say more, depositing her bag by the door, not opening it or helping her in. The situation was awkward enough as it was. She touched the side panel and the door slid open. Hoisting her bag, she stood silent for a moment, obviously nervous, a reaction he could detect by the way she brushed back an errant lock of hair from her brow.

He stared into the face of Janice, finding it nearly unchanged after nine years. The same wayward curls, the same fiercely independent chin, the same eyes, though slightly more resilient now than they had been. He hesitated on a thought, unsure of the timing. *Just leave it be, Riker,* he told himself, and yet questioned anyway.

"After all these years, Janice, I still wonder at times."

She blinked, eyes dropping for a moment, cheeks flushing. Yes, he could see it: the thought had haunted her as well. It had not just been a summer romance; it might have been far more, and it still troubled her.

"Wondering doesn't change the past, Will," she said softly. "We both have to live with the consequences of our choices."

"Yes, of course," he replied stiffly, vowing now not to let his feelings show. "After all, you are a historian, you know those things."

She looked up at him, features set. Riker cursed himself. *It was going so well,* he thought. *Why did I have to open my big mouth and take a dig at her?* "Janice, I'm sorry I said that, can't we just . . ."

With a calmness that appeared strangely out of place amid the tension of the earlier conversation, she interrupted him. "Just remember, Will, you never asked me to stay."

With that, she disappeared into her room.

Harna Karish settled down in the chair, noting that it had been designed with room for his prehensile tail. Yet another sign of the lengths those of the Federation would go to in order to make him comfortable. Again, a sign of their willingness to accommodate, and a sign of their weakness.

The one who was the second, Riker, his pronunciation was atrocious, the attempt of a fumbling underling to appease one of greater stature. Yet he was considered almost as powerful as the commander of this ship. One could see the interplay between the two; there was no abject lowering of Riker's head to acknowledge Picard's superior position. Odd . . .

He stood up and went to the computer-input board for the ship. His inquiry in Tarn gave no response, so he was forced to access through Federation Standard, a loathsome tongue that he had studied for years in preparation for this assignment. He began to scan through the logs, the information about the ship, randomly searching back and forth.

Surprisingly, the information was open: design systems, maps, histories. Eventually, it could be subtly altered, filtered to appear real but actually laden with misinformation. But first he would have to download the data; it might prove useful.

Out of curiosity he accessed the computer's information on the Tarn. Their version, at least, was extensive: first contact, the undeclared war, the settlement and establishment of a neutral zone for both . . . interesting that they left such information available. It was one-sided to be certain, yet readily accessible if he so desired. Why was that? Was this

all a façade, the computer controlled and programmed so that he alone would think they were
being open, and thus he would report favorably?
Or perhaps it was a part of their elaborate preparation to convince the Karuuki, the First Circle, that
the intentions of the Federation in seeking a per-
manent treaty were honest.

Harna smirked without pleasure. The Karuuki
circle would soon fall from power, and when his
own circle, also of the royal line, the Kala, took
control, then the Federation would see once again
the power that the Tarn could extend, for was it not
their destiny to rule? There were other races who
bore no love for the Federation yet still sought
alliances. The Kala would be more than happy to
make similar alliances, playing one against the
other, weakening each so that their own rightful
destiny to expand could be fulfilled. The question
was, how did he expand his own position in the
meantime?

"Captain to the bridge."

Picard stirred, drawn from a peaceful dream.
Quickly focusing his attention, he stood up, trying
to stifle a yawn.

"On my way."

He pulled on his uniform and shoes.

Stepping out of his quarters, he advanced into
the upper area of the bridge. Data, in command of
the watch, approached the captain as he entered.

"Sir, sorry to disturb you, but I think you had better look at this."

"What is it, Data?"

"We were passing within point zero three parsecs of the Torgu-Va system and did a standard sweep of the area."

It took Picard a moment to orient himself. They were into their second day of passage through the Tarn Neutral Zone, the first Federation ship in this position in over two hundred years. With the initial protocol reached between the Federation and the Tarn, the No-Entry Zone was now open to both sides, and Starfleet wanted one of their best ships in there as a show of force. Standard scans of any nearby systems were part of normal procedure, but in this case the scans were essential. After all, this was all unexplored territory.

He looked at the plot board. Only a single planet showed on the screen, the data scrolling by indicating that it was nothing more than a scorched rock. No sentient life-forms.

Data pointed to a small blip orbiting Torgu-Va's sun, almost directly opposite the position of the planet.

"What is that?"

"It appears to be wreckage, sir, a derelict ship."

Picard looked crossly at Data. There were thousands of wrecks in space, the flotsam and jetsam of hundreds of years of exploration, colonization, and wars. Why had he been awakened for this trivia?

"I believe there is something significant about this wreck," Data said as he pointed at a high-gain magnification of the scan.

Picard leaned over to look at the screen, his curiosity suddenly aroused.

"Order helm to bring us about. I want a closer look at this."

Picard stepped back from the screen and watched as the starfield display on the forward scan shifted. The pinpoint of light that was the harsh blue-white sun of Torgu-Va appeared in the lower corner. It'd take them an hour off course, but still . . .

The minutes passed slowly, the way they always seemed to idle by monotonously when one was standing watch at three in the morning. This was probably just a phantom, a bit of minor wreckage. Still, there was something about the configuration. He was tempted to call for their new historian, but decided against it. Let the woman sleep. She had been aboard now for four days and he wondered about the wisdom of the transfer, the personal tension that was so evident between her and Riker. An assignment that Picard first thought would please his Number One was in fact distracting and troubling him, and the captain wasn't pleased with that effect.

Funny that he even remembered Will mentioning her. It must have been more than a year or so back, when he had called his first officer's attention to one of Eardman's articles in the journal *Starfleet*

Historical Review. Riker had looked uncomfortable at the mention of her name, and said little more than that they knew each other at the Academy. When her name had come up for field assignment, Picard had been delighted on a personal level; history had always been one of his passions. He had expected a similar reaction from Riker, judging from how well Riker got along with Counselor Troi. He wondered now if he should have steered Dr. Eardman to another ship.

An updated scan appeared on part of the screen and Picard looked over at Data. This was starting to get interesting. At the very least, it was a break from their usual routine.

Here could be found dragons and unknown lands, Picard thought with a smile. It was good to have an anomaly presented, even if it was 3:25 in the morning.

The wreckage was dead ahead, the range closing down to the tens of millions of kilometers, the sun of Torgu-Va off their port side, the undistinguished planet, typical of the vast majority of uninhabitable worlds, nearly eclipsed on the far side several hundred million kilometers away.

"Bring us to impulse power, Mr. Data."

"Shifting to impulse, sir. . . . Captain, we are closing in on the core of the wreckage. I think you had better look at this."

Picard left his chair and walked over to Data's display panel at the back of the bridge.

"We have two distinct wrecks here, three point

nine thousand kilometers apart. We have scattered wreckage spread across several tens of millions of kilometers."

"Focus in on that central mass," Picard said quietly.

Data pushed the magnification up to maximum. Computer analysis took over, a flood of information coming back, and then there was a flash on the screen as a computerized outline was superimposed over the wreck.

Startled, Picard looked over at Data.

"It can't be," Picard whispered.

"Sir. I think it is. The hull configuration matches with the computer outline."

"The other wreck?"

Data manipulated the computer screen's information again.

"Far less distinct, sir, heavily damaged. Our information on Tarn ships is sketchy, but it looks like the Tarn ship *Rashasa,* reported lost two hundred and four years ago."

"Shift us back to the other one."

Picard stared intently at the image, which was now coming into sharp detail as they closed to less than a hundred kilometers and slowed to a stop. The entire aft section was blown off, the warp nacelles were gone, the main deck area was flame-scorched, and the ship was hulled in several places . . . it was the ghost of a distant past.

"Data, have Commander Karish report here to

the bridge. Then wake Riker and Eardman to serve on the away team. Brief them and go along. I think they're going to find this interesting."

"Transporter room." Janice gave the command within the turbolift and waited impatiently as the machine slipped into action. She caught a wayward curl that inevitably strayed from its pin and shoved it absently behind her right ear. The wake-up call had pulled her from a deep sleep with an order to report to the transporter room within thirty minutes with her historical recording gear. There had only been time for a quick sonic shower, leaving her feeling rushed and slightly disheveled. The rush of shipboard life was unsettling, but then again, the order for her to report had stated that it was a high-priority mission and that she was to don an environmental suit, which would be found in her closet. When she had inquired about details, Captain Picard had merely replied that she would be briefed before transport. She had sensed a note of excitement in his voice, as if there was a pleasant surprise in store.

The turbolift came to a smooth stop at the transporter-room deck. Janice took a long draught of air in an attempt to settle her stomach before entering the room. She slowed at the sight of Will, who was deep in conversation with Data. He had canceled their date for strawberries, claiming ship's duties came first, and had pointedly avoided contact with her since. She caught his gaze following her as she came in, and she made a point of greeting him with a polite nod and then immediately breaking eye contact.

He looked up at her and nodded. "We're in luck. The scan indicates that there's airtight integrity on the main bridge of the wreck. We won't need suits but we'll keep them on just in case. You can keep your helmet visor up, but if there is a decompression you'll need to lock it in place."

"Yes, Commander."

He approached her, casually checking the helmet clips and air supply.

"Fine." He stepped away, turning his back to her.

"Data, are you prepared?"

"Yes, sir."

"Good. Now, with the doctor here, we will be ready to leave soon. Doctor?"

"Yes, sir." Janice assumed that, amid company, it would be wise to address Will as the superior officer that he was.

"Data is already informed of our mission so I will fill you in briefly. It seems we have come upon the wreckage of the *U.S.S. Verdun* and a Tarn ship which apparently fought them, the *Rashasa.*"

"Captain Murat's *Verdun?*" Janet asked incredulously.

"His is the only one I know of."

"But the *Verdun* was reported missing and assumed lost with all hands. . . ." Her words trailed off into stunned silence.

"Janice? Are you all right?"

"The *Verdun?*"

"That's what we've found. Why?"

"My God, Will. It was reported lost two hundred years ago."

"Actually, it was two hundred and four years ago, according to our historical records," Data supplied generously.

Her heart was pounding as she struggled to maintain an outward display of professionalism. The *Verdun!* Not a single ship of that design had survived. All were either destroyed, reported lost, or scrapped.

"But it was reported lost . . . destroyed," she finally whispered, realizing that everyone in the transporter room was looking at her after her exclamation of disbelief.

"It was not destroyed, entirely," Data replied. "Many of the lower decks remain . . . as well as the main bridge."

Janice's eyes widened. The main bridge. That would mean records, data storehouses, access to personal logs. The historical significance of such a find would be phenomenal.

For a second her eyes met Will's and she could see that he was genuinely pleased for her sake, that he understood just how excited she would be and was happy about her pleasure.

"It's ours, or should I say yours for the exploring," he said with a smile. "You're the historian. We'll take our cues from you once aboard."

"Ready for transporting, sir," the ensign at the console offered.

"Are we ready?"

Data replied in the affirmative; Janice could muster only a nod.

Will brushed his insignia slightly. "Captain, the away team awaits your orders."

"Very well, Number One. Beam aboard."

Will looked over at Eddies.

"You're certain the diagnostic checked out all right, Eddies? I'd hate to find myself floating outside that ship rather than inside."

"It's running fine sir," Eddies replied nervously.

Riker gave the final command. "Whenever you're ready, then, Ensign."

Transporting was still something she found slightly unsettling. The flash of light, the momentary sense of disorientation, and the instant shift from one reality to another as if one simply blinked one's eyes and the entire world changed. She had been looking at Eddies as he activated the beam and now, in a flash, two hundred years had been transcended.

A dimly lit bridge was the first thing she noticed, followed by a sense of surprise that somehow a power system was still operating. Artificial gravity was still active but weak, maybe one-half Earth standard. And the air: stale, reminding her, of all things, of opening a refrigerator at her family's summer home after it had sat empty for months. A flood of sensations started to wash over her . . . the swirl of dust motes in the light, a flicker from a display panel, the tomblike silence . . . and she wanted to seize and embrace each detail, knowing that somehow she was walking into the past, that this moment must be remembered and held as if it were a precious gift.

The historian's job was to rummage through the dusty pages of the past, to uncover, to explore ancient truth. Janice had always found the investigative aspect of her job to be fulfilling. Yet even that had its moments of clinical detachment. Computer records, after hours of poring over information, became tedious; logs could only be deciphered after weeks of breaking codes; even personal memoirs could become odious, detailing dietary supplements and exercise schedules far more often than poignant details of an individual's life. But to walk the corridors of the ship that housed so many lives was exhilarating. She was reminded of her student years, when she spent hours at a time wandering the open rooms of ruined abbeys or crumbling shrines. She found a sweet thrill in occupying the same space as someone hundreds of years before her, attempting to capture the intensely personal air of physically placing herself in the haunts and hideaways that other people thrived in. Records were vital, of course, imperative for documentation; but they couldn't give one the same sensation as watching fuzzy light streak through the window of an ancient turret, or the ache of cold concrete against bare toes. In a field of data accumulation and accuracy, Janice reveled in moments in which she felt she could share nearly the same breath as those she studied.

So now, standing on board the bridge of Captain Lucian Murat, Janice trembled with the responsibility she bore. No one had stood where she stood for nearly two centuries.

"Lieutenant Eardman?"

"Hmm?" Shaken out of her reverie, she realized that Will and Data had been standing patiently, waiting for her directions. Will was grinning.

"Your orders, Lieutenant?"

The professional finally snapped back into place.

"Nothing's to be touched," she said softly, "nothing. I want to keep this site in situ. Hold on just for a moment."

She pulled out her recorder unit and held it up. The system recorded details of the bridge along with data analysis. She saw that Data was doing the same thing. Good, a backup was always nice to have.

She tentatively stepped forward and started to circle around the bridge while motioning for her two companions to remain stationary. She paused for a moment and looked down. Skeletal remains, still clothed in the uniforms of two hundred years ago, were scattered in clumps. She steeled herself, thinking that it was no different than opening an ancient tomb, that one could be detached, that the skeleton was merely an object of curiosity, but this *was* different somehow. The remains of what had once been a woman were draped over a flame-scorched position. It was the ship's navigator's post. Her uniform was burned, her blond hair curled and scorched from the fire, her skeletal arms and legs curled up in the position the dying assume when burned alive.

Tears came to her eyes. It was obvious that the dead on this bridge had died in agony. Though the air was now breathable, her imagination took hold. She could almost feel the flames, hear the screams and gasps for breath as the room was flooded with smoke and poisonous fumes. With a trembling hand she pointed her scanner at the body and then at what was left of the navigator's position, then moved on.

Her eyes took in everything. The flame-blackened overhead paneling was blown out, revealing the upper bridge section . . . most likely the concussion from a blow to the hull had reverberated throughout the ship, cracking the supports. She pointed up.

"I don't know if that's stable or not. Data, could you scan it?"

"Support beams are eighty-five percent destroyed, but it is safe to walk under, Lieutenant."

She continued her circuit, amazed at just how small and cramped the bridge was compared to the *Enterprise*'s. And yet, there were positions for nearly three times as many personnel, who had occupied their posts sitting almost shoulder to shoulder. Every cubic meter on the old ships had to be purely functional.

She finished her walk around and then nodded to her companions.

"Fine. I think I got a good scan. Data, see what you can do with downloading the computer files. If memory serves me right these ships ran on a Gotherin Eight computer system."

"Gotherin Eight-B," Data replied.

She felt a bit of professional jealously as she looked over at Data. Of course he would have perfect recall on the information, but still . . .

"Will, could you run a scan on the other decks, but don't set foot off the bridge yet. This is an incredible find, but I want to go slow with it. Disturb as little as possible."

"Aye, aye, Lieutenant."

She finally approached the center of the room . . . the captain's chair.

She stood silent before it, filled with an almost reverent sense of awe. It was here that Captain Murat had once sat. It was here that he had so boldly commanded his legendary journeys. She wanted to touch the arms of the captain's chair, to feel the smooth indentation near the end where he was reputed to have pounded so often in fury. And the series of engineering consoles in the back of the bridge. They had belonged to Commander Pready. He was rumored to have been quite the philanderer, yet he devotedly wrote adoring letters home to his wife and four daughters living on Terga VII. These men had felt what she felt now, had gazed upon the same surroundings. Perhaps their last sight of the bridge was similar to what she now saw. But their attitude had not been the same. Had they envisioned their deaths moments before they occurred? Had beads of perspiration coursed across their foreheads, while their fingers clutched smooth panels in terror? Or had they stood firmly, feet solidly planted on the polished floor beneath her, and defied death to come their way?

So many memories clouding the thin air of the room; so many lives inexorably wound within the fabric, the materials found on board.

"Why don't you try the chair out for size?"

She turned and saw Will standing beside her.

"This is a historical site, Will," she gasped, scandalized at the mere thought of what he was suggesting. "I couldn't possibly."

He gave her a knowing smile.

He winked at her. "Data and I will never tell."

She looked back at the chair. It wasn't professional, it simply wasn't done. It would be like grabbing hold of a precious document with dripping, muddy hands. And yet . . .

She turned and nervously sat down. She took a deep breath and settled back in the chair. The darkened viewscreen was before her.

" 'Bring me a map and let me see, how much is left to conquer all the universe,' " she whispered.

"What was that?" Will asked.

"It's Marlowe, from his play *Tamburlaine the Great,* though the actual word was 'world,' not 'universe.' It was one of Murat's favorite quotes. I can imagine him saying it, as he sat here, right here, as they leapt forward into the unknown. It was here, right here, that he did it all. . . ." Embarrassed, she looked away; the emotion was simply too much. She was ashamed that Will would see that, or for that matter, any emotion, be it professional or personal.

She was startled when he reached out and lightly touched her on the shoulder.

"Enjoy your moment, savor it."

He stepped back and away. *He's doing it again,* she thought. Though history was not his field, he nevertheless understood just how deep the emotional impact of it all truly struck the core of her soul. It was one of the reasons that now, after all these years . . . she pushed the thought aside.

"Lieutenant?"

Data interrupted Janice's thoughts, catapulting her into the present.

"It will take time to gain a solid interface with *Verdun*'s computers. Apparently, there is a security lock on them. Any attempt to tamper or gain access will cause a core dump of all information."

"Right, I should have thought of that. It was standard security procedure when one of these ships went to battle stations. If they lost and were boarded, no one could gain access to information."

"I would like to run a double check on the unlock code before trying it, Lieutenant."

"Fine, Data, proceed as you see fit."

"There is something else, Lieutenant. We have received a scan update from the *Enterprise*. Initial information is showing the remains of two hundred and eighteen bodies on board. That leaves over seven hundred missing."

"Seven hundred?" Riker asked.

"Yes, sir. Even with decomposition, and the possibility of bodies being lost outside of the wreckage, the number of bodies missing is unusually high. Probability statistics would indicate that, including these factors, some four hundred and seventeen bodies should still remain somewhere on board this surviving section of the ship."

"So where are they?" asked Riker.

"We have scanned the planet for life-forms, haven't we?" Janice inquired. She quickly regretted the question. Of course they had.

"We did an initial sweep of the system as we came through. That is when the wreckage was picked up. The first scan of the planet showed a rotational axis inclination of less than two percent, a low magnetic field, high surface radiation as a result, and extreme temperature, reaching nearly eighty degrees Celsius. No human or Tarn life-forms. The wreckage of the Tarn ship is far more extensive. There is little evidence of physical remains."

In her preoccupation with the *Verdun,* Janice had not given much thought to the wreckage of the Tarn ship. She would love to explore what little was left, but that would require diplomatic approval first as, according to Federation rules, a derelict ship, or wreckage, was the property of the race that had owned it, and could not be touched without their permission. In any case, she had quite enough on her hands with the *Verdun.*

"It is very odd that Captain Murat's remains are not here," Data said.

"This command center took a lot of damage," Janice replied. "He may have moved to the secondary bridge area."

"Which is missing," Riker replied. "They either died there or on the way to the shuttlecraft to escape. Unfortunately, that entire bay area was blown apart."

She looked back at the blank viewscreen, trying to imagine what Murat felt in those last moments. Did he order the shuttlecraft away in the vain hope that somehow they might be found? For his sake, she hoped that he and his comrades had died in the destroyed part of the ship rather than drifting for days or weeks until supplies had at last given out.

She looked back at the curled-up body at the navigator's post. Though the woman had been dead for two hundred and four years, Janice could not help but mourn. She wondered how old the woman had been. Ship's records would show. Yet she could almost guess already . . . there was a scorched piece of a pale blue bow in the hair, something someone who was young would wear. A gold band of an engagement ring dangled from the skeletal third finger of her left hand . . . was her fiancé on this ship, or did he mourn her for a lifetime, wondering what had happened to the focus of all his dreams?

She turned away. Murat had sat where she now sat, time had spun out its course across two centuries, and nothing could be changed. She looked over at Will and saw that he was patiently waiting. For a moment all the old barriers were down between them.

"Come on, Janice, let's explore the rest of this ship."

31

Chapter Two

"YOU KNOW, I HAD AN ANCESTOR who died in the Tarn conflicts," Geordi announced with a touch of pride in his voice. "Was an ensign aboard the old *Constitution.*"

Picard acted as though he were ignoring the conversation and was instead engrossed in a game of chess with a young cadet who had been assigned to the *Enterprise* for the summer session away from the Academy. He could tell that the boy was thrilled beyond words that the captain would actually challenge him to a match. Picard would never admit it, of course, but he was simply looking for a convenient place in Ten-Forward to sit and keep an eye on Karish.

"Many of my circle died with great glory as

well," came the hissing reply. "My circle holds their names in honor. . . ."

"That's check again, sir."

"Hmm?" Picard looked back down at the board, and then at the cadet, who seemed to be proud of his latest maneuver, which had forked Picard's king and one of his rooks.

"Good move, Midshipman," Picard said absently, moving his king out of harm's way.

"Sir, do you really want to do that?"

Picard looked into his opponent's eyes. He could sense that the boy was trying to be polite—was, in fact, a bit nervous that he was so thoroughly trouncing his captain. Picard smiled and looked back at the board.

"Ah, I see. Move there and you have me in mate next turn."

"Yes, sir."

"Well . . ." He fumbled for a second trying to remember the name. "Well, Forsyth, rules aboard this ship are: You let go of the piece, you've moved it."

"All right, sir," Forsyth replied while taking the rook that would place Picard in mate.

The boy looked up at him nervously and Picard laughed.

"Mr. Forsyth, I'm not Napoleon."

"Sir?"

"Oh, just an old family story. I had an ancestor who fought in the Battle of Trafalgar. He claimed that he once beat Napoleon at chess and that it was months before the Emperor forgave him. My compliments on your game. It shows you have a quick mind, Forsyth."

"Thank you, sir!"

Picard felt a slight tinge of irritation. It bothered him at times how easily he was able to maneuver some of the youngsters new to the Fleet. They came fresh from the Academy with the exuberance of children, so eager to ingratiate themselves into the way of life on board the *Enterprise*. The captain marveled at how a smile, a simple compliment, was enough to send them grinning into the path of death without a moment's hesitation. The line between duty and idealized notions of sacrifice was rarely understood by the first-year officer.

". . . and I tell you that incident was provoked by your Federation!"

Picard shifted his attention away from Forsyth and back to the conversation going on behind him.

"I can understand how you might see it that way," Geordi replied, trying to sound diplomatic, yet scarcely disguising the touch of annoyance in his voice. "But the record shows that the *Constitution* was fired on without warning. Two hundred crew members died."

"Your ship, this *Constitate* or whatever, was coming as a reinforcement and had to be stopped."

"We were answering a distress call, which later turned out to be a false alarm, put out by one of your ships . . ."

". . . Another game, sir?"

"Ah, no thank you, Mr. Forsyth, losing two in a row is enough for tonight. Thank you for your time."

Picard stirred as if getting up to retire and Forsyth, not used to the rules of informality which existed in Ten-Forward, sprang to his feet, snapping to attention, drawing bemused smiles from many at other tables, at least those who were not listening in on the debate between Karish and La Forge.

As Picard stood up he scanned the room. Riker was nowhere to be found; he could imagine why but was slightly annoyed nevertheless. There was, after all, the duty of keeping an eye on Karish rather than on attractive historians. Troi was not in the room either, but he did see Data, who was looking at him from across the room. All it took was a subtle motion of the eyes and Data was rising from his seat and making his way toward Picard.

Picard turned and, as if feigning surprise, looked straight at Karish.

"Commander Karish, I hope you are enjoying the hospitality of our lounge?" Picard said.

Karish stopped in midsentence and looked up.

"They do not serve *Hammasi.*"

"I'm sorry, I'm not familiar with that."

"It is a rather potent brew of the Tarn," Data interjected, coming up to Picard's side. "One of the ingredients is fermented blood of a creature rather similar to a tiger on Earth."

"Well, Mr. Data. Perhaps you can share your

knowledge with Guinan, and we'll see if we can come up with a reasonable facsimile of this *Hammasi*. And while you're at it"—he paused—"since I was talking about the Emperor, a bit of that special Napoleon brandy for myself, if you don't mind."

"Certainly, sir. I think I shall try that as well."

Picard moved to a chair between Geordi and Karish and casually sat down as Karish continued the conversation, addressing the newest member of the group.

"I was just instructing one of your junior officers as to the true history of the War of Federation Aggression," Karish announced.

"I see. You're speaking of the *Constitution* incident."

"Our defense against that ship."

Picard shifted his gaze to Geordi.

"You know, this is all rather interesting," Picard began, adopting an almost professorial tone, "especially in light of the wreckage we've just found. *Verdun* was a proud ship, her captain famous in our history."

"As is Qiva in ours, though we do not hold the same view of your Captain Murat, a butcher of hundreds who could not defend themselves."

"Old history can be troubling, but it can also be learned from. Wouldn't you agree, Geordi?"

"Yes, sir." Picard could sense that Geordi most definitely did not agree, at least as far as their difficult guest was concerned.

"For example: Geordi, I think you had an ancestor who died fighting the Tarn?"

"On the *Constitution*," Geordi said coldly.

Picard looked back at Karish. "You see, Commander Karish, there's more to Lieutenant Commander La Forge's family history than his family's service on the *Constitution*. At one time his ancestors were slaves in a place on Earth called America."

Karish looked at Geordi, and Picard could sense that Karish was confused. To the Tarn, the admission of a family line of slaves was something to be ashamed of.

Picard looked back at Geordi. "I remember you telling me about it once, Geordi, how your family escaped and one of them fought in the American Civil War."

"The Twenty-Eighth United States Colored Troops out of Indiana," Geordi replied with a touch of defiance in his voice. "He carried the regimental flag and lost his arm at the Battle of the Crater, July 30, 1864."

"Slaves?" Karish interjected, a note of disdain in his voice.

"Yes, Commander Karish. You will see in your time with us that both Commander Riker and Lieutenant Commander La Forge had ancestors who fought in that war to extinguish slavery. Both of them are proud of their family histories. Their ancestors fought for future generations and their freedom."

"And I take it that I should learn a profound lesson from this?" Karish replied coolly.

"I hope the *Hammasi* meets with your approval."

Picard looked up gratefully at Data, who was offering a gilded horn to Karish. Karish took the horn and tentatively sniffed it. A faint whiff of the drink drifted over to Picard, who steeled himself not to react. Gagging, he determined, would not be the most diplomatic of responses. Will still relished telling stories about the various Klingon dishes he had sampled while serving aboard the *I.K.S. Pagh,* and Picard was forever grateful that his first officer had drawn that assignment rather than himself. The thought crossed his mind that in some cultures it was an act of friendship, and also proof you weren't poisoning your guest, to take the first sip from the other person's cup. Fortunately, that did not seem to be the case with the Tarn, as Karish raised the horn, closed his eyes, and with a ceremonial flourish let several drops of the drink fall on the floor before putting the horn to his lips. He took a tentative sip, paused, and then actually drank more.

For the first time Jean-Luc sensed that Karish was genuinely surprised.

Smiling, Picard took the brandy snifter offered by Data and motioned for him to sit down on the other side of the table. Picard raised his glass and let the drink swirl around, coating the sides. Data studiously imitated him. Karish watched the two. Picard raised his glass in a salute, then took a sip, Data doing likewise.

"I understand you are a machine," Karish said, looking at Data.

"Some could define me that way."

"Yet you consume food, drink?"

"I process food and liquids for energy the same way that humans do. Also, for the experience of tasting them. I take it that the *Hammasi* was satisfactory?"

"Where did you learn the secret? Who told you?"

Data smiled. "I am interested in cooking and culinary traditions. Our food-replication system can be programmed to create any molecular pattern, so once I knew the formula, the rest was quite simple. I came across the recipe some years back. The recipe is most interesting, particularly the step during which the bartender must allow the blood to congeal under the sun, drain the remaining liquid, then mix it with fermented milk from a Yaktu. One wonders who thought of it first and why."

If he didn't know better Picard would have said that Data was expressing a certain sarcasm as to who could be sadistic enough to create such a drink.

"It is the next step, though, that truly captivated my attention," Data continued.

"Actually, Data," Picard interrupted hurriedly, more interested in the previous conversation than in the finer details of Tarn cuisine, "we were talking about a fascinating historical point . . . how descendants of former enemies transcend the past."

"You are the descendant of slaves?" Karish asked again, looking straight at La Forge.

"Yes." Picard smiled inwardly, knowing that Geordi was tempted to add a few more comments.

"Riker is a descendant of those who owned you?"

"My ancestors, not me."

Karish sat back for a moment while draining off the rest of his drink.

"Killing him would be a redeeming point of honor for you."

Geordi looked at him, incredulous, and actually laughed.

"Will Riker's one of my closest friends."

"Then you are without honor."

"How is that?" Picard asked hurriedly, leaning forward so as to block Geordi's view of Karish.

"When a circle has been defeated it is without honor until it has fought to redeem itself. It is simply part of a circle, and does not carry the standard of the circle with it. If it is ever defeated a second time, it is cast out forever."

"It is an interesting point of Tarn culture," Data interjected. "Similar in some ways to the traditions of the Klingon warrior code."

"They were worthy enemies," Karish replied. "We enjoyed fighting them."

"And if Lieutenant Worf were here," Picard

replied, "he'd tell you he is still proud of his family, his culture, and his own honor. We once fought bitterly, we came to the brink of war on a galactic level more than once, and yet now we've found a way to live together.

"Maybe those two ships over there are a case in point," Picard continued. "We can see in them a reminder of what both the Tarn and we of the Federation value: honor, self-sacrifice, and what in my native language we called *la gloire*. . . . But it's also the past, Commander Karish, the past. You might call Captain Murat a butcher—"

"He was."

"—and I dare say from your perspective he was. But there is another side of him. He was one of the very first generation of starship commanders, a fellow classmate of Christopher Pike, Akiko Torunaga, and the Vulcan Kadish. He explored more than a hundred worlds, contacted and established treaties with eight societies, and, might I add as a Frenchman, bears an illustrious name from our history."

"And yet—" Karish began.

"And yes, Commander Karish. From the perspective of history we might say he was wrong according to how your society sees him."

Picard pointed toward the window and to the flashing beacon marking the position of *Verdun*. "That's history. I've received orders, which your government has agreed to, to spend an extra three days in this system, documenting the wreckage, retrieving both for your side and ours historical artifacts that we both might treasure. So let's just look at our conflict as history, Commander, and not the present."

"Does your Guinan now know how to make *Hammasi?*"

Caught by surprise, Picard looked over at Data.

"She has the ingredients now."

"I shall have another, then retire," Karish announced. He stood up and left the three. Picard was slightly annoyed at how Karish had so abruptly killed the conversation rather than continue to explore the point. Karish approached the bar and placed his order. Picard could not help but admire Guinan and how she took the order without the slightest sign of distress.

"He certainly is a hard case," Geordi said.

"That he is," Picard replied. "Paranoia seems to be part of the psychological makeup of the Tarn. It's hardwired into their system. The world they evolved on was a carnivorous nightmare; they were the smaller species, hunted nearly to extinction by a species which had gained what we would consider a classical period technology. They came back, wrested control of the planet away from their foes, and then turned on each other when there was nothing left to fight. They learned to trust absolutely no one but their own particular clan, which they call a circle."

"How they gained space without self-destructing

is fascinating," Data interjected. "There are only four other recorded cases of societies still at war with themselves who at the same time achieved the power of interplanetary flight without then using the power to destroy themselves."

"Us, for example, Mr. Data?"

"Of course, Captain."

Picard looked out the window.

"You know, personally I'm fascinated with Murat, though I wouldn't admit that in front of our guest."

He looked back to the bar. Karish drained a horn of *Hammasi* and then, after putting the empty container down, he walked out. Guinan gingerly took the horn.

"Nationalistic feelings, Captain?" Data asked.

"Well, I do have to admit there is a bit of Gallic pride there. The first Murat of fame was one of Napoleon's most capable marshals and his descendant one of the finest starship captains ever. When I was at the Academy I remember attending a lecture by one of the Vulcan officers who had served under Murat. It was amazing: even from a Vulcan you could almost sense a note of pride in being associated with a legend." Smiling wistfully, Picard said, "I dreamed of being another Murat, of having a ship and, as Masefield said, 'a star to steer her by.'" He chuckled softly, and then his features hardened as he looked back out the bay window.

"If the behavior of our guest is any indicator, I

fear that there might be some who will cite the discovery of the *Verdun* and the *Rashasa* as proof that our two societies will not get along."

"I find that hard to believe," Geordi said, then paused. "At least on our side."

"I hope I didn't embarrass you with the example I offered," Picard replied.

As Karish cleared the door Will came into the room and, spotting the group, came over to them.

"Ah, Will. It's nice of you to join us," Picard offered with just a hint of irony in his voice.

"Captain, Data, Geordi," Will responded while pulling up a chair in the back section of Ten-Forward. "Have I missed anything interesting?"

"Not unless you consider a conversation with a rude lizard interesting," Geordi mumbled.

Riker raised his eyebrow and contained a smirk. The engineer was a good friend, but he was hardly skilled in the art of diplomatic speech.

"Mr. La Forge refers, of course, to our Tarn guest. The two of them were discussing the early skirmishes between the Tarn and the Federation."

"Hmm. I see he's made a good impression on you, Geordi?"

"Sure. In fact, I'm going to talk to Guinan about that drink of his. *Hammasi,* was it? You know . . . might as well do my part to cross cultural barriers. Anyhow, I want to check in with Eddies and run another diagnostic on the transporter."

Geordi rose and nodded good night to the two officers. While he made his way across the room, the two heard his frustrated reply: "Maybe I can jam the replicator system; that stuff was awful."

The seated men exchanged a grin.

"Sounds like I missed the party."

"I'm sure you were enjoyably detained elsewhere."

Riker looked at his captain in curiosity before feigning shocked disappointment. "Of course not, sir." Then, with a sheepish smile, "Actually, I couldn't find the good doctor. You know, this is an awfully big ship and if someone wants to avoid someone, it's rather easy."

Picard chuckled and shook his head. The question was who was avoiding whom, but he felt it best not to bring that point up. Will could have, of course, asked the computer to locate her, but shipboard etiquette didn't allow that sort of thing.

"Ah, then I wasn't too far off the mark, I see."

"No, but getting back to the Tarn . . ." Will attempted to steer the conversation elsewhere.

He received a chuckle in return, though it was short lived. Picard's good humor drained from his face as a look of concern slowly took its place.

"Captain?"

"I'm a bit more concerned about this evening's conversation than our friend Mr. La Forge, I'm afraid."

"The discussion of past fighting?"

"More particularly the *Verdun* and its fate. The legends of warfare between the Tarn and the Federation will continue to ignite the passions of extremists on both sides. And legends carry little power to dissuade the concentrated effort to restore peace. In fact, in this case, I'm afraid that renewed interest in old war stories might actually interfere with the peace process. The discovery of the *Verdun* and the *Rashasa* is of incalculable historical value, but it may cause problems as well. . . ." Riker raised an inquisitive eyebrow. Picard continued. "The establishment of the No-Entry Zone was in many ways a wise decision on behalf of the leaders on both sides. Frankly, the Tarn knew we could beat them in a standup fight, and we fortunately weren't interested in a fight, so we agreed to cordon off a couple of hundred thousand cubic parsecs of space as a buffer zone between us. It effectively closed the discussion as to who was at fault."

"Probably both sides," Riker interjected.

"True. But the zone left that undetermined. It afforded a cease-fire, saving the lives of many. The hatred and discord were appeased for the time being. Peace, though shaky and untried, resulted."

"And the downside?"

"Legends without historical accuracy are sleeping mines. Provide a few artifacts, evidence of foul play or slaughter, and the mines are irretrievably armed."

"And you think that the mystery of the *Verdun* will produce such an outcome?"

"Would you gamble on a mine?"

"Captain Picard." Worf's voice interrupted the conversation.

Picard tapped his comm badge.

"Picard here."

"Captain, could you please come to the bridge at once."

"On my way."

As he stood up, Riker's comm badge beeped; then Data's beeped as well. The three looked at each other; if Worf was paging all of them, something was up.

"Gentlemen?" Picard said, and the three headed out of the lounge.

As Picard stepped onto the bridge he could immediately sense the tension in the room.

"Captain," Worf reported. "We just picked this up a few minutes ago. I think you should see the replay of it."

Worf motioned to a viewing screen. It was a magnification showing the glowing rim of the system's sun, the lone planet Torgu-Va barely visible in the shimmering corona.

A spark of light erupted on the surface of the planet.

"Automatic sensors detected it, sir, and triggered an alarm."

Riker leaned over to look at the information, reading it off: "Detonation, atomic weapon, thirty-kiloton range." Surprised, he looked up at Picard.

"Helm, take us out of this position so we can get

a better view of the planet. Put us on a heading over the northern pole of the sun. I want a clear view of that planet as quickly as possible."

The helm responded in seconds and the image began to shift.

"Data, could we have an interference readout from the sun's corona?"

Data was already at his station reviewing the information.

"Negative, sir. It is interesting that our instruments picked it up at all from that range with the sun nearly eclipsing the planet. I am starting to get a better view now. Sir, there was definitely a detonation on the planet's surface. The shock wave is still spreading out through the atmosphere."

"Range to the planet?"

"Four hundred and twenty-three million kilometers, sir."

Picard went over to his captain's chair and sat down, impatient with the time it would take to get a clearer view of the planet.

"What about our first sweep of the planet as we came into the system?" He asked the question in general, but his gaze was fixed on Data. "There's something down there; how come we didn't pick it up earlier?"

"Sir, we did a standard sweep, and nothing was detected on the surface, or in orbit above the planet. No signs of sentient life. Then we focused in on the wreck, sir, with the sun all but eclipsing our view so we could not monitor more closely."

"So, who's there?"

Even as he asked the question Picard had an uneasy feeling.

"I don't think we need a full alert yet, but I want our weapons and shields ready now," he said.

"Suggestions?"

The room was silent.

"Two hundred years ago, when the treaty was signed, this entire region was known to be devoid of sentient life," Data said. "Therefore, whatever is down there has arrived since."

"How would they have gotten past the monitoring systems that we and the Tarn set up along the borders?" Riker asked.

Even before the first officer had finished his question, Data turned away, his attention rigidly fixed on his display.

"Sir, now that we are clearing the interference from the sun, I am starting to pick up something." He hesitated. "Sir, it is in old-style sublight signals. The wave is distorted, but it is coming from the planet's surface."

"Patch it in," Picard replied.

The forward viewscreen filled with a static display of flickering streaks of light. The audio was indistinguishable, filled with cracks and hissing.

"Filter it, Data."

"I already am, sir. The frequency is prone to interference from solar activity. It will be another couple of minutes until we clear the sun."

The wavy static on the screen continued to shift.

Picard could sense now that there was something in the interference, and then, in a startling instant, a blurred image appeared on the screen and the static died away. Shocked, Picard stood up.

"Delta Three, Delta Three . . ." The image faded, a feminine voice disappearing back into static.

Picard looked over at Riker.

"She was wearing a Federation uniform," Picard said.

"A uniform I've only seen in museums," Will replied.

The image suddenly came back into focus. The woman was looking straight at the screen, wide-eyed, her face blistered. Behind her was chaos, people shouting, cursing, all of them speaking Federation Standard, but in a style, a tone, that seemed somehow arcane.

"Alpha One, this is Delta Three. Repeat, we have just sustained a nuclear attack. They have the bomb, repeat, they have the bomb!"

"Get Lieutenant Eardman on the bridge right now," Picard snapped.

He felt as if he were looking at a film from hundreds of years past. The personnel, in what he thought must be some sort of bunker, were all wearing Starfleet uniforms, several of them the old Fleet-issue blues, others in the uniform of the old Starfleet Ground Attack Marines. The image flickered and died.

As Eardman came through the door she slowed,

obviously wondering why she had been summoned.

"Play it back," Picard ordered, and the image of the woman reappeared on the screen.

"The missing personnel," she announced, her voice soft with disbelief as she came up to Picard's side.

"What's that?"

"The bodies of seven hundred people from the *Verdun* were missing. We thought that they must have been destroyed in the fight. That woman's wearing a standard-issue uniform from when the *Verdun* was in service. Somehow, survivors must have gotten down to the planet's surface."

"Are you saying that's them?"

"Well, sir . . . their descendants."

"Wearing uniforms?"

"I know it sounds strange, sir, but there are numerous historical examples of cultures in isolation rigidly clinging to old traditions."

"But who are they fighting?" Picard asked.

"Sir, I have a clean image coming in now," Data interjected, and the recording snapped off, simultaneously replaced with a live feed.

The interior of the bunker was on fire. Picard watched in silence, concealing his horror. They were dying, and dying horribly. The woman was still looking at the screen, the fear and rage in her eyes evident. Picard wondered who she was talking to and admired her strength, her courage, to stay at her station, even as the fires erupted around her.

"This is Delta Three. We're finished! The Tarn have the bomb, repeat, the damn Tarn have the bomb. Long live the Federation. Avenge . . ." The image snapped off.

"The signal is gone," Data announced, his voice echoing in the silence that enveloped the bridge.

"The Tarn have the bomb?" Picard asked, looking over at Janice.

"Sir, I think the descendants of the *Verdun* and the *Rashasa* are still fighting their war."

Picard looked back at the blank screen.

"Get Commander Karish to the bridge immediately."

Chapter Three

As soon as the Tarn walked off the turbolift, Picard turned away from the forward viewscreen and motioned for him to come closer. Then the captain turned back to watch the chaotic events unfolding down on the planet. The main screen had been divided into a dozen smaller images, each of them a transmission emanating from the planet's surface; all of the people on the screen were wearing old-style Starfleet uniforms.

It was obvious that a major battle was unfolding, and the Federation side was taking the worst end of it. Further reports regarding the nuclear detonation had been intercepted; the entire base had been destroyed. Another base was reporting that it had launched chemical weapons in response to the attack.

A side image showed a computer-generated map of the planet with flashing green dots marking where the signals were emanating from; nearly all were clustered around the planet's southern polar region.

"You ordered me to the bridge, Captain," Karish announced, but his attention was fixed on the screen.

Picard sensed that this was going to be difficult.

"Riker, Eardman, and Data, please report to my ready room and start reviewing this situation."

As the three stood up to leave, Picard watched as Karish cast a distrustful glance in their direction.

"There's a war going on down on Torgu-Va," Picard replied, motioning to the screen as the three exited.

Karish silently watched the images and then looked back at Picard.

"Obviously . . . and the reason you requested my presence?"

"Sir, we have another signal," Data's replacement at the conn interrupted. "This one thirty-three kilometers away from where the blast took place."

"Patch it in on the main screen."

A hiss of surprise escaped Karish. The image on the screen was of a group of Tarn; even to one unfamiliar with the language or body gestures it was evident that they were jubilant, shouting. The

Tarn standing in the foreground spoke excitedly. He looked over at Karish.

"That's why," Picard said. "What are they saying?"

"They are reporting to a circle commander. They are announcing the destruction of a target called Delta Three with an atomic weapon." Karish hesitated. "Captain Picard, their uniforms, they are old, from long ago."

"The same as the Federation uniforms," Picard replied, pointing to the other images on the screen. "We believe that these people are the descendants of the crew from the *Verdun* and the *Rashasa* who shuttled down to the planet. They're continuing the war down there."

Karish made a decidedly human gesture of nodding his head, as if slowly understanding the entirety of the situation.

Picard turned away from the screen and looked over at the ensign at the conn.

"We're going to stop this madness," he snapped. "I want you to lock on to their main frequency, boost our signal, and override it. I'm informing both sides right now that we are coming into orbit and that a cease-fire is in place. Commander Karish, if you would be so kind as to convey the same information to the Tarn I would appreciate it."

The ensign started to punch in the necessary information, but it was several seconds before Picard realized that there had been no response from Karish.

He turned back to look at him.

"Commander Karish?"

"Captain?"

"I'm asking you to help me end this. They're slaughtering each other down there. This is insanity."

"No, Captain."

A stunned silence swept the bridge, all eyes turning on Karish.

"I'm not sure if I heard you correctly, Commander. Would you repeat that, please?"

"No, Captain, I will not send the signal. I am invoking your own Prime Directive. I will entertain no further discussion regarding the contact of any forces on the planet."

Picard stood silent, concealing the anger that was welling up inside. The image of the dying woman was still fresh in his mind, as were the terror and chaos playing out on the other screens. There was another factor he had observed in the minutes since they had first picked up the signal . . . one of intense rage and hatred for the Tarn. He was used to the trained, detached, and very proper language used in all Federation transmissions. To see personnel in Starfleet uniforms shouting with rage, openly voicing the darkest obscenities when mentioning the Tarn, had shaken him. It was as if he had wandered into a darkened alley and was witnessing a bitter fight to the death, the combatants grappling in the muck and filth with their bare hands. As a starship commander, it was his duty to bring order out of this chaos.

"Commander Karish . . ."

"Captain. I am a representative of the Tarn government while I am on this ship. My status is as an officer in our Imperial Fleet. My title of Commander aboard this ship is merely an honorific term conferred on me while I am on board. I have not sworn a direct oath to you or to the Federation. Therefore, I refuse."

Karish paused for a moment, then stepped closer to Picard.

"I am also stating that the crew of the *Rashasa*, since they failed in their initial battle and lost their ship, are cast out of their circle. They are no longer a part of our government. As such, their descendants are of a different culture that has yet to achieve spaceflight. Therefore, you would be in violation of your Prime Directive if you contact them either directly, or indirectly, by establishing contact with the humans down on the planet."

"Commander Karish, this is outrageous," Picard snapped in disbelief. "There are people dying down there, and not just members of the Federation. There are reports of a chemical weapons strike on Tarn positions in retaliation."

"It would be typical of your Federation to use such things."

"Let's just stop it now."

"My position is the same."

Picard stood speechless as Karish slowly made his statement, as if he were a judge addressing a mob of lowly supplicants standing before his bench. Picard looked around the room and knew that everyone was waiting for his command. He looked back at the conn.

"Ensign, are there indications of any more weapons about to be fired?"

"No, sir. No indications of radioactive material other than from the debris plume of the detonation."

He looked back over at Karish. "Stay here," he snapped, and without another word, started for the door. Passing Worf, he slowed.

"I need to discuss this further," he whispered. "If there's any indication of another weapon being prepared, call for me at once. Meanwhile, see if you can talk some sense into him."

"Me, sir?"

"He likes Klingons. He claims you two have the same warrior instinct."

"I am not sure if I should take that as an insult or not, sir. It is one thing to fight, weapon in hand, another thing to use such weapons on an opponent who cannot strike back in kind."

"Just see what you can do, Worf. I'm not getting anywhere with him at the moment. Perhaps you can make some headway while I talk with the rest of the staff."

"Yes, sir."

* * *

"Dr. Eardman's theory that the inhabitants of the planet are Federation survivors is entirely plausible," said Data. "Two hundred and four years—that would mean a total of seven point three generations. If we postulated an average of four point two children per couple, factoring in certain variables such as sterility and infant mortality per cycle—"

"Yes, Data. The numbers would be great, I'm sure," Riker interjected tiredly. He wondered when, if ever, the android would fully grasp the concept of a rough estimate. Data cocked his head slightly.

"Something wrong, sir?"

"No, nothing at all. I'm just wondering why, if it's obvious that Federation forces live on the planet, we didn't pick up something, anything. We did an initial sweep of the planet; nothing significant was located."

"Initial sweeps of the planet included only the planet's surface, sir. Also, given the rotational period of just over thirty-two hours and an inclination of the axis of eighteen degrees . . . well, sir, in actuality we only saw sixty-two point one percent of the planet."

"And they were on the other side?"

"Yes, sir. Furthermore, there were no transmissions taking place at that time. It appears that the inhabitants live within a series of tunnels and subterranean dwellings."

"An underground city?" Eardman asked with interest.

"It would be a reasonable explanation. Surface temperatures, even at the poles, can approach sixty degrees Celsius during the day and plummet to below freezing at night."

The group looked up as Picard came into the room.

"Captain, are you all right?" Riker asked, sensing the tension.

Picard smiled, but to Riker, the expression looked forced. He wondered if something else had happened in the three officers' absence. Not that they needed any more excitement that day.

"Number One. Your assessment?"

"Well, sir. It would appear that the Federation forces on Torgu-Va are in need of immediate assistance. Of course, there is the delicacy of the current political situation with the Tarn both down below and with the higher levels of negotiation."

"Elaborate."

"Might this situation not play into the hands of militants who are against the current state of peace initiatives?"

Picard nodded.

"I would assume though, sir, that were we to simply inform both forces of our presence, neither side could misconstrue our intentions, while at the same time dispatching all the data we have to both Starfleet and the Tarn government," Riker said.

"Yes, that was what I had thought. It seems,

however, that there is an objection to our suggestion."

"An objection by whom?"

"Commander Karish. He claims that such action would be a violation of the Prime Directive. He is threatening to inform his commanders of our violation of that directive if we insist on making contact."

"That seems a bit far-fetched. He's stretching the Prime Directive a little too far, isn't he?" Eardman replied.

"Mr. Data, your assessment, please," Picard asked. "What legal precedents are there for Karish's claim?"

"Sir, Commander Karish could cite the incident with the Betelgeuse sleeper ship one hundred and twenty-eight years ago. They had departed from Earth at sublight speed in the middle of the twenty-first century. They were caught in a wormhole effect, transported far off course, and crash-landed on Henson's World, then degenerated to a primitive culture without any memory or records of their origins from Earth. It was finally ruled that they were to be left alone."

"But surely—" Riker snapped.

"No, I am afraid Mr. Data is right," Picard interposed. "Under any other circumstances, it would merely be a technicality. With negotiations between the Federation and the Tarn as precarious as they are, however, a minor breach such as this could ignite a multitude of diplomatic disasters."

Picard's experience as the commander of the *Enterprise* had taught him the necessary craft of disguising his feelings. Nevertheless, Riker could see that he was hard-pressed in this instance to contain his anger. The petty and disruptive nature of Harna Karish's demand was obviously based solely on the Tarn's hidden agenda: to created a rift so great that the Tarn ruling elite would be forced to defer to their isolationist party's unrelenting denouncement of the Federation as a pack of "expansionist warmongers."

If it had been a legitimate request, if Karish had truly been concerned about the welfare of the Tarn descendants, Picard would have undoubtedly heard him out more graciously. But as it was, Riker questioned whether the planet's inhabitants had even crossed the reptilian's mind.

"Captain, these are Captain Murat's men," Riker said. "We thought the *Verdun* was an incredible discovery. But now we have the chance to . . . to step into the lives of an entire population living in the past. This isn't a reenactment, some paltry attempt at reviving the past, this *is* the past. These people live and breathe, fight in a world that we forgot two hundred and four years ago. . . . We forgot them, sir. . . . And now it's our responsibility to do something."

Janice, smiling, looked over at him and nodded her thanks.

"They aren't Murat's men, nor are they warriors of the ship *Rashasa,* simply their descendants, the same as you or I. Granted, they are living as if it is the past, but we are dealing with the present, and all the political ramifications of this discovery."

"Captain, to focus on that present," Data interjected, "the Tarn have the advantage in this situation. They are in possession of some level of nuclear capabilities—primitive warfare, of course, but deadly nonetheless."

"All the more reason why we should contact the Federation forces," Janice countered.

"Because they are losing, Dr. Eardman, or because we have a moral obligation to stop this fight?"

Janice bristled slightly. "The latter, of course, sir."

Picard nodded. Riker noted that the captain seemed glad to see her touch of anger over his question.

"Then if there is no question that we have a moral obligation to stop this fight, the next question is how to approach Karish's objection to our desire to inform the forces of our presence along with our wish to broker a cease-fire." Picard rubbed his eyes in apparent fatigue. Riker looked down at the conference table and saw that his own fist was clenched.

"Sir, there is an interesting clause that we could cite," Data interjected.

"Well, Data, since you gave the argument against, I hope this is one in favor of ending this war," Picard replied.

"Certainly, sir. Again, it relates to multigenerational sleeper ships. The one I cited earlier was pre-Federation. It was an American and Russian effort. It was a private venture and thus not officially part of a pre-Federation government program. That, sir, was one of the legal considerations that influenced the final judgment to deny contact. However, shortly after the founding of the Federation, a sleeper ship departed for the Magellanic Cloud, a journey of several hundred years. The crew was put into suspended animation, but they were specifically chartered with the statement that their descendants were to be defined as Federation personnel and must obey all rules and laws of the Federation. You will recall, sir, that that ship was recovered by the previous *Enterprise* starship and that there was never a question regarding noninterference. The personnel on board that sleeper ship were Federation personnel.

"Citing that incident, we could argue that the line of command down on Torgu-Va, having maintained a direct link to the Federation through custom, is subject to Federation orders. The woman we saw said, 'Long live the Federation.' If they therefore perceive themselves as Federation, they are indeed Federation, and thus subject to orders."

"Orders, Captain? What are we ordering them to do?" Janice asked.

"To cease fire, of course."

"Forgive me, sir, but can we do that?"

"Where are you leading with this, Doctor?"

"Captain, the forces on Torgu-Va may not welcome our order to make up and be friends, to let bygones be bygones. If they resist our command, we are left with a situation in which our hands will be tied."

"Why do you think that there will be resistance?" Will interjected.

"The Tarn refuse to acknowledge their forces on the planet. Without intervention, their forces might continue to attack the Federation forces on Torgu-Va until they are annihilated. The *Enterprise* cannot allow its own forces to perish needlessly. However, we are in no way in a position to challenge the Tarn on the planet; to do so might very well trigger a war with the Tarn Imperial Government. Sir, I am certain the antirapprochement factor will construe a unilateral intervention as a *causa belli*. And on the other side, if we do force a unilateral cease-fire on the Federation forces down there, but do not back it up with force, we might actually trigger a bloodbath."

Picard looked around the room, and the others nodded their agreement with Janice's prediction.

"Suggestions?"

"My first thought would be to contact the Tarn government, ask them to send out a starship and help negotiate a cease-fire," Riker replied. He furrowed his brow and went on. "Of course, it could take days for them to get here. How many thousands might die while we wait?" he said, shaking his head with frustration.

The thought of one more human being, or for that matter a Tarn, dying in a senseless gutter fight of a war was sickening. It had to stop now. "Data's suggestion is still valid," Picard announced. "If we define those people down there as active members of the Fleet, we are at least entitled to make contact. If he stands on his objection with regard to contacting the Tarn, let us agree with him."

"Captain?" Will asked, for a second losing the thread of Picard's logic.

"I imagine, though, that once he learns that we will contact the Federation forces, he will be eager to let his side in on the secret as well, Prime Directive or no."

"I would agree, Captain," Riker commented. "The Federation forces must be told that our war with the Tarn, and their war with us, was resolved two hundred years ago."

Janice surveyed the men quietly, then finally said, "Their war is far from over."

Riker desperately didn't want to agree, but he already knew what she was driving at. And he had to admit, at least to himself, that the point she'd soon make had merit.

"Our comrades down there may wear the uniform, but be prepared to face a very different kind of Federation personnel. They may have actually developed a taste for war. Captain, to be blunt, I suspect you have two hundred years' worth of bred killers down there."

Picard seemed taken aback. Riker wondered

which surprised the captain more, Janice's words or the cold vehemence with which she spoke.

"Is it possible that the historian in you might be identifying too much with your subject?" Will asked quietly.

Janice looked over at Riker. "It's my job to understand that passion, Will."

Another good point. Riker decided that, from now on, he would think twice before questioning her judgment in her own area of expertise.

"Your hypothesis is noted, Dr. Eardman, and we'll discover soon enough if it is valid," Picard interjected. "But for now each second of delay might very well mean another life lost. I will overrule Karish's complaint and argue that the people down on Torgu-Va are subject to Federation recognition. I will order the Federation personnel to cease fire. Number One, you and Dr. Eardman will be the away team to meet with whoever is in charge down there. Be ready to go within the hour."

"Sir, what will you do if the Federation forces down there tell all of us to go to hell and keep on fighting?"

"First the cease-fire from our side," Picard replied. "Then we shall take the next step."

Karish waited impatiently on the bridge as Captain Picard and his three officers met in the ready room. The obvious exclusion from the private meeting was an irritation. Did the captain not trust him? He was the sole representative of the Tarn government on the site; it was his place to participate in such meetings. As it was, he had been left on the bridge and soundly reprimanded to boot! Karish rankled with the humiliation he had received.

It had been this way from the beginning: Federation diplomats dictating orders to the Tarn. Years ago, the Tarn were permitted the honor of exploring new territories, mapping out sectors of unclaimed space, attaining glory for their circle. War with the Federation was merely an extension of this. Given time, they would have triumphed, paving the way for generations of Tarn warriors to pay homage to their clan through the practice of skilled warfare. Peace with the Federation had brought an end to this. Peace, they called it. It was nothing more than the sectoring off of the Tarn into an area carefully controlled by the Federation. They referred to it as the No-Entry Zone. Its design as a neutral area to maintain peaceful negotiations was simply a façade; its true purpose, Karish believed, was to cage in their race, leaving them to police areas they already ruled and stagnate to a point in which they were reduced to fighting members of their own kind to achieve honor.

He looked back over at the Klingon, who appeared to be glaring at him. Strange, a Klingon as a lackey to the Federation. It was humiliating to contemplate. Picard had obviously whispered something to this Worf, most likely a command to befriend him, to convince him to change his path.

As he stared at him the Klingon approached.

"I had a grandsire who once had the pleasure of meeting with those of your circle."

Karish was tempted to rebuff the statement with silence, but his curiosity was aroused.

"Really?"

"Yes, at Garamora."

"My circle fought there."

"I know, it was a good fight. Much glory for both sides."

"More for ours. We won, if you remember."

Worf frowned. "That was not how the events were described to me. But nevertheless it was a good day at Garamora."

"That was when fighting was pure, not these ways now, this talk and talk and talk, then the secret slipping of a dagger into your opponent's back."

Worf looked up at the viewscreen. More data was coming in, a primitive video image of atmospheric flyers, ancient war planes powered by crude internal-combustion engines, sweeping low down a canyon. Another image, alongside, was from the high-gain tracking systems of the *Enterprise:* the images zeroed in on the planes, following them from above.

The first image, broadcast from a Tarn camera on the planet's surface, followed the planes as they swept overhead. Dark cylinders detached from the bellies of the planes, tumbling end over end, and slammed into the side of a mountain. A wall of fire splashed against the hilltop, hoarse cheers erupting from a group of Tarn standing in front of the camera. As the planes banked up and turned, a streak of gunfire bracketed one of the flyers, tearing a wing off; the plane spun out of control and slammed into a cliff.

Seconds later the camera fell, its operator shrieking and gasping as explosions erupted around him and green coils of poisonous smoke swirled out from the detonations. Data analysis on the screen clicked off the numbers of casualties for both sides, the image closing in on a group of Tarn thrashing in the clouds of chlorine gas.

"This is not war, it is genocide," Worf snapped bitterly.

"Yes, genocide for my people," Karish snarled, then barked with approval as an *Enterprise* camera closed in on yet another napalm strike hitting the mortar crew that had been firing the poison-gas shells.

"This must stop," Worf interjected.

Karish looked over at Worf with his cold, lifeless eyes.

"And who should presume to stop it?"

"You and the captain."

"Are you his lackey? Is that what he asked you to convey to me? Since when have Klingons been the boot lickers of the Federation?"

Karish said the last words loud enough so that all on the bridge could hear them. All eyes turned to Worf, who bristled.

"Tarn," Worf hissed softly, "if you were not under Federation protection, I would kill you where you stand for speaking such dishonorable words. No Klingon is a servant of the Federation. We are allies and equals."

"Any time, Klingon, I could spill your guts out here and now," Karish replied, touching the ceremonial blade dangling from his belt.

The two stood silent for a moment, glaring at each other.

"Honor forbids it," Worf replied.

"What, a Klingon afraid of a fight?" Karish shot back, again speaking loud enough so that all could hear.

"I am never afraid of a worthy fight." He hesitated for an instant and lowered his voice to a soft whisper, "But you do not offer a challenge. I could split you open with a flick of my finger if I so desired it."

"Oh, it is only worthy when your master Picard tells you it is. You hide behind words and your hairless Federation overseer."

Worf's gaze swept the room. He could see several half smiles over the reference to Picard as hairless, but the smiles died under his withering glance.

"He is not my master. He is my commander through oath and through the honor and respect he has earned in my eyes. Thus I follow his orders,

Karish. I would die for him, as I am certain he would die for me. That is the bond between Klingon and Federation. Learn that lesson, Tarn, and you will understand why Klingons and the Federation are allied now. And if it is war you wish, realize that in that bond is the strength of the Federation you so foolishly wish to fight."

He smiled softly. "And if it is war, know that we Klingons will be there for the kill. Our blades will glitter with the blood of Tarns."

Worf turned to see Picard coming back into the room. The captain's gaze was fixed on the viewscreen, but it was obvious that he had overheard the last statement and was curious.

The return of Picard, followed by his lackeys, interrupted Karish's retort to the Klingon's challenge. Too bad; he had actually been enjoying himself. The ritual of word challenge was a time-honored one and had been the first fitting diversion since his arrival aboard ship. He saw a quick look pass between Picard and Worf, the Klingon shaking his head and growling something unintelligible. Picard walked past the Klingon and approached.

"Mr. Karish," Picard began. "We will attempt to make contact with the Federation forces on Torgu-Va."

"I have already voiced my protest to this," Karish cried angrily. "I believe it to be a violation of your own Federation rules."

"Mr. Data, would you please repeat for Commander Karish the ruling you cited to me?"

Data reviewed the decision regarding the Magellanic Cloud expedition, then threw in a couple of other similar cases for good measure.

Karish could feel Picard's gaze of triumph.

"As officers, enlisted men and women who are direct descendants of Starfleet personnel and who currently wear the uniform of that organization," he replied calmly, "the people down on Torgu-Va are technically a part of the jurisdiction of the standing Federation. It is, therefore, our prerogative to initiate a line of communication. In no way whatsoever does the Prime Directive apply to them."

The Tarn bristled. "And the broken circle of Tarn, your rule does not apply to them?"

"Commander Karish, I am not denying to you in any way whatsoever the right to contact them. What you choose to do with the Tarn forces is up to you and your government. You may inform your leaders that we will be sending an away team to the planet. If you wish, Data will open a secured channel for you so that you may send your message in private. I will wait until you have done so before sending my own report back to Starfleet."

"I can see that there is nothing I can do to change this," Karish said.

"Commander Karish, you are correct on that assumption," Picard replied, a smile creasing his features. Karish had been briefed that the human tendency to smile was a complex one, and was not merely a showing of teeth as an indicator of hostility. Yet he sensed a mocking hostility in the smile and he wondered if there was blood challenge.

"Picard. I must speak with you."

"You are never denied that right, Mr. Karish."

"Now. In private, away from these." At this, he extended his taloned hand in a sweeping motion, disdainfully noting the various ensigns and officers present on the bridge.

Picard compressed his thin, soft human lips and replied, "This way, Mr. Karish."

The two entered the captain's private office, Picard turning on Karish as the door closed behind them.

"Yes, Mr. Karish?"

"I object to this decision, Picard."

"Yes, I had supposed you might."

"Well, what do you plan on doing?"

Picard fixed Karish with an intent gaze.

"I know you don't care for me, my crew, this ship, and the entire Federation," Picard replied. "I can, in fact, accept that. But what I cannot accept on this ship is rudeness. You were greeted with full honors, we went out of our way in our attempt to make you feel comfortable, yet you feel free to insult my crew, and myself, in public."

"Insult?"

"Data is a member of this crew, he is not a 'talking machine' as you put it. On more than one occasion his friends have risked their lives to save him. Second, I am captain of this ship, and when you address me, at least in public, I expect to be called Captain."

Karish found the moment interesting, the hairless one acting like the leader of a circle, asserting control. He was tempted to accept challenge but then, remembering his own orders, finally lowered his head.

"What do you plan on doing . . . Captain?"

"Precisely what I indicated on the bridge. A landing parting will leave the *Enterprise* sometime this evening. I would do it immediately in order to try and stop the fighting but I will grant you time to contact your government before proceeding." Another useless show of courtesy. Another sign of human weakness. Karish knew the situation was too serious for Picard to offer up some sort of frivolous joke, but his offer was too absurd to be taken any other way.

Karish exhaled slowly and began to explain in a tone he usually reserved for very young, very dim-witted hatchlings.

"Our government will have nothing to do with the Tarn on the planet. They are *obduli* . . . outcasts from their race. They have brought shame upon their circle by falling from power. They are not to be considered Tarn."

"But if they decide upon peace, they will not have lost."

"Their very presence on Torgu-Va is proof of their defeat. They should have annihilated Murat's forces two hundred years ago."

"And so the descendants of an ancient battle are to wear the stigma of defeat forever? The Tarn who fight now on Torgu-Va had nothing to do with Murat's battle." Karish stared at Picard for a moment. Truly, had this man absolutely no notion of honor?

"It is their duty, as members of the Katula circle, to make it their battle."

"And if they do not? If peace is negotiated instead?"

"Unless they destroy the Federation forces, Captain, they are of little consequence to the Tarn government. They would be better off dead, rotting as partial atonement for their dishonor. There are but two conditions in war, Captain, return with victory or die."

"So, if the Tarn government will not recognize the Tarn on Torgu-Va, there should be little problem with our contacting them," Picard interjected hurriedly, seeing an opening. "It should be no concern of theirs what move we take with individuals they do not consider to be Tarn."

Karish grunted, a chesty sound that resembled one choking on his own fluids.

"You attempt to cleverly manipulate your way into an advantage, Captain. A wise maneuver. It will not work, however. Members of the anti-Federation faction will interpret your actions of intervention negatively, regardless of how adroitly you disguise them."

"But if you were a part of a landing party to the planet, a Tarn representative to the Tarn forces, neither party could misinterpret the situation. The ruling party would herald your attempts at peace-making, the anti-Federation party would be appeased knowing that one as hesitant as you concerning open negotiations were to be in charge of an away party. They would feel that their interests were being protected by your presence."

Picard had boxed him in and there was no way out.

"The purpose of such a mission?" Karish asked skeptically.

"Simply to ascertain the condition and progress of the Tarn forces on the planet. And, of course, to inform them of present conditions between the Federation and the Tarn, including our strong suggestion to the Federation personnel on the planet to cease all hostile actions immediately."

"Who would accompany me on such a journey?"

Picard hesitated. He was tempted to send Worf if for no other reason than to keep an eye on Karish, but given the xenophobia of the Tarn, anyone not of their race might trigger a violent reaction the instant they were sighted.

"You shall go alone."

Karish was silent, then finally nodded. "It is an interesting proposal, Captain. I agree to go. I must state again that I still advise you against such action. However, as my position would indicate, I will serve as an ambassador in this confrontation."

Picard nodded, and once again showed his teeth in what Karish could only assume was some sort of victory grimace.

"Very well, Mr. Karish. I take it then that I can expect your cooperation in ending the warfare."

Karish nodded, again saying nothing. He was not sure how much longer he could withstand viewing this insufferable human's smug face.

"Mr. Data will arrange a communications link to the Tarn forces down on the planet. I will leave it to you to inform them of our presence, the current political situation, and our suggestion to the Federation forces to cease hostility."

"Yes, that is acceptable," Karish replied.

"Fine then," Picard replied hurriedly. "Once that is accomplished, prepare to depart. Our supply officer will draw whatever equipment you deem necessary, including a phaser. You and the other away team will beam down simultaneously."

Karish inclined his head gruffly. He found taking orders from a human particularly repulsive. His plans, however, were best served by playing the part of reluctant agreement for the moment. There was time enough for other things later.

Chapter Four

THERE WERE NINE STEPS to the top of the platform. The man took them slowly, ascending methodically, laboriously, though gaining energy, as if, with each step, he shed years of responsibility and toil from his body like an old snake skin. A gathering of nearly ten thousand was assembled in front of the platform: women with tired looks and bodies that seemed drawn to the ground, the product of too many children housed in the womb and too many tiny fingers continually pulling on skirts and breasts and arms; men with sinuous frames, eyes glassy hard, hands molded and callused by a gun stock or digging pick; and the elderly and small children seated on the ground, weaving a tapestry of seashell pink and withered gray against the earth.

As he cleared the final stair, the crowd reared up with a single shout, a thunderous roar that echoed and reechoed through the vast underground caverns. He raised his arm, sweeping back a lock of black hair speckled with gray before saluting his people.

Walking to the edge of the platform, he made his address:

"This morning when you awoke, what was your first thought? . . . Note it. When you left your homes, making your way to your stations, what new impressions crossed your mind? . . . Remember them. . . . Every nuance, every detail of this day is to be harbored in your souls for all time. For on this day, my people, we have gained victory over the Tarn."

His words jolted the crowd like an aftershock. Emotions, surprise, disbelief, pathetic appeals for hope, rippled across the faces of those who, moments before, had worn expressions of cured concrete resigned to the fact that the race of two hundred years had been lost, that they would perish in the final apocalypse.

"Yesterday's attack brought desolation; today we find redemption. . . . The Federation lives!"

There was a moment of silence and he realized that their motto, which had carried them down through the generations, was now seen as a desperate last cry.

He smiled and pointed upward toward the rough rock ceiling, then raised his hand further still.

"Above us, my warriors, my comrades. Above us. At this very moment a starship is in orbit above this world; a ship that voyages across the endless heavens has descended as our redeemer. We have kept the faith, and our faith has been answered . . . the Federation has returned!"

It took a moment for the reality of his words to sink in. Smiling, he nodded reassuringly, showing that this was not some religious trick, a promise of final redemption to those standing at the door of death. Rather, it was a clear and solid reality.

A ripple of excitement swept throughout the assembly. There were gasps of astonishment, disbelief.

"At the beginning of the last watch a message was received from a Federation ship orbiting this planet. They are here! You have lived to see the fulfillment of prophecy, the Deliverance from Evil. The Day has come!"

Wild shouts now erupted; hardened warriors bowed their heads, tears in their eyes; women grasped their children, who, but hours before, they had assumed would face death in the final assault of the Tarn.

"'Away all landing craft, away!' The command is echoing yet again in the corridors of a great ship that goes in harm's way. And it shall be as it once was, assault troops swooping out of the heavens from which we fell so long ago, falling upon our enemies, who shall tremble and wail with despair."

He lowered his head, as if in a prayer of thanksgiving for the day of deliverance. The room fell silent and then he looked up again.

"I see so well those days," he whispered. "Warriors marching to their landing craft . . . and the weapons they will carry!"

He held up his own gun, battered and worn.

"Phasers, chain guns, multiple-burst lasers. These they shall bring and put into our hands and we shall drive the Tarn before us, and rather than the cries of our young, it shall be their lamentations that we shall hear!"

Men before him held up their weapons in salute, roaring to be led into battle.

Tears streaming down his face, he held his own gun aloft in reply.

"Long live the Federation!"

Picard anxiously scanned the faces of the two away teams. Riker was accustomed to these kinds of missions, but it was evident that Dr. Eardman was filled with excited anticipation, while as for Karish, as ever the Tarn was an enigma.

This will not be easy, he thought as he looked over at Karish, wondering about the nature of the exchange between him and the Tarn leader down on the planet. He was annoyed with himself for almost giving in to the temptation to run the conversation through the computer for translation rather than purge it out of the system in accordance with his agreement of security. Something wasn't right, but he had to let the game go forward. What was more troubling, though, was the reaction of the Federation forces down below.

The Federation side had initially been filled with exultation, calling on the *Enterprise* to annihilate the Tarn. Picard had briefly wrestled with the notion of simply telling them the war was over, but then felt that such information was best conveyed face-to-face. The announcement that an away team was coming down, to discuss the situation further, had caused a wary reaction from the commander down below, Lysander Murat, who claimed to be a descendant of the captain of the *Verdun*.

On the Tarn side . . . that was a complete mystery.

"You all know your missions, now be careful," Picard said. A protective instinct always took hold whenever he sent someone into a doubtful situation. He nodded to Ensign Eddies. An instant later they were gone. When the last of the beams faded, Eddies looked up nervously at Picard.

"Captain, one of the targeting scanners is acting up again."

"Did they get down all right?" Picard asked, barely able to contain his anxiety.

"Yes, sir, but the system is down."

"Then fix it, Eddies, and fix it right this time."

Picard stalked out of the transporter room with yet one more thing to worry about.

Riker's first sight of the surface of Torgu-Va came in the early hours of twilight. The land was desolate. Miles of dry, raw acres lay prey to an abrasive wind that swept eastward from the mountains, ravaging all that lay in its path. The wind, fierce enough to challenge the balance of both Riker and Eardman, instantly wicked away the slightest drop of moisture. The searing blasts felt as if they were coming from a furnace as the wind howled down out of the ragged range of mountains that stretched to the sky like shards of glass.

Several miles to the east, a muddy stream ran in the shadow of the mountain range. Its spidery trail stretched thinly, woven into the contours of the valley as finely as a thread. The combination of arid soil and harsh wind left the trees emaciated, limbs blackened, leaves folded and lifeless. Their bows bent harshly to the left in continual submission to the elements. Other forms of vegetation were sparsely scattered across the landscape, hidden for the most part within crevices of rock and shade. All carried the disfigured bend to the west; all appeared parched.

Torgu-Va, on first impression, had a certain Dante-esque quality to it. Riker tried to remember which sin would cause someone to be cast into such a place. It was a land devoid of hope.

"No reception committee," he announced, carefully scanning the area around them while holding up his tricorder. He finally motioned off to the valley.

"There, do you see it?"

Janice shaded her eyes from the blazing sunlight and looked toward where he was pointing and shook her head.

"It's an opening, a tunnel."

He started down the rocky slope and she moved up alongside him. The air was rarefied, reminding him of the first day out on ski trips to the Rockies where, after a ten-minute run, you panted for a half-hour. Of course, the difference was that this air was roughly seventy degrees Celsius warmer.

"It's definitely an entrance to something," Riker announced, holding his tricorder back up.

"These are the coordinates they gave us?"

Riker checked his tricorder again.

"This is it."

"I don't get it. If they are hiding from the Tarn, why not a set of blast doors, a camouflaged entrance? It seems as if anyone has an open invitation to stroll on in."

Riker studied the entryway, then scanned the horizon before glancing back at Janice. "An open invitation. Maybe that's the point. Set your phaser on stun."

The two approached the tunnel, Riker leading

the way toward the black enclosure. As they entered the opening, they were immediately drenched in darkness. A chill tickled at the base of his neck. "A bit cooler in here," Janice whispered.

Riker ignored her comments. The two advanced farther into the tunnel, the light behind them receding far too rapidly for his comfort.

"Perhaps we should . . ."

Riker's hand shot up in the air, interrupting her suggestion. He strained his ear for a moment, struggling to distinguish a sound in the distance. "Our welcoming committee," he stated quietly.

What gave them away was not sight or sound, but rather the smell, the cloying stench of unwashed bodies. He slowed to a stop. Janice almost bumped into him. He knew she smelled it as well, and together they stood waiting.

"Identify!" A voice barked to the left of the two officers, shattering the silence.

"I am Commander William Riker of the *U.S.S. Enterprise* and this is Dr. Janice Eardman. We are here to contact the Federation forces on Torgu-Va."

"Ship identification number?"

"U.S.S. Enterprise NCC-1701-D, ancestor of the *Verdun."*

There was a quick flicker of red light that blinded him as it shined in his face, shimmered on Janice, then flicked off again.

Silence followed Riker's reply, agonizing silence.

He held his breath; his ears strained to determine where exactly the voice had come from. Silence, and then the quietest of whispers: "My God, it's true then, you're here."

Before Riker and Janice could locate the direction of this new voice, light began to weed its way through the darkness. A moment later, the corridor was dimly illuminated by a covered lantern emitting a pale red light revealing eight men encircling the two officers no more than two meters away, weapons still poised.

"Commander Riker of the *U.S.S. Enterprise?*" a man in his late teens reiterated, as if still doubtful. His head moved quickly, glancing from the eyes of Riker and Eardman to the left, to the passageway behind them, before again addressing the away team. He seemed nervous, on edge.

His uniform was indeed Federation. The boy was dressed in the dark, desert camouflage pattern of an old Federation branch of service long since out of existence. An old-style bullet-firing assault rifle was poised lightly in his hands. The weapon caught Riker's eye for a second. As something of an aficionado of antique weapons, he had to fight down the absurd urge to ask the boy if he could try the gun out.

The boy was burdened down with battle webbing, from which hung ammunition pouches, several canteens, and half a dozen round objects, which Riker took to be ancient fragmentation grenades. Most remarkably, the kid was carrying a primitive knife; an actual bayonet, Riker suddenly realized.

On his helmet, Will noticed a single vertical black stripe, and he ventured a guess.

"Yes, Lieutenant. Commander Riker of the Federation ship *U.S.S. Enterprise.*"

The boy snapped to attention and to Riker's confusion offered an old-fashioned hand salute. What was even more disconcerting, though, was the fact that the boy was crying.

Riker drew to attention and calmly returned the salute.

"It is the Day! The Day!" a voice from the rear of the group whispered.

"Sir. Welcome to Federation Battle Station Torgu-Va, sir," the boy stuttered, struggling to control his voice. "We are . . . well, we are thrilled to have you."

The small group murmured agreement, nodding among themselves. Riker couldn't recall a time in which he had been greeted with such naked appreciation.

The tonal inflections were subtly different, the military style of address and greeting archaic and touching.

"Silence! Officer on deck!" the lieutenant barked, and the group came to attention and snapped off salutes. Following Janice's lead, Riker came back to attention and offered the same hand salute to them as well.

There was an awkward moment of silence as the group before them stood in rigid formation.

Janice drew close to Riker and whispered, "Stand, at ease."

He nodded and gave the command.

The group responded with sharp precision to his order, left foot stamping the ground, hands going behind their backs.

"Relax, soldiers," Janice announced.

Excited whispers broke out.

"You really from the *Enterprise?*" a woman's voice called from the group.

The lieutenant looked over his shoulder.

"Miller, no talking in the ranks."

"Sorry, sir."

The lieutenant looked back, embarrassed.

"Yes," Riker announced with a smile, "the *Enterprise.*"

"I heard it's as big as the old *Verdun,*" the lieutenant finally asked, unable to hide his boyish enthusiasm.

"That was the old Constitution-class *Enterprise.* We're up to the Galaxy class now, just a bit bigger."

Heads bobbed up and down, grins creasing dirt-stained faces, several of them whispering about the "Galaxy-class" and speculating on the tonnage.

"I know you all have a lot of questions," Riker said, "but my captain's ordered me to report directly to your commander. Perhaps afterward we can get together to talk."

The lieutenant, called back to his duty by Riker's gentle prodding, came to attention.

"Yes, sir. Right this way, sir. Miller, point, Kochanski rear cover, Fenderson move ahead to deactivate mine systems three through six, then reactivate once the rest of the party's passed."

The lieutenant then hesitated, looking over curiously at Riker.

"Sir?"

"Yes, Lieutenant?"

"Where are the others?"

"Others?"

"The assault troops. Your heavy-weapons units, the landing craft? I was told that an away team was coming in to land."

Janice stepped forward slightly.

"We're the advance recon team," she said quietly.

"Oh, of course. Right this way."

Janice shot a quick glance at Riker, who looked as if he was about to say something. He paused a moment, returning Janice's look of worry, before deciding to remain silent. The two followed the lieutenant and his squad through a labyrinth of rough-hewn corridors. Each turn they made was followed by another until they had no idea where they were headed, or which direction they had come from. Occasionally, the lieutenant would call out a whistle of sorts that had an odd resemblance to the sound of a bat in flight. A hundred meters later, the group would come upon a small band of men and women, clutching their weapons with looks of joy on their faces. Each time they met with another group the reaction was the same, the point of interest was the same; the Federation fighters stared at Riker and Eardman with greedy looks, fearful that they would disappear more quickly than a mirage in the heat.

Will only broke the silence once, holding up his tricorder for Janice to see in the dim light.

"We've lost up- and downlink with *Enterprise.*"

"We must be going deep, you can feel the air, it's cooler, damper."

"Still, there must be a high lead content in the soil. I don't like this."

After nearly a mile, the lieutenant led the party through one last passageway into a large room, at the end of which stood three men guarding a set of steel blast doors.

"Lieutenant?" the man stationed farthest to the right questioned.

"We have an appointment with Commander Murat, Sergeant."

"Yes, sir. He'll be expecting you, I'm sure." The sergeant grinned recklessly, stepping aside to allow the party through the opening blast doors.

"Your blast doors, Doctor," Will whispered to Janice as they entered the doorway. Janice raised an eyebrow in acknowledgment.

Will could not help but admire just how cunning

the defenses were. If anything, these people wanted the Tarn to come down below, then to get lost in the maze of tunnels.

Janice turned to examine the blast doors more closely as they passed through. The doors were primitive, old-fashioned steel, no plasta lamination. In a small niche next to the doors a woman sat hunched over a glowing green screen. Janice and Will both slowed as they passed her.

It was hard to tell her age. Will sensed that the woman was in her early, maybe mid-twenties, but somehow she seemed older, lines already creasing her features, which looked deathlike in the light of the glowing screen.

A radar screen, he realized, standard radio frequency system. The technology of the *Verdun* was a hundred years beyond that. The survivors must have lost ground and only now, two hundred years later, were moving into late-twentieth- or early-twenty-first-century technology.

The lieutenant paused and looked at the woman. She raised her head.

"Area where they landed is still clear," she announced. "Watch Station Zebra reports a Tarn patrol of platoon strength is heading in their direction, but not in range. Battle group Carnelli is maneuvering to engage."

"Good. And the landing craft?"

"Nothing, sir. Maybe they have some sort of shielding."

Will knew that they were talking about landing craft from the *Enterprise*. Beaming technology was still new when the first *Verdun* ventured out into the unknown. It was still risky, and inappropriate for any type of large-scale landings. Assault transports therefore carried space-to-surface attack ships capable of carrying several hundred troops apiece. That's what they were waiting for, and it was a troubling realization. Picard had been careful in his statement that they were simply sending down an away team.

As they entered through the doors, the lieutenant's men left their handheld lights with the men on guard, the doors sliding shut behind them with a hollow menacing boom. A dim light glowed from a turn in the corridor ahead as they stepped into the next tunnel. Riker looked over at Janice and smiled. "Welcome to the past," he whispered.

Janice Eardman paused, struggling momentarily for control, her nose tingling from the myriad of scents. The primary one was the overpowering stench of unwashed bodies, the air so thick with the smell as one of the soldiers walked past her that she struggled to suppress a gag. There were other strange smells as well: leather, gun oil, a faint whiff of cordite, and a garlicky scent as the lieutenant exhaled nearby. History, she realized, was not clean.

"After you, Doctor," Will offered as they moved

through a press of soldiers lining either side of the corridor. It was apparent that they had just come back from some sort of combat mission; many of them were slumped against the corridor walls, exhausted, pale faces drawn. Several were asleep, others were eating a pasty-looking concoction out of battered iron pots, while yet others were hard at work cleaning their assault guns. More than one had a bloody bandage wrapped around a limb or forehead, and shockingly, there were half a dozen bodies lying in a narrow alcove, camouflaged ponchos covered the broken remains.

Even the wounded struggled to come to their feet at the approach of the party, and Will's right hand was almost constantly to his forehead, returning salutes, a buzz of voices whispering behind them as they passed.

"How did you construct all this?" Will asked of their lieutenant.

"We dug it ourselves," came the reply. "Still digging—everyone. Even our elite combat teams still give a day of the week to the making of space."

"By hand?"

"What else?"

"Murat must have been hard-pressed to get the first level built," Riker suggested.

"When the Elder Ones came to Torgu-Va they thought they were the only survivors. Going underground was an escape from the heat and background radiation, not from the Tarn. This area is limestone close to the surface but the underlying strata is granite, thus we can't get down too far."

"And the Tarn?"

"They touched down several hundred kilometers away, but neither side knew where the other was. It was nearly twenty years before we stumbled into each other. They found a scouting team of ours surveying an area fifty kilometers west of here. The damn lizards waited until the team had fallen asleep and slaughtered the group."

"Thus beginning your war?"

"Our war? You mean the Federation's war, of course. We are merely doing our duty, as are you. The Tarn started this damned war long before the scouting-team incident, long before the *Verdun.*"

Janice thought of the scouting team. This one incident had sparked a renewal of a conflict that would last for centuries.

"Food supply," Riker asked. "How do you feed yourselves?"

"We harvest the Garthin cactus up on the surface." The lieutenant fingered the sleeve of his uniform.

"The fibers make our clothes, the pulp inside is ground into flour. We can even make a rather potent brew out of it," he added, and the rest of the group chuckled.

"We also grow food in caverns below, now that we have electric lights. We generate the power from geothermal springs. And iron, this is rich ground for iron. We also use caves, the droppings from a type of bat found there we refine for the nitrates."

"Nitrates?" Riker asked.

"Explosives," Janice replied.

"How many Tarn have you slaughtered?" the lieutenant asked Riker, his guard slipping as curiosity took hold. "To be a commander, you must be a good killer."

Riker hesitated. "Yes, I've killed," he finally replied.

The lieutenant nodded eagerly.

"Tell us."

Janice could see that Will wasn't sure how to respond and was grateful when they reached yet another set of blast doors. Their arrival at this destination cut the conversation short as they went through the ritual of clearances before passing to the other side.

"Tight security," Janice whispered.

"We lost Delta Seven two months ago to a Tarn ground-assault unit. Near as we can figure, they gained the primary entry, forced a traitor to punch the proper security numbers in. Once down in the lower level they burst through the door and held it till more assault forces came down. It was a massacre, nearly three thousand died."

"Traitor?" Will asked.

"She talked, didn't she?" the lieutenant said disdainfully.

"But most likely they tortured her," Janice replied.

"The Federation Code of Conduct expressly forbids revealing information, no matter what the scum do to you. Her spouse committed suicide to atone for the dishonor; their children's names were changed and they were given to other families."

Will was about to speak but a light touch on his arm from Janice stilled him.

The tunnel went through a series of dogleg turns.

"Blast deflections," Will said softly while Janice nodded up to the ceiling. Rows of sharpened sticks, mounted on iron beams, were suspended overhead. The lieutenant, noticing what they were looking at, smiled.

"Does it meet with your approval, sir?"

"What?"

"Our defensive systems. You can't see it, but there's a crawl space above the ceiling. See those pipes jutting out? They're connected to vats of acid or boiling water diverted from the geothermal springs. All a child needs to do is crawl up there, turn a valve, and we melt some Tarn. Wonderful when we catch them like that."

"Charming," Janice said softly, the defenses reminding her of something from the Dark Ages.

"Early in our war it was often hand-to-hand, raiding parties striking each other's shelters. Those were glorious days."

The sharp turns finally ended. There was one last barrier, a sliding steel door which slid back at their approach. The sight before them was overwhelming, the street widening out into an underground city. It seemed as if the entire populace was out to greet them, and the crowd surged forward at their approach.

Janice could not help but smile, feeling as if she were a general returning in triumph to some ancient city. The crowd thronged around them, shouting questions, laughing, reaching out to touch them. The first impression of an ancient triumph hit her even harder as she tried to press down the street. The reality of living in a technological society was the norm of her life. The air was washed clean, clothes were clean, finely cut, individually tailored by laser-scan fitting. Diets were finely tuned to meet the metabolic needs of each individual and, above all else, people were clean.

She was all but overwhelmed by the harsh smells of unwashed bodies, stale air, oil and leather. The faces were different as well, extremely pale, drawn, looking as if all lived just a step away from starvation. All of the clothing had an early-Federation air to it. The weave of the fabric was coarse and the cut of tunics and trousers was straight out of Federation manuals from two hundred years ago. The vast majority wore the combat fatigue uniform of the old marine-assault units, but here and there in the crowd she spotted the old red of engineering, yellow of command, blue of medical, pale gray jumpers of enlisted personnel with trousers tucked into leather boots. Even the children were dressed according to regulation standards. She was glad to see, though, that the absurd microskirts and black stockings for female personnel had been abandoned for the more practical standard-issue trousers worn by the men.

The ceiling of the tunnel was cut high; it reached more than twenty feet up. Apartments were carved straight into the walls, with narrow doorways, windows that were just simple openings lining the upper level, all of them crowded with spectators, leaning out, shouting, pointing. She noticed how each of the entry doors had a plaque, inscribed with names, hanging from nails. She paused to look at one . . . Karuna, Ashobi, Gunnery Sergeant, Company C, Fourth Assault Battalion, Active Reserve, Legion of Merit, Five Kills, Wife Corporal Akiko, One Kill, Seven Children.

As she paused to read the plaque she heard a clicking of heels. Looking to the doorway, she saw a bent-over man, struggling to stand erect. He saluted with his left hand and she was surprised for a second until she realized that Gunnery Sergeant Ashobi Karuna had no right arm. My God, she thought, they don't even have regeneration or synthetic replacements!

Solemnly, she returned the salute.

"Are the landing craft here, sir?" Sergeant Karuna asked.

"Not yet," she replied. Then, embarrassed by her half-truth, she moved on, catching up to Will.

How old was Karuna, she wondered—bent with injuries, missing an arm, yet still on active reserve.

Yet again it was hard to tell age. She could see an

occasional flush of young beauty, usually in girls she suspected were into their first bloom of womanhood. The women who struck her as being nineteen and twenty, most of them were either pregnant or already carrying a young child. She wondered if Data's assumption concerning reproduction rates was, in fact, far too conservative.

Women who she assumed were in their late twenties already looked as if they were forty, teeth missing, hair dull. And as for the elderly, when she looked around she saw precious few.

Their lieutenant was having a hard time holding the crowds back. Embarrassed, he looked at Will, who was smiling, nodding, shaking hands as if he were a politician on a walking tour of a friendly city.

"This is outrageous," the lieutenant hissed. "I'm sorry for the breakdown in discipline."

"It's all right," Will laughed.

Janice smiled, remembering back to the Academy and how Will had indulged her in several holodeck walking tours of ancient times. One evening, to her surprise, Will had insisted that they actually do Rome rather than what was already his favorite, film-noir San Francisco. Once in the holodeck she had understood why. Will had reprogrammed it so that he was a Roman general returning in triumph. He had roared with childlike delight as they rode a chariot, the multitudes cheering him wildly. And as for the scantily clad slave girls parading on either side of the chariot, that had been the cause of their first serious fight. It had also resulted in Will being called in by the counselor for a talk to consider if he might be suffering from delusions of grandeur. It had taken all his charm to explain that it was just a simple evening of fun with his date who was a history major. It was the last time they had visited Rome.

She saw a bit of that delight now as the crowd cheered him on, heralding him as a triumphal savior. To her confusion, it kindled a warmth that she had been struggling to control ever since her arrival on the *Enterprise*.

The street finally broadened out into a small plaza, the rough stone floor giving way to a polished surface. A formal-looking delegation stood in the middle of the plaza, each member dressed in the yellow uniform of command.

Janice knew Commander Lysander Murat at once. Whereas the majority of the delegation stood at attention, backs ramrod straight, Murat paced slowly, staring at the ceiling. Five steps down the length of the plaza center, a clipped, sterile turn, and then the same five steps back. The motion was repeated several times while Janice and the escort team made their way toward the area. The man she observed was not what she had expected, and yet Janice was sure that this was the leader of the forces on Torgu-Va. He was short, or at least shorter than she had pictured him. He had heavy shoulders and black wavy hair that came together in a low widow's peak just above his bushy eyebrows. His movements, from what she could glean as she approached, were not fluid with the grace that comes from acknowledged prestige, or vicious, like a tyrant's, but rather stealthy; he moved like a street fighter.

His concentration appeared undisturbed. It was not until the group had nearly reached the plaza center that he turned, focusing his attention on the Federation officers.

As she and Will approached, the throng grew quiet and drew back. A command echoed across the plaza.

"Ship's company, attention!"

Instant silence reigned, broken only by the echo of a thousand heels clicking together. Will slowed and came to a stop half a dozen feet away from the line of officers.

"In the middle, salute first," Janice whispered, feeling all the while like a director of protocol advising someone who wasn't quite sure whom he was meeting.

Will stopped, came to attention, and offered the old-style salute.

"Commander Will Riker, Federation starship *Enterprise,* sir."

The man stepped forward and Janice felt as if she actually recognized him.

"Captain Lysander Murat, Federation ship *Verdun,* welcome aboard, sir."

At his words a loud cheer erupted.

"The Day of Deliverance!" Janice heard repeated from hundreds of voices. The way it was said seemed to have a ritual overtone to it, and to her surprise she saw more than one soldier drawing a bayonet from his or her belt and holding it aloft. The sight was chilling. She stepped behind Will and waited for him to take over.

Several seconds passed while Murat and Riker stared at each other—Riker curious, patient; Murat with the look of a convict just set free, hesitating behind the gate, pondering whether to step with confidence into the free world or to bolt. Were it not for the jaw muscle working steadily on the face of Murat, Riker would have thought the man was indifferent to the situation, so still was his form. He uttered nothing, neither moved nor flinched; even his ice blue eyes remained steady. All was a study in intensity, save the slight flinching of his jaw. Finally, he spoke.

"You came. My God, you finally came. We're going to win after all."

Riker felt a sudden rush of anxiety. He had been prepared for an onslaught of excitement, fully ready to stifle the cries of joy with a pragmatic excuse that his hands were tied. The Federation was not here to fight this war. But Murat's response was steeped in the intensity of the desperate; it was a bleak cry of need.

"This is Dr. Janice Eardman," Riker finally interjected, motioning to her.

"A medical doctor," Lysander said. "Good

heavens, we need your help. We have the texts stored away, but the ability to use many of them . . ." His voice trailed off.

"Our medical team will be down shortly," Riker said. Then he hesitated, wondering if their true mission might be seen as patronizing. "Dr. Eardman is a specialist on the war with the Tarn, among other things."

"A tactician, good, my staff will want to meet with you."

"There are other things first," Riker said.

"Yes . . . yes, of course. It's just that it's difficult to take in that, well . . . you came."

Lysander lowered his head.

Before Riker could reply Lysander continued, "When we received your captain's message we thought it was the Tarn. We have intelligence that they've been experimenting with frequency masking and naturally thought this was a ploy to ascertain our whereabouts if we replied. In the last ten years nearly half our bases have been destroyed and we thought they were looking now for targeting acquisition for their atomic weapons. You will forgive my men if they seemed at all wary upon greeting you. Every precaution had to be taken, you see."

"Of course."

"I have made the necessary arrangements. We can support nearly three thousand troops immediately. Rations are stockpiled, so you can use the additional transport space for munitions. We think we know where their nuclear production capabilities are located, but it's heavily fortified and below the surface. I assume your captain will want to hit there first. Antimatter space-to-surface penetrators should take them out, but a lot of this fight will still be old-fashioned ground action."

Riker furrowed his brow slightly.

"Phasers. Do you have surface-to-space phasers? A battery of those would neutralize their air power. And atmosphere ramjet interceptors, just a dozen, even a half-dozen, would sweep the skies. We've only dreamed of such weapons and now we'll have them. Once we get air superiority we can annihilate the rest of them." His voice was filled with excitement, as if he were a child sharing a Christmas wish list.

"Just to get my hands on a Falcon interceptor. I've seen their specs in the memory downloads. Guess they're outdated now, aren't they?" he said, shaking his head.

"I can't wait to see the weapons you have. We're both fighting with prop-driven planes. Thank God we had some specs on old twentieth-century aircraft in our files, at least the Mustangs we're making now are a match for anything the damn Tarn here have built, it's just that we don't have anywhere near enough of them." And he laughed as if embarrassed to reveal the primitiveness of their weaponry.

"Is there somewhere we could talk, Captain? Privately."

"What am I talking about?" Lysander continued. "We have command of space now that you're here. We'll upload the coordinates of their bases and you can take care of them all right now!"

Cheering erupted at his announcement.

"Though, we do ask that you not finish them. Our honor demands that we do that with our own hands. Honor and revenge demand it!"

"Captain, we need to talk first," Riker said quietly.

Lysander Murat seemed taken aback, surprised at such a request; then, with dawning understanding, he nodded his head curtly.

"Security, of course. This way, Commander Riker."

The two men and Janice left the pavilion and made their way toward a narrow building five hundred meters down the level's main artery. They entered a room constructed of a rough stucco and mortar mix, with a low ceiling and no windows.

Lysander took an earthenware jug down from a corner cabinet, uncorked it, and put three mugs on the table. Pouring out drinks, he held his mug up.

"To the Federation and death to the Tarn."

He downed the mug. Riker hesitated and Lysander looked over at him cautiously.

"To the Federation," Janice replied. Riker followed her lead, delighted with the burning punch the drink delivered. He stopped after the first sip, though, suspecting that the brew was easily a hundred and twenty proof. Now was not the time to cloud his thinking.

"When do you start unloading troops?" Murat grinned, warming the chill that seemed to linger perpetually in his eye. "It's your call, gentlemen."

"Captain, the *Enterprise* is not a combat transport," Janice said. "We have no ground troops on board."

There was a moment of silence.

"Don't tell me you're just a survey ship."

"We are a heavy cruiser, Captain, but we carry no ground-assault troops."

"So you must be escorting transports then."

Riker hesitated, looking over to Janice for support. She nodded and he took a deep breath. It was amazing how the personnel down here so completely misunderstood the nature of this contact. Now was the time to break the bubble.

"Sir, I think you misinterpreted the communication from our captain."

"How so?"

"Captain, the war is over," Riker announced quietly.

There was a long moment of silence, and Riker pressed in.

"Sir, the war between the Federation and the Tarn is over. It was resolved two hundred years ago."

Lysander Murat stood immobile. His face wore the bland expression of a man who waits patiently for someone who has made a mistake to quickly turn around and rectify it.

"I'm afraid you are mistaken, Commander Riker. Less than twenty-four hours ago I lost one of our main underground cities to an atomic weapon, more than eight thousand dead or dying at last count. Even now we are dealing with a strike on one of our primary outposts just half a dozen kilometers from here; you saw some of the troops engaged in that fight on the way in. The Tarn have the bomb and used it without hesitation, and we shall respond. No, sir, the war is not over yet by a long shot."

Riker sighed and took another sip of his drink before continuing.

"Sir, two hundred and two years ago the Federation and the Tarn entered into peace negotiations."

"How could that be? The Tarn are animals! We could never share space with them."

"Sir, please let me explain."

"You damn well better, Mr. Riker."

Riker stiffened slightly at the belligerent tone.

"There was a cease-fire in place and both sides have observed it ever since."

"Next thing you'll be telling me we're friends with the bloody Klingons too."

Riker let that one pass.

"So what about us? We were here. What about us?" Riker explained the Tarn Neutral Zone to an increasingly pale Lysander Murat.

"No one got a signal?" Murat finally said.

"Signal? No, sir, neither side ever received a word. In fact, we did not even have any knowledge that a battle had been fought."

Riker looked over at Janice. Maybe she'd have better luck explaining the rest.

"The official entry read that the *Verdun* was reported overdue and presumed lost either due to mechanical failure or hostile action," she said. "We inquired during the peace negotiations but the Tarn denied any knowledge. On their side, they asked about the ship you encountered and we had no knowledge of it as well."

"And so you abandoned us," Murat said quietly.

"No, sir. If anyone had known they would have come for you. It's just that this system was in the middle of the No-Entry Zone and, therefore, it was cut off from any future contact until now."

"Why now?" Murat asked bitterly. "We thought that perhaps one of our old sublight carrier signals had finally been picked up."

Riker started to say that it was simply an accident they had been found but stopped himself.

"Only within the past several years has the Tarn government indicated its willingness to develop open communications with the Federation, allowing for mutual visits to command locations and, just recently, an officer-exchange program. The *Enterprise* is the first Federation ship into this system since the *Verdun.*"

"So, you knew we were here?" Murat responded to Riker's explanation.

"No, we had no idea of your existence until we picked up sensor readings of the nuclear detonation."

"But you knew of the *Verdun,* yes?"

"Only when we found your ship orbiting this sun did we know for sure that there had even been a fight. As for the actual cause of the loss of the *Verdun,* our records indicated nothing conclusive, merely speculation. Remember, there were simmering conflicts with several races at that time, including the Klingons. It was impossible to attribute blame to the Tarn for certain."

"Klingons. Another bunch of animals," Murat spat out.

Will said nothing, glad that Worf wasn't along.

"All we had was a broken signal from Lucian Murat whom, I assume, you are a descendant of," Janice continued. Riker silently thanked her for getting the conversation back on track.

Murat nodded his head.

" 'Enemy in sight. His strength is superior. I shall close and engage,' " Janice said.

Murat looked over at her.

"Every cadet at the Federation Academy knows those words," she said. "They're legendary. The signal was picked up by a remote unmanned monitor. The monitor's relay was broken, so the message was simply stored. We had no indication of direction and could only guess within a hundred thousand cubic parsecs where it might have come from. A repair ship didn't pick up the monitor until the treaty was already being negotiated and it was assumed that it was Murat's final signal."

"Assumed? No, Commander, the Federation opted to shelve the lives of over three hundred men and women, the ancestors of whom just greeted you as heroes. It negotiated itself a pat on the back and a clean slate for a conscience."

Murat gave a sigh of disgust, an audible response that was as palpable as a nasty shove.

"The Federation may have found what they believe to be peace with the Tarn, but that doesn't change what is here. We are at war here and we expect support."

"We can't offer military assistance without violating the treaty with the Tarn."

"For God's sake, Commander, we're dying. Do you honestly plan on doing nothing to help?"

"You are fighting a war that has been resolved. There is no purpose in continuing. It accomplishes nothing."

"Nothing." Murat spit the word out, dismissing the notion with an angry sweep of his hand. "Commander. This war is what keeps us alive."

"Alive? If they have atomic weapons and you don't, it's all but finished for you."

"We'll have them soon enough as well, and until then we have new nerve gases and biological weapons. We will even the score."

Riker stared at the compact, clenched body of the man in front of him. He sought for something to say, something to bring reason to the situation.

Reason, however, seemed to be the farthest thing from Murat's mind. This was not a Federation officer with whom logic and decorum held any sway.

Janice stood back up and formally came to attention.

"Sir, I regret to have to say this but our own orders are clear, as are yours. By order of the Federation you are required to institute an immediate cease-fire. The same message is being communicated at this very moment to the Tarn forces on this planet."

Lysander stared at her coldly. Riker said nothing, realizing that Janice was playing on her knowledge of the military system that existed here.

"Go to hell," Lysander snarled. "It's over when we win, and not before."

"That, sir, is an order," Riker chimed in.

Riker was spared a response when the door to the command center was thrown open, revealing the stocky form of a woman in her sixties.

"Lysander. There's been a penetration in Delta Eleven, the West Complex. Battle group Bamberg was overrun. Bamberg's dead. You're needed."

Lysander stood up, glaring at the two.

"Did you give them our coordinates?" he cried.

"Of course not."

"Well, so much for your cease-fire, Riker. They're hitting the perimeter of this city. Stay here . . . perhaps we can send a few of our dead back with you to remind your captain of what he seems so easily to have disregarded."

The messenger stood in the doorway with a slight frown as she watched the retreating form of Lysander. She paused a moment in reflection before turning to Janice and Riker. The three surveyed each other quietly.

"You've frustrated my son; not an easy accomplishment."

"Your son?" Janice asked.

"I'm Julia Murat." She said nothing more, her features fixed.

"I'm afraid we weren't exactly what your son was expecting," Riker offered.

"No?" Her response questioned, curiosity merging into distrust. Riker had the sudden sensation that he was on trial, losing the support of his last juror. Was he to disappoint each man and woman on this planet one by one?

He explained the situation and told her in conclusion that they were there to help bring about a cease-fire.

"Cease-fire? Then why are the Tarn still attacking?"

"They've most likely not yet received word."

"I doubt that," she replied coldly. "And there is a battle on and I am needed. Excuse me, our people are dying. I must go with my son."

The door shut behind the woman, leaving the two officers alone in the unfinished room.

William R. Forstchen

"Get the feeling we're the bad guys here?" Will offered dryly.

Janice grimaced in response.

"So what now, Commander?" She kept her voice light in an effort to temper the magnitude of the situation.

"Well, we start by breaking a direct order."

"And which order would that be?"

"We're going for a walk."

"A bit rebellious there. Dare we?"

"Sure. Care to join me?"

"What lady could pass up an opportunity like that?"

Riker grinned as Janice passed through the doorway in front of him.

The two left the partially completed command center. The two guards at the door looked at them but said nothing as they continued on and walked slowly down the center artery of the complex.

"Do you realize that this is the most fascinating thing we've ever seen?" Julia remarked. "It's us, two hundred years ago. The tunnels would have to go, of course, but their uniforms . . . they're perfect. And those men, did you see them?"

"The two who stared at us back there?"

"Those were copies of Garand carbines! Can you believe it? This is not a holosimulator, this is real."

"And real people are dying. I thought we'd pass the word, and that would be it. I never expected this response."

114

"I did," Janice replied.

Will looked at her in surprise.

"Two hundred years of war, Will. This entire society is bred to war and nothing else. We can't switch it off like one of those ancient lightbulbs."

The two continued down the street, which was roughened by uneven cobblestones and gravel. They came upon a series of several open pavilions, men and women hunched over what appeared to be ancient fuse-activated explosives.

"Our friend Julia Murat?" Janice noted, nodding her head in the direction of one of the open-faced buildings.

"Appears so," Riker commented, observing the woman as she clipped out sequence patterns for the men and women to follow.

At that moment, Julia Murat glanced in the direction of the two officers. Her voice paused in midsentence as she cast an indifferent look in their direction. The group, diligently scrutinizing red and black wires in front of them, noticed the hesitation in her voice and began murmuring in curiosity as they recognized the officers.

"Ripley!" Murat spoke sharply, bringing the attention back to the task at hand. "Red to—"

A slight rumble could be heard in the distance. A tremor, no more. Murat stood rapt with attention, head cocked, eyes alert. A second tremor displaced a cup perched on the edge of a nearby table, which tumbled off and shattered. A third rumble, louder, echoed, dust sifting down from the arcing roof of the cave.

"Cover!" Murat shouted.

The tremors quickly changed to ear-shattering explosions, rattling everything in sight. Riker grabbed Janice's arm and flung her against a wall near a drainage ditch. A man fell against her, a boulder crashing from the ceiling just yards in front of him.

"Hang on!" he cried. "It only lasts a few moments." It was as if he were describing the sting of a shot, or something else equally momentary.

Janice burrowed into Riker's arms, trembling as a long string of explosions rocked them.

And quite suddenly, it was over. The din rumbled into the distance, echoing upward, downward, he couldn't tell. The dust was thick, visibility barely a meter or two.

"You okay?" Riker whispered.

Janice nodded. The man who had offered reassurance was lying against their sides, blood trickling down from his shattered skull.

"Will—" She trembled.

"I know." He moved around her and gently eased the dead man off of her leg. He drew his fingers across the man's eyes, closing them.

"Commander. Commander Riker." A voice cut through the silence.

"Over here."

"Hmm. Good. So you're alive." Julia Murat's

voice became more distinct as she approached them. "So much for your cease-fire." She nodded to the dead man. "Karlson, good warrior, perhaps you want the assignment of telling his three children, they lost their mother only yesterday in the atomic strike. Tell me, how do we classify those who die when a war is supposed to be over?"

"What was that?" Janice asked.

"Air strike. Penatrator rounds, designed to collapse underground tunnels. They've been closing in on us for months now, tightening the ring, wiping out our outposts and secondary cities. Looks like they know where we are."

With a brisk motion, she rose. "I must see to the ventilation units; there's work to be done." And with that, she walked quickly, determinedly away.

Riker, with the skill of a first officer, quickly assessed the situation for himself. A man, thirty, no more, had been hurled to the ground on the other side of the drainage ditch during the force of the attack. Riker watched as he stood, wavering only the slightest bit, and quickly brushed off his sleeve. He stooped, retrieved his weapon, and walked determinedly down the alley, his face inscrutable. Likewise, the young and old around him collected themselves and, without comment or hesitation, began sorting through the damage. He was amazed at the fluid nature of the attack. When the *Enterprise* was under fire or in danger of any sort, time had an odd distortion to it. Moments were dragged out, delayed. The atmosphere tense during, electric with relief and joy afterward. Above all, there was a decided change in the crew upon the conclusion of the skirmish, each member thoughtful, appreciative, some even reckless. And yet here, time seemed unscathed. The initial confusion over, normality shifted back into place with hardly a missed beat. Riker heard no cries, panic was nonexistent. The scene was a study in industriousness.

A young woman caught Riker's attention as she ran up to the area of most severe damage. Determined rather than frantic, she studied the wreckage intently, moving quickly in and out of the debris. She was looking for something, someone. A moment later she found it, a girl of four or five, standing perfectly still amid a swarm of measured activity. She ran to the girl, her sister, perhaps her daughter. And there, with people perfunctorily clearing the rubble around them, noise surrounding them but very little talking, the two simply stared at each other. Without a word, the older girl knelt to a child's eye level. With a single finger she moved a strand of hair, glued with tears and grime to the child's cheek, and gently curved it around her ear. For a single minute she stared at the child, a foot away. She studied her as if counting every freckle, memorizing the curve of cheek into upturned nose, noting the lashes separated with moisture. And then she nodded, one quick, hardly noticeable movement. And the child, equally undemonstrative, nodded once, no more, in return. The woman stood, having never embraced or spoken to the child, turned, and walked away, the little girl following a step behind.

Riker thought of Janice's comment, "bred to war." *A world bred to war, and how do we stop it?*

Chapter Five

HARNA KARISH STOOD EXPECTANTLY near the entry-way into the shelter. It was good to breathe air again that was almost like home, hot, dry. His nostrils distended, as if searching for prey. In front of him the red sun hovered in the sky like a burning ember in a sea of burnished brass.

Evidence of battle littered the ground: craters dotted the area, torn fragments of cloth, a shattered helmet, twisted bits of unidentifiable metal, a scattering of brass cylinders which he realized were ancient cartridge casings. . . . Wonderful, fighting was still good here, close and direct. On a rock wall he saw several curious forms. Drawing closer he realized that they were human skeletons, the bones held in place by stained and tattered remnants of uniforms. The bodies had obviously been hung from the wall as trophies or warnings. He nodded approvingly.

Karish's attention shifted as a grating sound echoed in the narrow canyon. Looking over his shoulder he saw, to his surprise, that a field of boulders seemed to be moving. They rolled back smoothly, one of the larger boulders apparently splitting down the middle. Behind the boulder a dark cavern appeared.

Several dozen Tarn emerged and he looked at them in open amazement. All were wearing the dark green uniforms, black leather crosshatching, and brown sash of their Imperial Era, the ruling circle of which had fallen from power following the disgraceful treaty agreement with the Federation two hundred years ago.

The warriors spread out, ancient assault weapons held at the ready. They approached warily, carefully scanning the ground. One of them stopped for a moment, bending over to probe the soil with his bayonet. He finally stood and looked back into the cavern.

"It is clear."

A lone warrior now appeared, his brown sash worn from left shoulder to right, the mark of a clan leader, with a gray circle in the middle of the sash. Within the circle was a gold embossed talon, claws extended.

The circle of the gold talon, Karish realized. The warrior drew closer and stopped before Karish. At his approach, he warily stepped to one side so that his shadow would not touch Karish. For a brief instant he moved to exhale, to offer greeting, but was halted in his attempt as Karish flinched slightly, stepping back in refusal. The warrior altered his approach, falling to his knees with head lowered in the dust.

"The circle is broken," the warrior hissed. "Our ancestors, lost in the hell of forgotten names, beg for redemption. Do unto us as you will."

Karish stood silently, looking down. He drew the ceremonial dagger from his belt and held it above the warrior's head, paused, and then, with a lightning-like swing of his arm, slashed the nape of the neck of the warrior kneeling before him. A trickle of blood rose to the wound, and a sigh drifted up from the other warriors. The ceremonial kill had just been performed, removing for Karish the onus of speaking to one of a circle which was without honor. For the moment it was as if Karish were speaking to someone who was already dead.

The kneeling Tarn stood up.

"I, Gadin, commander of those of the *Rashasa,* of the Broken Circle, greet you who are still of the circles of the chosen."

"Karish," he said in reply, for his clan markings were evident and to explain them further was to imply equality between their clans.

"Your ship, if I might ask?" Gadin replied.

Karish was silent. How to answer this? To his amazement, Picard had opened the initial contact to this circle without any indication that they were a Federation ship. He had allowed Karish full discretion on that point. The only image Gadin had seen on his primitive video screen was that of Karish, who had simply announced that he was in orbit above the planet and planned to beam down.

Strange, very strange, Karish realized. With the power on board the *Enterprise* Picard could have annihilated this dishonored circle in a matter of seconds, and yet he had refrained. Of course, there was the issue of war. In spite of his statements regarding the outcast nature of Gadin's circle, their annihilation would have been a direct provocation for war. Was this Picard's sole motivation for restraint? Could he even make such a decision without first consulting a higher authority before proceeding with an attack?

Perhaps that was what was really going on. Picard was waiting for a response from his Starfleet Headquarters. He would want backup, additional ships. There was another lingering thought as well. Could it not be that Picard knew about the existence of Torgu-Va from the very beginning and that the "accidental" find was a sham? If so, this was nothing more than an elaborate ruse, the finding of a provocation to launch a war which would not cause dissent within the Federation ranks. The rescue and vindication of the humans on Torgu-Va would be the rallying point for an all-out attack.

Yet, why was he allowed to send a message to his own command? Or was Picard's assurance of a secured channel a lie as well? If so, then Picard most certainly must know what the response to that signal would be.

It was a game within games, Karish realized. Wonderful—such intricacies were the joy of the Tarn.

Karish realized that he had not replied to Gadin's question.

"Inside," Karish finally said, motioning to the entry to the tunnel.

Gadin bowed. "Of course. They might have patrols beneath us even now."

Gadin snapped an order, the squad deploying around them. Entering the tunnel, Karish followed the lead of Gadin as they wove their way through a series of defensive barriers, guard posts, and concealed traps.

An open gateway to their right caused Karish to pause. To his amazement, he saw a huge open cavern. Lined up inside were a dozen aircraft, ancient machines of wings and propellers.

"Made by our own hands," Gadin announced proudly. "We started with nothing but the material salvaged from our landing craft. Four hundred and eight survivors, barely enough food to last thirty days. The first years were the Times of Struggle: digging shelters, raising food, learning the old arts as revealed in our stored computer records. We suspected a Federation ship had crashed nearby but it took years to find the animal scum. Then the

War for the Redemption of the Circle began. For once we confirmed they still lived, we knew our victory was not complete, and thus . . ."

His words trailed off, for it was far too bitter to admit that they had lost a ship without achieving total victory.

"Go on."

"First it was with knives, bows, primitive single-shot powder weapons, and two phaser guns which still held their charges. From there, down through the years, we made rifles that could repeat shots, artillery, radio, radar, aircraft, missiles, armored vehicles, short-range rockets, and now, now you have arrived at our moment of triumph. Yesterday we succeed in unleashing our first atomic weapons, destroying one of their cities. Even now we are searching for their underground capital. Once that is shattered the war will be won."

It was evident that Gadin was reciting their accomplishments with the hope of gaining approval.

"Yes, I saw that," Karish said.

"And you were pleased?" Gadin asked hopefully. "We slaughtered thousands. Even now we are finishing preparations for two more strikes."

Karish said nothing. How bad the timing of all of this. Another half-year and this circle would have completed its war in triumph. He stepped into the cave that served as a hangar bay. Slowly he walked down the line of aircraft, putting a hand out to touch the tapered aluminum wings, pausing to smell the oil, gasoline, and dripping hydraulic fluid.

An armorer, at the sight of Karish approaching, froze in place, head lowered. Karish ignored him, slowly walking around the plane. It was something of legend, not used in half a hundred generations; never had he seen one before. He scrambled up on the wing, peering into the open cockpit. The instruments were primitive, nothing computerized at all, an old-fashioned ball floating in a curved tube to indicate pitch, another one to show artificial horizon and a compass, that was it.

He looked back down at Gadin.

"Now we have this," Gadin exclaimed, his pride evident, his tone one of an underling seeking approval.

"And the humans, the Federation?"

"They have them too. They call theirs a Mustang. I believe it's the name of an ancient warrior god. We are completing our first jet and, within the year, we will have a missile that can loft a small atomic weapon into orbit."

"And you did this from nothing?" Karish asked.

"Our honor is at stake, my lord, our desire to restore our circle by any way that we can."

"You could have killed yourselves," Karish replied coldly.

Gadin lowered his eyes. "Yes, my lord. But then, if we had done that, our enemies on this world would still be alive to spit upon our rotting hides."

Karish looked down in open surprise. There had been stories before of circles that had been dishonored; the tale of the Thirty Outcasts was a famous ancient play. Their lord had been dishonored by a courtier at the Imperial Palace. He had failed to gain revenge when he had attacked the courtier in front of the emperor and was forced to commit suicide. His circle of warriors, outcasts, had wandered for years, placed under an Imperial Injunction not to seek revenge. Yet there was the higher calling. After twelve long years of waiting, the courtier had returned to the Imperial Palace to receive an award. The Thirty infiltrated the palace, disguised as holy ones. And in the middle of the ceremony they fell upon the courtier and killed him, then turned their knives upon themselves in atonement for breaking the Imperial law. Thus, honor was restored in all ways.

Yet these warriors had waged war for over two hundred years. He stepped off from the plane's wing and continued down the length of the hangar, passing larger planes obviously intended for the dropping of primitive explosive-filled bombs and yet others which he realized were for the transporting of warriors who would jump upon their target.

He heard the tramping of feet and, looking back down the length of the cavern, saw a line of warriors marching in, burdened with heavy packs and weapons, wearing uniforms that would blend with the desert landscape.

"A team to be dropped near where we suspect an

enemy city to be hidden. If they discover it, we'll place our next atomic weapon there to collapse the city. The setting and detonation of a bomb is the highest honor."

"And the ones who set it die?"

"But of course, they are *Tacig,* the Chosen Ones of Glory."

"You speak as if your circle had honor, for only a circle that is complete may name its warriors *Tacig.*"

"Forgive me, my lord, but in all these years there has been nothing."

Gadin hesitated, head lowered again.

"Go on."

"My lord, we wondered if all the circles had been defeated and if, perhaps, we were the only ones left."

"How could you imagine that?" Karish snapped angrily.

"Forgive me, lord, but there was never an answer. We had, at least, destroyed their ship, the hated *Verdun.* We lost our ship in the exchange, our ancestors taking refuge on this planet. We thought there would be some reply to our last broadcast announcing the kill . . . but there was nothing."

He spat out the last words with bitterness. Karish remained silent.

"Then we stumbled upon them. When we took their first patrol, and realized that they were indeed survivors of the *Verdun,* we thought our victory was tainted and that we had been abandoned for not fulfilling our mission, that we were unclean."

Gadin stopped speaking, his gaze unfocused as if he himself had discovered the hated foe.

"And then," he whispered, and there was a moment of hesitation.

"Out with it," Karish snapped, half suspecting what was to come.

Gadin looked up at him, eyes flaming.

"And then, my lord, some came to think that it was we who were the unbroken circle and that all the other circles were the ones who were broken. Across the generations we have fought, waiting with dread but also with hope that there would someday be a sign that we were remembered."

Karish said nothing.

"Tell me, my lord, why do you come now, now when victory is so close? If you arrived but a year later we could have stood with heads held high, proclaiming our mission to be complete and our circle purified."

"Because we came, that is answer enough."

"Is it? Where is your ship, my lord?"

Karish hesitated for the briefest of moments and instantly realized that he had made a mistake. A subtle difference now showed in Gadin, as he raised his head level to look into Karish's eyes.

"There is much to talk about," Karish said, brushing the look aside. "In private."

Gadin said nothing.

With a hiss, Karish uttered with clenched teeth, "I will be obeyed."

The bark of command caused Gadin to finally lower his head, but only for a moment. As he looked up again Karish could see the dark suspicion in his eyes, the slight prickling of the spikes down the back of his head.

"For now, then," Gadin replied, waiting several seconds before adding with a hint of mockery, "my lord."

"My commander," a voice interrupted.

Gadin turned. A warrior wearing the star of a commander of a hundred on his breast stood at attention behind him.

"Go on," Gadin snapped.

"My commander. The Eighth Company of the Hadarish Command reports that they have located a tunnel which may be the one we have been looking for, the primary entrance into their main city."

"What?"

"Yes, my lord," the ensign announced, eyes bright with passion. "The commander of the Eighth just radioed in. One of his hidden surveillance posts saw two humans appear out in the open, as if materializing out of thin air, then disappear into what we suspected was an access tunnel. They have yet to reappear. Our team deployed a seismic probe and definitely picked up indicators of underground air pumps in operation. We might be on to a major site."

"Was the patrol seen?"

"The Hadarish are the best, my lord. They infiltrated the area weeks ago without being seen. The Feds don't know they are there."

"Let me see!"

Gadin followed the officer over to a room carved into the side of the hangar cavern. Karish, ignored for the moment except for several watchful guards, slowly followed him. One guard made as if to stop him but Karish cast him a sharp gaze and he lowered his eyes. Karish stepped into the room, dimly lit by a single incandescent lamp suspended from the ceiling. Gadin was leaning over a map table, the young officer pointing out a location.

Karish said nothing. Riker and Eardman had been spotted beaming down, that was obvious. Did Picard fail to do a proper scan of the site or were the Hadarish so well concealed that they had not been detected?

Gadin whispered some commands to those gathered around him, then looked back at Karish, motioning for him to step out of the room. Karish remained for several seconds as if to convey that if he was leaving it was by his own volition rather than by Gadin's command, then withdrew.

Gadin finally stepped out and with a wave of his hand dismissed the guards so that the two were alone.

"What do you know of these humans that appeared? It sounds like they were beamed down the same as you."

"What do you intend to do?" Karish replied.

"Do you know who these humans are? Are they from a Federation starship?" Gadin asked.

Karish sighed. He had not dreamed that his explanation of what was happening would take a track where he was on the defensive.

"Yes, I know of them. They are with the Federation."

A low rattling hiss escaped Gadin.

"And are you?" he snarled. "I have asked you twice about your ship and twice you have evaded my question."

"You forget your place in this universe, Gadin," Karish snarled.

He stared straight at the Tarn commander, but this time Gadin did not lower his eyes.

"Are you with these humans? I find it a singular coincidence that both of you arrive within minutes of each other."

"No!" Karish barked. "How dare you even imply such a dishonor."

"So why do both of you arrive at the same time?"

Even as they spoke, Karish noticed a sudden increase in activity in the hangar. Ground crews came bursting out of side corridors; an ancient truck, powered by internal combustion, rumbled past, stopping in front of a four-engine plane. What looked like electrical cables were run out from the truck and hooked into the plane. Within seconds one of the four engines on the plane coughed, propeller turning, then kicked over, the propeller blurring, engine howling. The truck was disconnected and then rolled onto the next plane as the other three engines on the first plane spun to life, filling the cavern with a thunderous roar.

Pilots, looking to Karish like actors from an ancient play or holostory, sprinted across the cavern, ground crews helping them to scramble up ladders into their planes.

"There is so much to explain," Karish finally replied. "So much to understand of all that was and now is."

"Then tell me!"

Karish briefly tried to explain all that had transpired, bending the information to make it seem as if he were an envoy sent to deal with the Federation, thus explaining why he was aboard their ship.

Gadin looked at him with open suspicion.

"And this Federation ship commander. He claims he sends his people down to the Federation on this planet ordering them to stop fighting?"

"He wants an end to the fighting."

"And do you believe it?"

Karish hesitated. "It seems doubtful."

Gadin said nothing, staring at Karish. Finally he stirred. "Victory is within our grasp. Our honor restored. And now you are here, you of the Imperial Circle that abandoned us."

"Ancestors of the circle, not I."

"And what will you do, you of the Royal Circle?"

"What are you planning here?" Karish asked.

Gadin turned and went back to his staff, bent

over, and talked softly with one of the radio operators. He waited for several minutes, then came back to Karish. All around them the pace of activity increased, columns of troops marching out of what Karish suspected were barrack areas, warriors bent over with heavy loads. There was expectancy in the air, the scent of the hunt, of the kill, and it stirred Karish.

"If your words are true, then this human commander sent his envoys down to meet with their leader, the one called Murat."

"That can be assumed," Karish said cautiously.

"Then now, for the first time, we truly know which of the compounds is their headquarters, a goal we have sought for years. In their arrogant stupidity they have revealed it to us."

Karish did not stir. He had no loyalty to the Federation, but still, he was bothered by this mistake of beaming Riker and Eardman down and thus revealing the location of the main city.

"I've ordered a strike with explosives and gas. It will cover the lifting of assault troops in to support the Hadarish unit. We've bombed the area before, because we suspected that there might be a city there, so another strike will not give us away. The bombs will not do much damage, the city is buried deep, but they will serve as a diversion.

"I'm going with the assault force. If we have indeed found the entry to their main city we will gain the entrance, secure it, then prepare for the final strike. Do you wish to see how the Circle of the Golden Talon fights?"

Karish could not help but notice that Gadin referred to his command as a circle and not as one that was broken.

It was a challenge offer. Karish nodded an agreement.

As if noticing for the first time, Gadin looked down at Karish's chest. There, tucked under his sash but with the edge protruding, was a communicator tab with the emblem of the Federation on it which could also serve as a locator. Karish looked down and saw it as well.

Without comment Karish removed it, let it drop to the floor of the hangar, and quickly ground it under his heel. He silently cursed. Hopefully Gadin had not clearly seen the emblem.

"Wait here then," Gadin replied, almost as if giving an order. He retreated back into his command center. All was now a mad bustle of activity around Karish. The first planes were taxiing out. The sound was deafening, the air so thick with exhaust fumes that he thought he would get sick. A column of troops marched past him, filing up the back ramp into a plane; more columns followed.

Gadin, followed by his staff, came back out of the command room. One of the guards approached Karish, bearing an extra set of battle gear, and set it down by Karish's feet. Karish looked at it in confusion.

"Are you going with us or not?" Gadin asked, the challenge in his voice evident.

"Of course!" Karish snapped. "This equipment is primitive. Show me its use."

Gadin motioned to the guard, who looked at Karish in surprise. The guard unrolled a battle jumpsuit, unzipped it, and handed it to Karish, who slipped it on and zipped it up. The fabric was heavy, close-fitting. Feeling the weave, he noticed that it felt slightly oily, and realized a moment later that it was designed to dissipate infrared signature so that one blended into the background. The color was red-hued, to match the terrain. The guard now helped him with his helmet and camouflage hood; next came the goggles, then belt, crosshatched webbing, canteens, a pouch of fragmentation grenades and flares. A heavy pack was strapped to his back. The guard hooked the webbing over Karish's shoulders.

"This is the pull ring," the guard said, taking Karish's hand and placing it over the steel ring.

"Pull ring?"

"For the parachute. Clip it onto the trail wire when you form up to jump."

"Parachute?" Karish asked after waiting for several seconds to make sure that his voice was under control.

"We're jumping, of course," the guard said, looking straight into Karish's eyes for a reaction. Karish said nothing.

More gear was strapped on: an ancient sidearm, an assault gun strapped across his chest, and finally another pouch, which, if its weight was any indication, carried yet more munitions.

"That's it," the guard announced. "Move, they're waiting for us."

The floor of the cavern was empty except for the dozen four-engine planes lining up, engines howling. Staggering under his burden, Karish struggled to the ramp of the plane, the guard having to help him up. An empty bucket seat was beside Gadin, who motioned for him to sit by his side. As he sat down the plane lurched, turning. Karish almost fell out of his seat and he heard several barks of amusement. Furious, Karish looked around, and heads were lowered.

"My warriors are amused by you," Gadin announced.

"I am not here to be an object of amusement," Karish snapped angrily.

The plane lurched again. Engines howling, it staggered forward, picking up speed, the vibration and lurching bounces blurring his vision.

"They want to see how a warrior of your circle fights."

"I know how to fight."

"Like this? In the manner in which we have fought for hundreds of years, forgotten by the other circles? Tell me, Karish, how do you fight?"

"What do you mean?"

"Do you fight like us? Can you fall from the sky as we do? Can you crawl down one of their filthy tunnels with nothing more than a knife in your hand, knowing they wait for you around the next bend? Can you spot their traps, weave through their underground mazes? Have you ever had a tunnel blow on you, or found a comrade nailed to a tunnel wall with his throat slit? Can you survive those things, Karish?"

The plane lifted off, then banked sharply, rolling up on its starboard side so that Karish was hanging by his seat belt, looking straight down at the warriors strapped in on the port side.

The plane flipped over onto its port side and then finally leveled out. As it slowly climbed it bounced violently, soaring up and down on the hot air thermals created by the scorching late-afternoon heat.

The taunt in Gadin's voice was clear, but for the moment Karish was forced to struggle with the fear that the violent maneuvers of the plane might make him sick, a humiliation that would be unbearable.

Gadin watched him casually.

"You ask how the Federation personnel arrived at the same time."

"I was waiting for the answer, the answer to many questions."

Karish began to explain. There was no sense in hiding the truth; Gadin would find out soon enough, and to plead mere coincidence would lower his position even further when the truth was revealed. Gadin listened, saying nothing. Karish stayed focused on him in order to distract his mind from the violent rolling ride and the cold fearful anticipation of what was to come.

A yellow light suddenly blinked from the ceiling above Gadin.

"More later," Gadin announced as the warriors around them struggled to their feet.

Karish followed Gadin's lead, fumbling with his drogue line clip until Gadin finally reached around and snapped the hook onto the wire trailing overhead.

The back doors of the plane parted; a hot howling wind swirled around Karish. The plane nosed over, blue red sky filling the opening before him. With a stomach-lurching bounce the plane leveled out and Karish saw dark canyon walls to either side of the aircraft.

A klaxon boomed, startling Karish.

"Ready!" Gadin roared. "Karish, just run for the door when I give the word!"

Karish swallowed hard, staring straight ahead. The rim of the canyon was racing past to either side, the clearance so close that he thought the wings would touch.

The thumping boom of the klaxon stopped abruptly.

"Go, go, go!" Gadin roared.

Karish froze for an instant. He felt a hand shove violently against his back. From the corner of his eye he saw that the warrior at his side was already out the door, disappearing.

Taking a deep breath, he started forward; better to die than to suffer the humiliation of cowardice.

Lying on his side, he wasn't sure what to do next. He felt rough hands grab him by the shoulders, unsnapping the harness. Gadin pulled him to his feet.

"Injured?"

Karish shook his head. Looking around, he saw that the second wave was already touching down. Within seconds they had started to form. Gadin motioned for Karish to follow.

"We know this canyon is secure from their observation. The planes will form in with the bombers, pass over the target, then return to base. Meanwhile, we link up with the commander of Eighth Company, try to gain the entrance, and see if this is just an outpost or the main access into the city."

"How?"

"We raid it." Gadin slapped the assault gun strapped to Karish's chest. "That's why you brought this along."

Gadin broke into a loping trot, units forming up behind him, skirmishers deployed forward, dodging from rock to rock as they moved. The warriors moved with a steady catlike ease, weapons at the ready, heads turning back and forth as if scanning every inch of ground as they passed. Karish struggled to keep up.

He suddenly felt a rumble pass through the soles of his feet. Bits of dust swirled up from the ground, a few small rocks came sliding down from the canyon wall to his left. He looked over at Gadin.

"The air attack on the suspected city."

"Gadin, something seems out of the ordinary here."

"What?"

"You are the commander of all forces here?"

"Yes."

"Then why lead a raid like this? Surely there are lower ranks just as capable."

"The fact that this Federation commander beamed his people down here is the clue we have sought for years. Perhaps it is where their main city is located. Tell me, these Federation personnel, did they beam down to meet Murat?"

Karish wanted to reply but for some reason felt he could not. He felt torn by the requirements of Picard, of his own circle, and now of this warrior of a broken circle.

"How can you not already know where their command center is? Surely a city is easy to find?"

Gadin looked over at him, astonished.

A skirmisher forward held his hand up and the group instantly froze, crouching down. Gadin raised a clenched fist, then extended it palm outward. The warriors around him went to ground. Karish followed Gadin's lead, lying down beside him.

"You understand nothing of this war, do you?" Gadin whispered.

"Yes, that you have fought them for two hundred years."

"No, the tactics, the challenge."

"Tell me, then."

"Look. We hold the surface. This world, I am told, is not too unlike the homeworld. For the humans of the Federation it is all but uninhabitable. As soon as they arrived they burrowed underground to escape the heat while we stayed, for the most part, on the surface. When we finally made contact the paradigm had already been set.

"Through all the long years of battle they have dug like vermin beneath the soil. Always digging, crawling, burrowing." He spat the words out with distaste. "As quickly as we find one nest and exterminate it, there are two more dug. Now there are thousands of miles of tunnels beneath us. They pop up in the darkness, often under our very feet to kill. Only forty days ago they raided the very command center where you beamed down—you saw the litter of that fight. They destroyed three planes and almost penetrated to the assembly area for our nuclear weapons before we destroyed them. The fight was good. I personally cut the throats of two of them."

Gadin grunted with pleasure at the memory.

"We, in turn, fight to dig them out. We search for airholes, trapdoors, places where they have harvested food. We now look for infrared signatures of exhaust vents, traces of chemicals from their manufacturing. When we find these clues we try to dig them out.

"We have found smaller cities, for they have dispersed over the years, but never the core of the hive, the nest where Murat and those closest to him live. That is the heart and, by all the gods, if we have found it I will cut it out and stop its beating.

"Now that we have atomic capabilities, if this is indeed their capital, we will set our next bomb here and collapse it with the blasts. It will be glorious."

While listening to Gadin, Karish watched as the skirmisher at the head of the column crept forward and then stopped.

"There might be something ahead," Gadin whispered. "Stay alert."

Two more skirmishers moved to either side of the first one, weapons raised. The first warrior seemed to grab hold of the ground and then pulled it back. A rattle of firing broke out, startling Karish. An instant later the skirmisher was flung backward by an explosion. Karish had seen death in many forms but never from primitive explosive powder. The skirmisher's body seemed to just disintegrate.

"Vermin, damn vermin!" Gadin snarled.

"I thought you said this place was secured?" Karish cried.

"Nothing is secure against these animals," Gadin shouted. He barked out a series of unintelligible commands. Karish looked around in confusion but the warriors around him seemed to understand what was expected. There was a flash of fire forward. A curious whistling sound clipped past Karish. He raised himself up on his elbows and then saw a plume of dirt erupt by his side.

"Down, you damn fool," Gadin cried. He turned away from Karish, grabbing what looked to be a microphone from an ancient radio off the back of a warrior who had been following them. Gadin started to shout into it.

Surprised, Karish realized that someone was actually shooting at him. It was hard to grasp. There was no trace of light, no high-pitched crackle of a phaser, just the curious whistle, puffs of dirt and shards of shattered rock. It was something straight out of ancient times and, rather than be afraid, Karish felt a curious thrill. Unclipping his assault gun, he looked at it for a second, somehow instinctively knowing that pulling back the handle on the side of the weapon would chamber a round. He heard the reassuring click and, rising up, he shouldered his weapon and pointed it up toward a canyon wall where he had seen a sparkle of light and puffs of smoke.

"Don't," Gadin snapped. "You don't know who to shoot at. Just stay still."

An explosion erupted from the side of a canyon

wall, followed a split second later by a deafening roar behind Karish. Warriors around him raised their guns and started to shoot at the concealed artillery position. Without bothering to ask Gadin's permission, Karish sighted his weapon, squeezed the trigger, and held it. He was startled by the violent recoil, the stuttering burst of fire erupting from his gun. A couple of seconds later the gun fell silent. Surprised, he removed it from his shoulder, burning his fingertips on the barrel. What was wrong?

"Fool, fire single shots!" Gadin shouted. Grabbing Karish's gun, he tore the clip off, fished in his own ammunition pouch for a replacement, slammed it in, and passed it back. Karish grunted with approval as the gun was again in his hands. Finding it hard to shoot lying down, he got up on one knee, ignoring Gadin's angry warning. Taking careful aim, he gently brushed the trigger, and the gun recoiled. He released, then touched it again.

The power was intoxicating. Roaring with delight, he continued to shoot, ignoring the whistle of bullets, the shriek of another incoming round.

Gadin rose up on both knees, cupping his hands around his mouth.

"Air strike coming!" he roared. "Pull back! Pull back!"

Warriors around Karish got up, still firing, and started to fall back, two of them stopping to drag off the dead body of the warrior in front of Karish.

Ahead, the two surviving skirmishers got up and ran, dodging and weaving. An explosion erupted under one, flinging him into the air.

Before he even understood what he was doing Karish was up, racing forward. Plumes of dirt erupted around him. Crouching low, he slid in beside the wounded soldier, who was clutching the stump of his leg, shrieking in agony. Karish grabbed him around the waist, hoisted him up over his shoulder, and, turning, staggered back.

Gadin was on his feet, shouting something, but in the thunder of battle Karish couldn't hear. Looking up, he saw a plane winging its way up the valley, twisting and turning through the narrow pass.

Gadin extended both hands, motioning for Karish to get down. Karish fell to the ground, and then to his own amazement he actually shielded the injured warrior with his body. The plane screamed overhead, twin dark cylinders detaching from its belly. The cylinders tumbled from the heavens, spinning end over end, dropping from the sky with grace. A second later a thumping whoosh swept over Karish, followed an instant later by a searing wall of heat.

The fire of the flaming napalm engulfed the valley floor. Another plane shot over, this one at a right angle to the canyon, the cylinders of napalm slamming into the wall where the concealed gun positions were located. Fire splayed out in every direction and Karish curled up, feeling the heat wash over him.

He felt someone grab him by the shoulders, pulling him up. It was Gadin.

"Come on! Gas is next!"

Together they helped to drag the wounded soldier back. Two more warriors came up, one of them wrapping a tourniquet around his leg. Clearing back around a turn in the canyon, Karish finally let go of the soldier, who looked up at him with shock-glazed eyes and then nodded a thanks.

Karish collapsed against the side of a boulder, heart racing. He understood now the calculated side of his action. He had been held in disdain until he could prove himself; saving the soldier was the necessary move to win that. But there was something more. He wanted to do it; to seek risk beyond the sterile, joyless, and tedious realities of life in court. This was a harsh reality undreamed of, and he wanted to grab hold of it with both hands and embrace the danger as if it were an illicit lover.

Gadin was looking at him warily.

"Why?"

"Why not?" Karish snapped back. "A warrior comrade was hurt. He could not be left."

"My comrade, my circle, not yours."

"Then why did you not go forward yourself to rescue him?" Karish replied coldly.

"Because he will die despite your vain act of heroism." Gadin hissed and nodded to where the warrior lay, shuddering spasmodically. Comrades around him were kneeling, looking one to the other.

"Plasma? You have that?" Karish asked. "A laser scalpel could open that wound in seconds and then clip off the bleeding."

"Your circle, not mine," Gadin whispered coldly. "Besides, there's no room for one-legged warriors on this world."

One of the wounded soldier's comrades lowered his head and whispered into his friend's ear. There was a feeble nod. The circle around him lowered their heads, each of them placing a hand on the soldier's chest.

The prayer for the dead of a circle, Karish realized. The warrior who had whispered something to his friend moved quickly, hand drawing dagger. Even as he did so the wounded soldier bared his throat and it was over in a second. The one who had performed the release of the soul closed his friend's eyes. The circle stood up and started to walk away, heads lowered.

Karish gazed at the body.

"At least you let him die within the circle of comrades rather than burn to death," Gadin finally said. "You have won the honor of their circle for that act."

Karish said nothing. Another plane came in, shrieking low overhead, banking sharply as it turned up the valley. The sound of the explosion was different, a soft *crump,* and he saw streamers of green rise up over the edge of the canyon wall, then settle back down.

"Gas?" Karish asked.

"Won't do much good. They're long gone, but we might catch someone."

"Shouldn't we have masks on?"

Gadin barked with amusement. "The wind is at your back, warrior. It will go the other way."

Karish heard the low thump of the gas bombs going off as two more planes winged in. The warriors around him were scattered into small groups, warily gazing at the sides of the canyon walls. Some were already cleaning their weapons, a few were eating or taking a drink. Karish suddenly realized that he was suffering from a burning thirst. Unclipping his canteen, he started to take a long drink but paused as a sidelong glance from Gadin told him to conserve. Taking but a short sip, he clipped the canteen back to his belt.

"You haven't answered one of my questions."

"And what is that?" Gadin asked.

"Why did you come up here? This is not a job for a commander."

Gadin grunted, staring straight at Karish.

"I wanted to see if your circle had the stomach to fight."

Karish felt as if he should be insulted, but he knew better. He stared straight at Gadin, realizing that the warriors around them had been listening to their conversation.

"For my circle I thank you for granting Jarah the

right to die within his circle," Gadin said, and Karish heard grunts of approval from those gathered around them.

"He died as one of a true circle, I shall honor his memory," Karish replied formally.

Instantly, he could sense the change around him. The wall was down. His statement carried with it the full understanding that he of the Royal Circle had passed judgment and had found these warriors to be pure . . . they were not outcasts.

One of the warriors stepped forward and raised his hand. Karish saw blood on his fingertips. It was the one who had helped his comrade to pass to the realm of ancestors. The fingertips brushed against Karish's forehead.

"Now you bear the blood of Jarah," the warrior announced. Karish felt a cold delicious thrill of emotion. He was now formally a part of their circle. Here was life as it was meant to be.

Drawing the bayonet out from his belt he closed his eyes, bracing for the shock, and slit his wrist open. Gasps of wonder erupted around him. He held his wrist up and felt fingers touching the blood. He opened his eyes and there was Gadin, looking down, nodding with approval. Gadin's fingertips were red and with a dramatic flourish he wiped them across his own forehead.

"Time to move," Gadin announced. "Masks on."

The warriors around him took off their helmets and camouflage hoods, pulled gas masks out of pouches and slipped them on. Karish followed suit, not embarrassed when Gadin checked the fit and then tightened a strap.

"Let us go kill Federation vermin and have our revenge," Gadin announced.

Growls of approval echoed around Karish and his heart froze. For a brief moment he had forgotten why he was here. What was it that Gadin expected? Was he to go with them, to hunt and to kill, perhaps to find the city with Riker and Eardman inside? If it was found, surely the next atomic weapon would be used. Then what?

He thought of the promise extracted by Picard, and beyond that, the promise made to the Council of Circles before departing on this mission. The warriors started to file past him, weapons at the ready. He cursed himself, allowing his emotions to get swept away by the thrill of the moment, the return of the hunt and the scent of the impending kill. Those who had gathered around Jarah motioned for Karish to fall in with their squad.

Yet here was a call to war as it once was in the glorious past. Here he could be alive, part of a circle that was not dishonored, perhaps the only circle still with honor as he had always dreamed. And for the moment he forgot all . . . except for the joy of the hunt and the kill.

Chapter Six

"CAPTAIN PICARD, THE TARN flagship is hailing us."

Picard stood up, studying the viewscreen closely. Three Tarn ships had entered the system an hour ago and were now moving into orbit above Torgu-Va. Their design reminded him of the old Romulan Bird-of-Prey configuration and he wondered if the Tarn had acquired some of their upgraded technology from the traditional rival of the Federation.

"I'll take it in my quarters," Picard announced. He sensed that this was going to be difficult, better handled alone for the moment.

He looked back over at Data.

"Data, as soon as you find out what is going on, call me at once."

"Yes, sir."

Picard wanted to explode with frustration. Everything, it seemed, had slipped out of control. Riker and Eardman could not be found. Apparently, they had moved so deep within the planet's network of caves that their sensors could no longer be located. Karish's location was even more mysterious; the signal had simply winked off as if his communicator had been smashed.

"Data, keep on Mr. Eddies. I want that transporter back on-line."

The door slid shut behind him as he paused for a moment to look out the viewport to the world below. Most planets, when silhouetted by the darkness of space, looked warm, inviting, even if the surface was cloaked in liquid ammonia or boiling sulfur. This one, however, even when viewed from space, seemed harsh, foreboding, a place that, given a choice, he would pass by without a second look.

"I have Admiral Garu Jord of the Tarn Royal Circle, sir."

"Patch him in."

The screen on his desk flared to life. Garu Jord's attention was elsewhere, his back to the screen as he spoke to someone standing behind him. It gave Picard several seconds to compose himself. The conversation seemed animated and Picard wondered if it was a bit of playacting for his consumption.

"Commander Picard?" Garu Jord finally asked, swinging his chair back around to look at Picard.

"I am Captain Jean-Luc Picard of the Federation starship *Enterprise*," he replied, concealing his annoyance regarding the slight in rank.

"I am Admiral of the Royal Circle Garu Jord, commander of this flotilla, sent to investigate events here on Torgu-Va. I expect a report."

Picard stiffened slightly at the imperious manner in which Jord addressed him.

"Admiral Jord, I will be happy to share all ship's logs with you. Once we have finished talking, my communications officer will download them to your ship."

"Fine. I wish to speak with Commander Karish in private."

"He is not back from the surface of the planet."

"Not back? Is there something wrong?"

"Commander Karish went to meet with the Tarn commander on the planet's surface. He has not reported back."

"I wish to speak with him now."

Picard hesitated for a moment. "Commander Karish is out of communication range."

"Out of range? Maybe for your system but not for ours."

"Sir. He is either too far below the surface or has removed his communications link. We have not spoken to him for nearly a day. I should add that the away team we sent to the human survivors on the planet has not reported in either."

"By 'human survivors,' you mean the Federation personnel, don't you?"

THE FORGOTTEN WAR

Jord was obviously laying a diplomatic trap. If Picard openly acknowledged the legitimacy of the command held by the personnel on the planet then any hostile actions they engaged in could be laid at the door of Starfleet Command.

"That designation is still being considered by Starfleet," Picard replied.

"Admiral, may I ask the reason for your visit?" Picard pressed, wanting to shift control of the conversation back into his own court.

"This is now free space, is it not, Captain? The Tarn have as much right to the access of it as you do."

"I do not debate that right, Admiral. Given the current situation down on the planet I know I can count on you to help bring about a peaceful resolution."

A gruff bark escaped Jord. A harsh comment erupted behind him and he turned in his chair. After nearly a minute he finally turned back.

"As per my advanced communication to you, Captain, I am expecting that you do not in any way offer assistance to the Federation personnel down on Torgu-Va. If you do so, we shall intervene immediately on behalf of the Tarn who are down on the planet."

"Admiral, I have not intervened but I think your sensors will reveal that a full-scale battle is currently in progress. We have been monitoring air drops of Tarn troops, artillery strikes by both sides, and numerous other actions across several thousand square kilometers of ground. Hundreds, perhaps thousands are dying and I wish to see it stopped at once. Can I count on you to do that?"

A moment passed in silence.

"Captain, I would like you to come aboard my ship."

"I must respectfully decline, Admiral."

"You don't trust us?"

"That is not the issue at all," Picard replied with ease. "I have two away teams down on the planet. I need to stay here in case there is a crisis."

Picard kept a straight face. Given what was evolving, there was no way that he would leave the *Enterprise* at this moment.

"Then I will come to you."

Surprised, Picard nodded an agreement.

"I should add that we are having difficulty with our transporter system. Could I ask that you use yours?"

Again a bark, which Picard interpreted as a laugh of amusement.

"Damn things, never liked them," Jord growled.

"Spacious, very spacious," Garu announced as Picard led him into the ready room. "One would think your ship was a royal barge for a princeling rather than a vessel of war."

Garu had maintained a stony silence all the way up from the transporter room. Picard was not surprised that the Tarn's first comment was sarcastic, but the captain was in no mood to rise to the bait.

Instead he merely motioned for Garu to follow him into his private quarters. The door slid shut behind them and Picard offered refreshments. Garu showed evident surprise when the replicator produced a horn of *Hammasi*.

"Where did you learn to make this brew?" Garu asked, obviously pleased with the drink's bouquet, a scent which Picard hoped to mask by ordering up a strong brew of Earl Grey.

"Commander Karish's drink of choice."

"Hmm. Very good. . . . So what is this concerning Karish? Where is he?"

"Down on the planet's surface."

"Why?"

Jean-Luc offered a quick briefing. Garu listened, saying nothing while sipping his drink.

"Captain Picard, what do you think of Karish?"

"He is a competent officer."

"He is of the reactionary circle."

"The internal politics of your government are, perhaps, not our most pressing concern," Picard replied guardedly.

Garu grunted—the equivalent of a chuckle, Picard surmised. The captain watched in amazement as his visitor drained his drink and motioned for another. Without comment Picard fetched another one from the replicator.

"The internal politics of the Tarn circles might very well become the direct concern of the Federation soon enough."

Was this a warning? Jean-Luc wondered. "Would you care to elaborate?" he asked cautiously.

"First, let me share with you my orders. My squadron was ordered here at maximum warp to assess the situation on Torgu-Va. My orders from the Ruling Circle are quite specific. We are to observe the situation. If the parties below should reach a peace agreement, independent of any influence from off the planet's surface, that will be acceptable. However, if you should move to provide any assistance to Federation personnel down on the planet I am authorized to provide full and unstinting support to the maximum of my ability to the Tarn."

"Full and unstinting?"

Garu nodded. "Up to and including the deployment of weapons systems down on the planet and fire support from orbit."

Picard said nothing for a moment, feeling slightly uncomfortable with the cold, almost lifeless stare of Garu as he finished the second horn.

"Admiral. We are facing a situation that could rapidly escalate out of control. If you should in any way interpret my current level of involvement as providing support, and decide to react with aid to Tarn personnel on the planet, I will undoubtedly be ordered to match your level of involvement. This will trigger a rapid slide downward into full-scale combat involving both of us."

Garu nodded.

"Tell me, Admiral: personally, off the record, do you want a war?"

Garu said nothing.

Picard did a quick calculation of the three Tarn ships in relationship to his own vessel. Chances were, he could cripple one, maybe two of them, but a knock-out fight with all three might result in the loss of the *Enterprise*.

"You know I outgun you," Garu announced as if reading his thoughts.

"Yes, I realize that. That equation, however, cannot be the deciding factor in the policy I might be required to follow."

"Your own death is not a deciding factor? Tell me, does the Federation train its officers to pursue suicide?"

"We are trained to fulfill our missions and to do so without regard to personal interests."

"And the crew for which you are responsible?"

"They understand the risks when they join the service, but that is not the issue before us at the moment. I want to see this situation resolved without the risk of war."

Garu offered a wry look, as if Picard's desire were mere fantasy, the dreams of an ignorant child. But a new thought was now visible on his face. He broached it with the captain. "Have you seen how the Federation news is reporting this crisis?

"You must know that there is more than one member of your government who is not at all pleased with the prospect of a full peace agreement between your side and ours. It seems some of them are using the *Verdun* as a means of stirring opinion against us."

"And your side?"

Garu smirked. "Yes, the same. Already our council has declared that the onus of the broken circle has been removed from those down below us. Some are hailing them as heroes who kept faith while cowards scrambled to seek peace."

"Why is it that those who seek peace are so often called cowards?" Picard sighed. "Often it is the harder course to pursue."

Again a chuckle erupted from Garu. Picard studied him closely. Though the Tarn seemed to display certain universal gestures, nodding the head, laughing when amused, even sighing, it was impossible to read their eyes, to sense what was going on beneath their mask-like visage.

"You realize that your decision to send teams down to the surface was viewed less than enthusiastically by certain members of the Royal Circle."

"I made my decision based upon the crisis of the moment. No hostile intent should be interpreted by those actions. I was attempting to stop the senseless killing."

"Some might not see it as senseless."

Picard stirred uncomfortably. There was a flare of temper inside and he struggled to control it. Did the Tarn really believe that there was a purpose to the primitive slaughter being waged down below?

The whole thing was an exercise in futility and to see it in any other light was beyond his comprehension.

"I suspect you are not pleased with my attitude," Garu announced.

"Why do you think that?"

"You pink-skinned creatures, so transparent. One can see the blood flowing below the surface. One can read that flow of blood to understand what is in the heart. Strange, the sight of it seems to arouse a certain hunting instinct for us."

"To my knowledge I don't think I've been contemplated in quite such a manner before," Picard replied.

"And us, what sort of primal sense do we engender?"

Picard looked down into his cup of tea and realized that it was empty. When he motioned to Garu's horn, the admiral nodded. The captain refilled it and handed it to the admiral, who came up to the counter where the replicator was.

"The scent of the drink troubles you, does it not?"

Jean-Luc smiled enigmatically.

"But you haven't answered my question, Captain Picard."

"Some theorize that wired into the psyche of my race is a dread of reptilian species. That, however, is simply instinct. The purpose of intellect is to transcend instinct."

"Very good. You are quite adroit in avoiding the

question. But perhaps we are arriving at the crux of the problem, Captain. The sight of you arouses the instinct of the hunt, the sight of us arouses the instinct to kill as well, to destroy the hunter before he strikes. Our compatriots down on Torgu-Va are therefore fulfilling their instinctive desires and, some say, pointing the way to what all of us should be doing."

"If you believe that, Admiral, then two hundred years of negotiation are for naught. You might as well take that ceremonial dagger on your belt and come at me," Picard answered smoothly.

Garu's hand slipped down to the dagger and he drew it out of its sheath, the sound of steel on leather sounding like the hiss of a snake.

"It is not ceremonial, Captain," Garu announced softly.

In spite of his training, Jean-Luc found his attention fixed on the blade. There was a flash memory of many years ago, the fight in the bar with the Nausicaans, the blade slipping between his ribs, slicing into his heart—and the drifting into the dark, to awaken with an artificial beat in his chest.

Garu stared at him and Picard wondered if indeed the admiral would come for him. The captain maintained an outward calm, intellect telling him that such an action was absurd, it served no purpose, no logic, but instinct screamed at him to strike first before the cold remorseless blade and the cold remorseless talons encompassed him.

Garu suddenly laughed, breaking the tension.

With a flick of his wrist the knife twirled through the air, slamming point first into the table by his side.

"You wondered for a moment, didn't you?" Garu asked.

"Would I be a soldier if I didn't?"

"That is what we are dealing with," Garu stated while contemplating the drink in the bottom of the horn. "You see, there is fear in our hearts too when we gaze upon the likes of you. The sense that you fear us and that in your fear you believe it best to strike first. Tell me, Captain, did you consider striking first just now?"

Picard nodded; there was no sense in denying the truth. Garu leaned against the wall and smiled.

"Captain Picard, surely you must realize what we have here. The negotiations of our governments are not something that is fully supported by many of the circles on my side. I am willing to venture that such is the case on your side as well."

Picard said nothing. The Tarn could fish all he wanted, Picard wasn't prepared to just hand over intelligence.

Garu smiled and nodded. "As I suspected. There are elements on both sides who would love nothing more than to see this incident on Torgu-Va provide the excuse, the flash point, for an escalation into a full-scale conflict. If it did, the policies of the Royal Circle would be shattered and another circle of royal blood, such as the one Commander Karish belongs to, would rise to power."

Picard raised an eyebrow. Sending Karish, had that been a mistake as far as Garu was concerned? Was he, even now, moving to another plan, hoping to use Torgu-Va for his own ends?

"May I have another?" Garu asked, nodding to the replicator.

Picard nodded and, taking the horn, refilled it and passed it over. The intoxicating effect of the drink seemed barely to touch Garu, he noted as he watched the admiral drain half the cup.

"Captain, I regret to tell you this, but the Royal Circle senses the precarious situation it is in. The balance of power is such that it could topple, plunging my planet into civil war. Torgu-Va might be the trigger for that. Though the Royal Circle wants to reach a fuller understanding with the Federation, it will not do so as an act of suicide. I will follow my orders, Captain. If you should try in any way whatsoever to increase your involvement, to stun Tarn forces or offer any aid to Federation personnel down on the surface, I shall attempt to block you by whatever means necessary to ensure the survival of my circle."

"And what do you think of all of this, Admiral?"

Garu smiled. "Madness, all of it madness."

Finishing his drink, Garu slammed the horn down, spilling some of the contents onto the table.

"I must return to my ship, Captain. It has been a pleasure meeting you. You were, after all, one of the humans I spent a good deal of time studying. It was interesting to meet you in the flesh, as they say."

Picard smiled.

"Admiral, a favor."

"What?"

"We are here. Our respective governments are hundreds of parsecs away. Let us see what we can do between us to ensure that this does not get out of control. Can we at least agree on that?"

Garu smiled, saying nothing.

"At least let us open up communication down there. You can sit in on the meeting, we can inform both sides that we are in orbit above them. I will request a cease-fire, nothing more."

Garu hesitated, then finally nodded. "If you think such a folly is worth it we can try, but I can assure you they will not listen."

"Work with me, Garu. I sense that you want to do that—you are a warrior of honor."

Garu said nothing, heading to the door and back out onto the bridge. Punching the communications tab on his shoulder, he called his ship and asked to be beamed up.

"Admiral, may I have your assurance?" Picard said.

"We must render unto Caesar what is Caesar's, Captain Picard. But we shall see what we can render unto the gods."

Garu disappeared in a beam of light.

Picard settled into his chair and the image of the

Tarn admiral, who had moments before stood on
the bridge of the *Enterprise,* flashed onto the forward screen.

Picard spared a quick glance to Data, who nodded to the forward screen. A sidebar in the lower
corner of the screen showed the tactical position of
the three Tarn ships, status lights indicating that
they were going to a higher state of readiness.

"You can see I've ordered my ships to condition
two, Captain," Jord announced.

"I see that and you will see I have not yet
responded."

For the moment there was no need to, but he
knew that behind him Worf was waiting, hovering
over the control boards, and that down in engineering Geordi had been alerted. There was a subtle
change in the air, his people were ready if need be.

"Open a hailing frequency to both sides, Mr.
Worf. Mr. Data, you may translate the Tarn language where it is appropriate."

"Understood, sir."

"Frequencies open, Captain."

Picard cleared his throat. "This is Captain Jean-
Luc Picard of the Federation starship *Enterprise,*"
he began. "I wish to speak at once to those in
command of the descendants of the Federation
ship *Verdun* and the Imperial Tarn ship *Rashasa.*
We are overriding all frequencies and I expect an
immediate response. Whoever is in command,
reply by voice radio on whatever frequency you
have and we will pick it up."

He settled back, waiting.

"Captain, your overriding of radio frequencies is an act of interference," Jord interjected.

"Momentary inconvenience applied to both sides," Picard replied. "I will clear the other frequencies as soon as we have the two leaders on-line."

Jord harumphed, shifting uncomfortably, but said nothing further.

"Sir, I have Gadin of the Circle of the Golden Talon on-line."

"Tell him to wait until we contact the other side, I will give the identical message to both sides at the same time."

Picard looked up quizzically at Jord, who finally nodded an agreement.

Another light flashed, at almost the identical location.

"Lysander Murat is on-line, Captain."

Picard nodded. "Put him through, Mr. Worf."

He drew a deep breath. "This is Captain Picard of the Federation starship *Enterprise,* maintaining orbit above Torgu-Va. I am here to inform you that all hostilities between the Tarn Empire and the Federation ceased more than two hundred years ago. I am therefore informing you that a cease-fire is in place."

He waited for several seconds. Finally Lysander's voice crackled back.

"Picard, Lysander Murat, commander of all Federation forces on the planet Torgu-Va here.

Captain, I do not recognize your authority to issue such an order."

On the main screen Picard could see that Jord was frowning while listening to the hissing reply of Gadin. Picard shot a glance at Data.

"Gadin's response is essentially the same," Data announced.

"Then, Mr. Murat, you must recognize the authority of my superior, Admiral Nagaru of Starfleet Command, who has conveyed the same order." Picard looked up at the screen again, his look somehow conveying his thoughts, and Jord nodded. "Gadin of the Golden Talon, ships of the Tarn imperial forces are in orbit above this planet as well, here to convey the same information."

Jord stiffened slightly but said nothing.

"That is a lie," Gadin shot back.

"It is the truth," Jord interjected. "Three ships of the Imperial Talon orbit Torgu-Va as well. There is a cease-fire."

"Captain, smash them now!" Murat shouted. "Strike first, don't make the same mistake as the *Verdun!*"

"Again the same response from Gadin," Data announced. "He is calling for Jord to launch a strike."

Picard sighed to himself. Any hope of negotiating, of talking sense, was breaking down.

"The away teams, I wish to speak with them," Picard snapped.

"They are elsewhere," Murat replied, and there

was a brief pause, "helping in our defense, unlike you."

Picard stiffened.

"I wish to speak to Commander Riker immediately."

"It's been lovely chatting, Picard, but there's a war to be fought. Murat out."

"Damn," Picard hissed under his breath.

"Picard, is it true your people are helping them?" Jord now asked coldly.

"Of course not, Commander Riker is my most trusted officer. Murat was deliberately trying to provoke a situation up here, Admiral."

"Sir, the same reply from Gadin, he said Karish is actively engaged in combat," Data said.

Picard looked accusingly at Jord, who seemed taken aback.

"Cut communications to the planet, Mr. Worf."

"Yes, sir."

Picard looked back at Jord.

Jord was still speaking, then looked at the screen and stopped.

"May I ask what you said?" Picard inquired.

"Suspicious, are we, Captain?" Jord asked.

"Just that, given the situation, I am required to know."

Jord chuckled again. "You seem to be playing your hand openly, so I will too, Picard. Just an inquiry to Gadin to reconsider." To one side Picard could see Data nod in agreement.

"Sorry, Admiral."

"If your Riker is indeed helping them, we shall be forced to respond."

"The same goes for Karish," Picard replied, ruing his own decision to send the away teams down. This situation was spinning further out of control by the moment.

Riker had had his fill of roaming after an hour. His primary responsibility to inform the Federation forces of the current status of their war accomplished, he was stymied as to how to fulfill the second: How was he going to convince Murat's people to accept the situation and establish a cease-fire agreement?

Janice had retired to the bunker she would be staying in with the hopes of speaking further with Julia Murat, which left Riker with nothing of any importance to do until he could arrange a second meeting with Lysander. His walk through the level for the past hour had left him disheartened. Word spread quickly throughout the city, it appeared. He had been greeted with far less enthusiasm than on his arrival. The people were polite, but wary. He had offered to help in the cleanup of the earlier bombing but had been met with firm smiles of denial.

Another rumbling wave washed through the corridors, not as severe as the previous bombardment. A battle group trudged by, obviously returning from the fighting, men and women, eyes unfocused, hollow, battle tunics torn and bloodstained.

One of them staggered past, dried tears streaking the dust creased into her face. Over and over she whispered the same refrain, "I told you to stay low, stay low . . . I told you to stay low, stay low."

Riker slowed, wanting to extend a helping hand, but a sergeant gently elbowed him aside, putting his arm around the woman's shoulder and leading her away.

Frustrated, Riker decided to make his way back to his bunker. He turned down a side street that led behind a series of houses, cubicle block buildings built with little attention to coziness. There were no people here. If he closed his eyes he could almost believe that he was in a quiet neighborhood back home in Alaska, where the old men sat outside on summer evenings and watched the sun still blazing high in the arctic sky, even at midnight. What would those old men think of a world where no one saw the sun, where all of their talk, all of their lives, revolved around slaughter?

A kicked stone behind him startled his attention away from thoughts of home. He turned quickly, surprised to find a girl standing merely inches behind him. She was small and delicately made, beautiful even at five or six. Stringy hair had been twined into two braids at either side of her head and she wore the same coarse clothing of the adults.

"You've been following me." Riker smiled as he said it.

The girl nodded but did not comment.

"Do you always follow strangers?" Riker asked.

The child cocked her head back to take in Riker's height. "I'm a watcher," she said proudly.

"A watcher? What does a watcher do?"

"Hide."

"Where do you hide?"

"All over."

Riker smiled gently.

"What's your name?"

"Alissia Murat."

Riker was surprised; this must be Lysander's daughter. "Well, it's been very nice to meet you, Alissia. I'm sure I'll see you later."

The girl did not move.

"Good-bye," he prodded. When she still made no comment he smiled again and turned away, walking down the way he had come. He wanted to turn his head and see if the child had moved, but thought against it—no need to frighten her. But halfway down the street, his curiosity overcame him. He cast a quick look behind his shoulder and was surprised to see that the child had followed him, again, so quietly that he had not realized her presence.

"Daddy said that you came to make everything right, but now you aren't going to."

Riker sighed. What was their notion of right, he wondered.

"I'm going to try," he said, infusing the remark with more optimism than he felt.

"Want to see where I hide?" she asked simply.

There was no excitement in the question, but then that was unsurprising. There was no time or place on this planet for childlike enthusiasm.

"All right."

Alissia reached up and took his hand, bulky in her own, and led him away. He noted her act of trust with surprise but said nothing, allowing her to lead him down several back streets. They entered a tunnel that led them away from the main level. Unlike the narrow tunnels that had brought them into the city, this tunnel was wide and dimly lit with emergency lights. It was not a tunnel designed to mislead, as were the series of passageways that he had originally encountered, but rather, formed for efficient movement. He concluded that it had been built as an escape tunnel, its dusty appearance indicating that it had not been in use for some time.

They soon reached a large circular room, the openings of more tunnels radiating in all directions like wheel spokes. Riker dropped the girl's hand and peered into the entrance nearest him. It appeared far more narrow than the tunnel they had come from but still maneuverable.

"What's down there, Alissia?"

"It's just my tunnel."

"Where does it go to?"

"Outside."

"Outside where?"

Alissia looked at Riker with a blank expression, as if she didn't understand.

"To them," she responded without affect.

"Do you mean that it's an unguarded exit? A way out of the city?"

"There are lots of them. It's closed up with stuff in front of it, there are mines and traps too."

She spoke as casually of the traps as other children might speak of dolls and favorite toys.

He turned his attention back to the opening. Clever, he thought. If the need for an immediate escape did arise, it would be foolish to herd the entire city out of one exit. Each of the side tunnels led to a different surface exit point, thereby dispersing the population over a large area of ground.

The child walked away from him, seeming to lose interest in the conversation. Riker watched with curiosity as she began to spin herself around in circles, sending her braided hair lashing out on either side of her. The activity seemed to occupy her, yet he found no signs of pleasure on her face.

"Will you take me up there?"

Alissia stopped suddenly, her gray eyes round with interest.

"We aren't allowed up there."

"You've been up there."

"I'm tiny and I can run fast."

Riker thought a moment. "Will I fit?"

The girl looked him up and down, as if sizing him up. She nodded an affirmative.

"Don't tell?" the child asked.

"I won't."

174

Alissia paused a moment. Riker could decipher nothing from the placid face. It remained curious, devoid of any other emotion.

"Come on."

Riker followed quietly, ducking into the small entrance to avoid the brush obscuring the opening. The tunnel was dank, dripping with moisture. A system of piping ran along the roof, making it difficult to walk without ducking to one side. The walls and ground of the portal were made of dirt and rock, held up only by a few support beams every hundred feet or so.

"It gets smaller up here. You're gonna have to crawl."

She was right. The tunnel narrowed significantly, sloping upward as it decreased in diameter. Crawling on all fours, Riker attempted to keep up with the child, who was agile and dexterous in the cramped area. They continued in this manner for some time before reaching a level area of ground. The tunnel opened upon a small room of sorts. Granite walls with metal plating covered the floor. In the right side of the room several boulders were piled up to make a stairway that led to a securely latched metal hatch in the ceiling. The way out, Riker supposed.

She pointed to several wires cunningly set across the bottom of the boulders and gingerly stepped over them. Alissia turned and held her finger in front of her lips, cautioning for silence. She scrambled up the rocks and motioned for Riker to do the same. "This way. You can see the blue thing from up here," the child whispered.

Riker nodded, cautiously moving over the wires and climbing the rock pile carefully. Once safely on top, he positioned himself awkwardly next to the girl.

"Look. Through there. The broken piece. Can you see it?" Riker peered through a half-inch slat of corroded metal tangled with brown weeds and gravel. At first glance he could make out little but a finely laid layer of red silt covering everything in sight. The slightest exhaled breath sent several grains into his eyes. Blinking to clear his vision, he looked away.

"Did you see it? Isn't it beautiful?" The child gazed with wide-eyed wonder at Riker.

"See what?" Riker blinked again, beginning to question what whim of his led him to follow the girl in the first place.

"The blue thing. It's so pretty. Daddy thinks so too." The child stared up again, drinking in the sight. Her animation, the first he had seen since meeting the girl, was contagious. She was captivated by whatever it was that she saw through the corroded metal. He craned his head up next to hers and took a second look through the narrow opening, squinting his eyes to see through the crack. This time he could see beyond the dirt and debris, past the dry weeds and up further. Puzzled, he pulled back and stared at the girl, who was waiting, eyes wide, for his response.

"You mean, the sky?" he said quietly.

"Sky?" she said reverently. "Is that what it's called?" And she stuck her tiny head up against the hatch again, nose peeking through the tiny slit, eyelashes brushing against the metal in her effort to be as close to the opening as possible.

Riker studied her little form pressed upward, straining to get a glimpse. He had the sudden urge to break through the exit and climb through, throwing her up onto his shoulders so that she could reach up her little fingers and laugh as she tried to tickle the clouds. He wished he could take her away from this world where children wore the eyes of old men and their only source of wonder was in a stolen, slivered glimpse of sky.

Explosions thundered in the distance and his first instinct was to pull her away but she didn't move. She was far more battle-wise than he; if there was danger nearby she was bred to sense it, so he let her stay. He silently cursed the fact that his communicator and Janice's had been confiscated. From here he could easily reach the ship, find out what was happening, report in, and yes, perhaps even beam this child up and away from hell.

Alissia apparently noted Riker's silence and turned to look at him. She moved so that her gray luminous eyes were inches in front of his own, their noses almost brushing against each other. With a voice no stronger than a whisper she asked slowly, "You don't like my sky?"

"It's the most beautiful piece of sky I have ever seen," he said truthfully.

She blinked once and then offered him the gift of a smile; it was the first sign of her childhood. "Good. I think so too." She spoke confidently, her face serious, her voice wise. And without another word, she scrambled down the rocks and left the room.

"Dear God, keep her safe," Riker murmured to himself before following, wondering where Janice was now.

Chapter Seven

As Julia Murat motioned for Janice to wait by the tunnel entrance, Janice second-guessed for the thousandth time that day her decision to join the platoon heading up to the surface. Perhaps "join" was not the proper word. For while she was certainly joining in the journey, she was most certainly not joining in any of this insane fighting.

"It's a climb to the ridge above," Murat announced. Moving swiftly she started out, weaving up through the boulders. Janice could not determine whether the woman was offering this comment as a note of apology or derision. Janice marveled at how Julia, who was surely approaching her mid-sixties, tackled the rough terrain with such adroitness. She hardly appeared out of breath, which made for a sad comparison to Janice's own labored attempts at climbing.

There was in Julia's eyes an intensity that Janice could not define. She gazed out upon the view that Murat was transfixed by and noted its beauty. It was indeed breathtaking, an eerie transformation from the parched land found during the day. Stretching for miles, the mountains extended to the northern horizon in folds of buckled land and shaded slopes tinged with the harsh, red light of the dying day.

The battle around the northern entryways raged far below in the valley: smoke, fire, concussive blasts still thumping into the lungs. Perverse as it seemed to her, the view was glorious, thrilling, and she felt deep guilt at the pleasure. This was not history, she had to forcefully remind herself. This was reality. Good men and women were dying down there.

Janice's gaze turned again to the sky, rising from the mountain peaks like a taut, platinum canvas. Streaked across the horizon were stains of crimson clouds, trailing their color as a reminder of earlier glory.

"The wounds of our people," Julia whispered softly.

Janice hesitated, cautious of the pain in her companion's voice.

"We could heal those wounds," Janice offered gently.

"Heal our wounds, could you? Tell me, Dr.

Eardman, with what would you propose to heal them?"

"With peace. Isn't that preferable to the killing?"

"Yes, peace . . . the magical balm . . . our elixir of salvation."

Julia stood immovable, drinking in the landscape as if its wild fierceness could temper the raging of her spirit. And yet she was obviously looking through a soldier's eyes as well. Removing her binoculars, she carefully scanned the ground beyond the river and then across the face of the next ridgeline.

"Watching post. They must have had one over there and called in the air strike. Maybe we'll see it from up here."

Janice refused to believe that was the only reason Murat had climbed up here. Maybe it was to share something, maybe it was simply to soak in the open air, the windswept heights. *God knows this woman deserves a moment of freedom from the dark confines below,* Janice thought.

"This can end, Julia. Please let us end it."

"You speak of a peace that my people do not understand. We have forgotten its meaning."

"You could learn it again. Think of the lives that could be spared."

With this, Murat turned and faced Janice. Her look was one of astonishment that slowly shifted to disgust.

"We are not barbarians simply because we fight, Doctor. We think of the lives that could be spared.

How could you assume that we do not? To do so would be inhuman. Despite our forced habitation with the Tarn, we have maintained our humanity. We may be machines of war, we may fight to survive, we may kill often and effectively, but we have a conscience. We love our people."

"I was not implying—"

"I know what you were implying. . . . But you're wrong. . . . I think of the lives that could be spared. I think of the lives that haven't been spared."

The air turned chill with the blue-black hue of night.

"I had four other boys beside Lysander. Good boys. Tillean, the youngest, he understood the heart of his people. He fought for them; he fought to live, not simply to stay alive. He was called to disarm a bomb three years ago in one of the western wings.

"The men," she chuckled gently, "they used to tease him about his skill as a bomb technician. Said he was better with wires and fuses than he was with a knife or planning military strategy. They were kidding, of course. Tillean could outmaneuver them all. Second only to Lysander. . . . They said the bomb was defused. He and his son, my first grandson, were shaking hands over their accomplishment when the warning light came on and the timer began ticking again. The room had been sealed off to prevent damage to the rest of the wing, so they were trapped inside. He had four seconds. . . . Four seconds to review his life."

Murat turned to Janice again with a look of appeal in her eyes.

"What can you recall in four seconds, Doctor? A lifetime? Surely not."

Murat's gaze dropped from the helpless face of Janice and sought the mountains instead, now a soft shade of mahogany beneath a sky just beginning to glitter with pinpricks of silver.

Janice watched as the look of tender nostalgia was replaced by anger on the face of Murat. Her body stiffened with bitterness; her fingers writhed with frustration. The carefully maintained rigid demeanor crumpled beneath the naked pain of the memory of her son's death. And then, suddenly, the tense muscles relaxed, the bearing softened. Julia Murat exhaled on a sigh of weariness.

Facing Janice, she said, "I do think of the lives that could be spared, Dr. Eardman. Those who have died, those who will die . . . their hearts beat alongside my own. I don't take a single breath without feeling them breathe along with me. But I alone do not decide their fate. I am with them but I cannot save them. If it were within my power . . . it is not within my power, however. Lysander is a skilled warrior, a brilliant strategist . . . and he is a good man, however hardened. He is my son. . . . He is my son, Doctor, my last son. And I will fight for him. I will die for him."

"So it's to continue . . . forever?" Janice ventured.

"We must win this ourselves, Doctor. Otherwise

183

all this was meaningless. You rush about thinking only of the gifts you bring, not of all the questions that will come afterward. This decision was made realizing that there would be such questions. If there is victory we must achieve it ourselves. Then we can hold our heads high and return to the Federation."

"And your son made this decision?"

She was silent for a moment. "I had hoped they'd get arrogant after the attack, get careless and reveal their position. I guess not. Damn."

Murat cased her field glasses and hoisted her rifle.

"Come, Doctor. You will get chilled if we stay much longer."

Again the motherly tone; then Murat stiffened. "In any case, it won't be safe here in a few moments. Their infrared systems are a lot better than ours."

Murat turned and began the descent, leaving her companion to follow her lead. Janice was left standing, amazed at the malignant tone the evening had adopted. She had embraced Julia Murat, the Federation on Torgu-Va, with the practicality of the historian. Here, in a clinical sense, was war as history, an eternal war. Yet one could not stay clinically detached, not when one felt the rush of boiling air from a napalm strike. In spite of the years of training she could almost feel hate for the other side, and she struggled to control it.

She felt the hypocrisy of her words flood over

her. How could she plead for peace so passionately and damn the enemy in the very next breath? There was no denying the insanity of this war. Yet here, in the wind, in the raw and hideous, poignant world of the Federation fighters, she dared to weigh the insanity against the hatred.

"The wounds of your people, Julia," Janice whispered to herself before making her way down the mountainside in pursuit of Murat.

Julia Murat moved quickly, her mind heavy, her body sore. They would be reaching the tunnels within moments; she must decide what to do before then. She turned her head over her shoulder. Janice was keeping up. *Not bad,* she thought. *The child is impulsive, young, but determined.* Julia smiled cautiously. Her people could use a bit of this young doctor's spirited temper.

The tunnel entrance was in sight. The women skirted the large boulders and found themselves in the dark mouth of the cave they had exited earlier in the day.

Clearing the outer guards, she led the way back down into the bowels of the city, and then, at the approach of the junction that led to the concealed chambers, she hesitated. She had been wrestling with the decision for two days now, ever since first contact. But the orders had been far too clear.

And yet there was something in the youthful idealism of the child following her that was disturbing. The offer from above was so patently simple, and so infinitely complex. Yes, there was the argument of history, of two hundred years of struggle that could not simply be turned off like a light. And yet there was something else, far more disturbing . . . the realization that the war was being lost. Six months ago they had been so confident of victory, the gaseous diffusion plant was on-line and within two years enough weapons-grade uranium would be separated to make the first bomb . . . but the Tarn had gotten there first. They were now at the very gates of the city; if they had a second bomb it would be used here. And when the Tarn used that second bomb, it was all over. A Federation victory was now impossible.

She stood silent, pondering, and then reached her decision.

"There has been a change in plans," Julia said quietly. "We'll not go back to the main level quite yet. I'd like to show you something."

Once again, Janice followed the woman blindly through the continually changing system of tunnels. They exited into a room with vaulted ceilings. The standard team of three men were guarding an elevator.

"Keep your mouth shut," Julia whispered as they approached the soldiers.

" 'Please' would do just nicely," Janice muttered, irritated. She thought she heard the muffled sound of one guard suppressing a laugh, but was unsure in the darkness.

"You, there. Stop." An imposing voice disturbed the monotonous hum of the night. "This is a restricted area. What are you doing here?"

"Soldier, I'm checking the security of the area. Orders of Commander Murat."

"Mrs. Murat? I'm sorry, ma'am, I didn't recognize you at first. I wouldn't have been as abrupt. . . . But, uh, ma'am, you still shouldn't be here. I didn't receive any orders from the commander to indicate that a security check would be in effect this evening."

"Well, of course you didn't. That would defeat the purpose of a check, now, wouldn't it, soldier?"

"Uh, yes, ma'am. I suppose so."

"Well, never mind, we're proceeding to the level below. This area is secure. The elevator, please."

"Yes, ma'am. Have a good night."

Julia Murat motioned to Janice to follow her onto the elevator. The two entered. Janice kept her eyes averted and stayed in the shadow of Murat. The doors began to close quietly when the soldier on guard quickly extended an arm to prevent the door from shutting. Janice drew in her breath sharply as Murat slowly cocked an eyebrow at the young man.

"Yes? What is it, soldier?"

"I just wanted to thank you, ma'am."

"Thank me? . . . It's just a security check. No thanks are needed."

The man smiled slightly. Janice took in his lanky form, his toothy grin. His smile took away the edge that the oversized clothing and military boots added to his frame. He must have been only nineteen or twenty, Janice imagined.

"My daughter was in the wreckage of yesterday's bombing. You pulled her out. . . . I wanted to thank you."

Julia's gaze of defensive effrontery diminished with the stark gratitude of the man.

And in an instant, Janice knew what it was that held this band of warriors together. It passed between the lieutenant and the woman; it made them equal. A look, a shared moment. The conveyance of that thing, more emotion than thought, more vague than definable. The essence of loyalty, the heart of bravery, that which embraces loss and nourishes sacrifice. It was there, hiding in their gaze, and they knew it was a thing to be felt and not mentioned.

With a pang of jealousy, Janice watched the two closely. She could not share their moment. Once again, she found herself merely the historian: noting, perceiving, processing.

And then the moment was gone. Murat nodded, breaking the mood, shifting it into the focus of real time.

"You have a beautiful daughter. . . . Good night, son."

"Good night, ma'am." The soldier stepped away from the doors.

As the doors shut another wave of explosions rocked the two.

"It's getting closer," Julia said absently. "I think they're moving to breach an entrance."

"And then what?" Janice asked coldly. "A slaughter?"

Before Julia could answer, the ancient iron-wickered elevator came to a stop, the door sliding open, and Janice gasped with astonishment.

Riker leaned against the rock wall, gasping for breath in the suffocating heat and smoke. They had sprinted all the way up from the center of the city. Lysander had not once slowed the pace as he led the company of troops up to point where the Tarn had secured a foothold inside an entryway. The invitation to join the group had been a taunting one and Riker had reluctantly gone along with it, frustrated as well by the knowledge that Janice had wandered off on a similar mission.

From the corridor ahead came a continual rattle of small-arms fire, explosions, screams of pain, triumphal roars of battle joy. Wounded streamed past, bearing word that the Tarn had gained a main access corridor and were fanning out.

Riker sighed at the inevitability of the situation. Murat's men waited, weapons raised, the sound of battle rising and falling. Murat—indefatigable, Riker thought—stood near a bend in the corridor, tense and expectant.

Without warning he spoke, Riker his only audience in the dark tunnel. "There are tales in my family, tales of Lucian Murat."

He hesitated for a moment then continued. "He used to sail ships on the oceans of Earth. I've seen pictures. Endless miles of open space all the color of a newborn's eye. He used to say, even with all of that water stretching so far to the horizon that it blended into the sky, there was always more; for in reality, you were only looking at the top."

Riker listened carefully. It was almost as if Lysander had talked to the legendary leader and the dreams of Earth had somehow been kept alive.

"I've been to the sea when I was a child."

"Really? Where?"

"On Earth. The North Atlantic Ocean."

"And it was like this?"

Will grinned with the childhood memory of an idyllic summer on the coast of Maine.

"Yes."

"So much space. What would one do with it all?" Lysander's arm swept in a stilted circular motion, indicating the tiny area they were trapped in. And the simple gesture conveyed to Will the longing, the instinctive ache to crawl up from under the ground, to feel the breeze coiling in from the sea, to smell the grass.

"The Tarn have free access to the surface while we rummage around in the ground like beasts," Lysander said roughly. "Forced to eat in the dirt, bathe in the dirt."

Lysander's voice reverberated with the frustration of one who is accustomed to futile arguments with himself.

"Don't you see why we must fight? The Tarn won't just simply go away and leave us. They enjoy the fact that we have been chased underground, forced into hibernation while they roam freely, ravishing the land that is already so starved that it has begun to turn on itself for survival. They are more warlike than we are. We just fight to survive. But they, they enjoy it. Their kind are vicious savages, nothing more. They'll never stop."

"And how are you different, Commander? How is it that your hatred is less savage than theirs? They have the upper hand, obviously. But how different would it be if you were above ground?"

"We are different, Commander, because we aim to end the fighting. We are not creatures of war at heart."

"No, you simply fight to extinguish the Tarn, to destroy their race or, at the very least, subdue them into slavery. You're not fighting for peace," Riker responded.

"There is no peace with the Tarn. Their kind are incapable of peace."

"Negotiations have proven successful in the past. The Tarn have been persuaded to cease their expansionist policies. We exist in peace with the Tarn. You are the Federation leader. If you made a stand, the Tarn would be encouraged to listen. Perhaps they would follow suit with the remainder of their people who have chosen to live in harmony with the Federation. It would at least open the door to communication."

"And then what?" Murat snarled. "Live on the surface of our lovely Torgu-Va with the Tarn . . . our new friends? The scaly beast that killed my brother would be invited to share my table, eat with my wife and daughter. Those who murdered our children would suddenly be our neighbors."

Riker remained silent. Murat's hatred filled the small enclosure.

A blast at the entrance to the corridor interrupted the moment of quiet. Two wounded soldiers came around the corner, one of them pausing to fire a long burst with an assault gun before dodging past Murat. "We're it," one of them cried, "they're behind us!"

"On your feet!" Murat hissed. "Chang, rear security, attack pattern eight! Let's go!"

Riker was momentarily caught off guard. The sound of the explosion was still ringing in his ears. The corridor ahead was filled with smoke. Lights flickered, the air alive with bullets, men and women going down around him, some dying, others crouching to fire back. An explosive roar erupted from a side corridor. Its concussion knocked Riker over. He lost sight of Murat, the others.

Wild confusion erupted, a tall shadowy figure rushed past, screaming, a Tarn, uniform on fire. More waded in, knives flashing out of scabbards, human and Tarn struggling hand-to-hand in the flame-lit corridor.

"They must not take this tunnel. Stand your ground!" Murat's voice rose above the din.

Confused, Riker scrambled back. A Tarn came at him, blade lowered. Riker dodged the blow using the butt of his assault gun to knock the Tarn out. He gazed down at the creature, confused.

"Finish it!" someone screamed.

Riker saw a young woman, wide-eyed with battle fury, glaring at him. He refused, shaking his head, backing up. Before he could react she lowered her gun and emptied a burst into the Tarn.

Riker wanted to scream at her, to scream at all of them, to damn all of them to this hell of their own making.

An instant later the woman collapsed, clutching her side. At least here was something he could do, Riker thought. Slinging his gun, he reached over, grabbed the woman, and started to drag her back out of the fray.

"Leave me be, I can still fight," she yelled.

Riker ignored her protest. Placing her gently on the ground, he turned and went back into the fight, pulling out a second soldier, who had a Tarn blade buried in his stomach. As Riker struggled to maintain a hold of the soldier's uniform, he felt a brand sear through his chest. He lost his breath with the pain and gasped for air. His legs felt buoyant, flimsy beneath the weight of his chest. He fell to the ground, the world around him becoming oddly dim and muffled. Feet ran past him. He heard a distant cry of retreat. Riker could see the Tarn filling the corridor, their clay-caked boots rattling the earth where his ear lay.

The Federation fighters must have fallen back, or maybe it was just that he couldn't hear them any longer. He could see the Tarn boots coming closer, a left shoe untied, a rare pair of shiny boots pausing in front of his face. He blinked quickly, struggling to remain alert as the Tarn in front of him knelt to his face.

"Not quite dead, I see," the Tarn hissed.

"Karish," Riker whispered. And then he knew no more.

Chapter Eight

"CAPTAIN, THERE IS AN AUDIO HAIL from the surface. It is Dr. Eardman."

"On screen," Picard snapped.

"Captain Picard, Lieutenant Commander Eardman reporting, sir."

"Yes, Commander?" Picard replied coolly. He fought down a temptation to take her to task for not reporting sooner. It had been nearly forty-eight hours without contact since the beam-down. But then, there was probably a perfectly good explanation for the away team's silence. And if not, there was plenty of time to reprimand both Eardman and Riker later. He hoped. Where in the world was Riker anyway? Before he had a chance to ask, Eardman continued breathlessly.

195

"My apologies for the delay, sir. We were required to leave our communicators down below. They were worried that the Tarn could track on them. Sir, I must keep this short, under one minute so it can't be triangulated."

"I see. Well, then, Lieutenant, shall we begin with Commander Riker. Where is he?"

"He's, uh, not here—sir, may I suggest that you come down to the surface."

Picard said nothing for a moment. Such a request, coming from a new officer on his staff, was highly irregular. So was the panic he heard in her voice. The captain took a deep breath and reminded himself that the young historian hadn't had much starship duty.

"Your reasoning, Commander Eardmann?"

"Sir, Commander Riker is wounded, his condition is serious."

Picard took a moment to compose himself. How bad was it?

"Give me the coordinates, Dr. Eardman, we'll beam him directly to sickbay."

"Sir, he is too far below and I've been ordered, um, I mean, well, asked not to do that."

"And who is giving you these orders, Dr. Eardman?" *Last I heard this officer was under my command,* he reflected sardonically despite the seriousness of the situation. *I really must have a talk with her once she's back on board.*

She hesitated, Picard sensed there was something more here and she wasn't going to say it.

"Sir, Admiral Jord is paging."

"On screen," Picard announced, knowing that Eardman could clearly hear his command.

Obviously she was being reticent out of concern about the Tarn monitoring.

"Dr. Eardman, stand by, please," Picard said, and nodded for Data to put Admiral Jord on while shutting off the commlink to Eardman.

"Monitoring our communications, Admiral?"

Jord grunted. "This creates a problem, Captain."

"One of my crew is injured."

"So I heard. Does that mean he was in combat? If so, Captain, this presents a very unpleasant scenario for me."

"The orders to my personnel were strict. They were not to be engaged in any way whatsoever."

"Yet one of them was injured. So it seems we must assume . . ."

"We must assume nothing, sir. Remember that the city where my first officer is located is currently under Tarn attack," Picard replied sharply. "I want to go down there to find out what is going on, Admiral."

He hesitated, hating the fact that he was forced to ask. "I know that you won't have any objections. This mission is strictly to check on my personnel."

"Interesting. Tell me, Captain, is it your policy to dash about looking for adventure instead of commanding from your own bridge?" Jord pressed, sidestepping the challenge in Picard's voice. "I understand that you had one or two other starship commanders who were famous for doing that."

Picard smiled despite himself. This fellow didn't miss a trick. One of these days, when this blasted war was over, they would have to have a drink together under more pleasant circumstances. As long as it wasn't *Hammasi.*

"Commander Riker is my second-in-command." Picard paused. He knew he really didn't owe Jord an explanation. Perhaps he was just trying to rationalize. After all, there was something to what the Tarn had said. Picard really could have sent someone else.

"Command Riker is also my friend," he added quietly. It was Jord's turn to pause.

"This is irregular, Captain."

Picard smiled. It was an objection, but a half-hearted one. Just as the captain had thought—the Tarn admiral understood personal loyalty.

"What about this mission is not, sir," Picard replied calmly.

"Indeed, sir. All right, Captain. Beam down, retrieve your wounded officer, and return."

"I will also attempt to convey the continued wish for a cease-fire."

Jord shook his head. "If you wish to appear as a beggar, that is your concern, not mine."

Picard shifted uncomfortably.

"Our transporter is still down, Admiral."

Jord chuckled. "So you want to use ours?"

"I was planning to use a shuttlecraft, but since

you've made the offer, I will accept. I also wish to take our ship's doctor."

"Two now?" Jord was silent for a moment, as if debating whether he could haggle something out of this favor.

"Drop your shields. Hail me with your communicator when you are ready, Captain."

"Thank you, Admiral." Picard hesitated for an instant. "You know, of course, that allowing me to beam down with your system will provide you with the exact location of the Federation city, quite a tactical advantage."

"We already gained that coordinate by tracking your lieutenant's signal. The information has been filed if needed for later use."

Picard said nothing as the image of Jord faded.

Picard and Crusher rematerialized in a shallow depression. Dry rock walls rising up in a bowl. Within seconds, sweat started to break out on Picard's forehead, and he squinted while looking up at the boiling sun.

And then he heard the sound of metal clicking on metal. The sound was very old, from another time, yet he knew it immediately. It was the sound of a round being chambered into a gun.

"Don't move."

Picard cautiously looked over his shoulder and saw three forms rising up from the boulders, their camouflage so perfect that for an instant it had seemed as if the rocks had come alive.

"Jean-Luc Picard, captain of the Federation star ship *Enterprise*," he announced softly while cautiously extending his arms out to show that he was unarmed.

"Just stay where you are."

A soft whistle echoed and he waited, looking over at Crusher, who offered a wan smile.

"You know, Jean-Luc, ten minutes ago I was fast asleep and having a most delightful dream."

"Sorry, Beverly."

"Captain Picard."

The woman's voice was sharp. Picard looked up to the rim of the bowl and saw her. She appeared to be in her late fifties or early sixties, maybe older.

Picard nodded.

Dr. Eardman appeared by her side.

"Captain Picard, I'm glad to see you," Eardman announced.

Julia Murat whistled softly and the three sentries closed around Picard and Crusher, motioning for them to scramble up the side of the bowl. Reaching the rim, the soldiers paused for a second, sharply scanning the cliffs, and then motioned their guests forward at a run.

Seconds later, Picard was in a tunnel entrance. Julia Murat paused, holding her hand up. Picard stopped by her side and looked back. A distant thumping echoed. The sound was strange and he looked over at her.

"Air strike on entry point Delta Five. They're airlifting more troops in."

Without another word she motioned them forward into the tunnel, and Eardman fell in by Picard's side.

"How's Will?" Beverly asked Eardman.

"Not too bad, Doctor."

"You said it was serious, Commander," Picard said sternly.

"Sir, I wasn't sure if we were being monitored. I felt it essential to get you down here but couldn't explain why on an open channel."

The captain frowned. That talk he was planning to have with Eardman would be even longer than he first anticipated.

As they circled down into the darkness, Eardman hurriedly recapped what Picard suspected was a heavily censored account of all that had transpired. He said nothing, taking it all in as they stepped around traps, pausing for a moment at an intersection of corridors where, from out of the darkness the distant thumping still echoed, sounding even stranger than before.

A platoon of assault troops rushed past them, laden down with bandoleers of ammunition, carrying heavy boxes marked GRENADES. Stretcher bearers came past in the opposite direction, carrying their shattered burdens. Murat looked over at Crusher, who watched them pass, her eyes wide with disbelief.

"Primitive, aren't we, Doctor?" Murat said coldly.

"I'd like to help."

"Ah, but for your fine noninterference clause."

Picard watched helplessly as Crusher chewed her lip. He could only imagine what she was restraining herself from telling Murat.

"Are we almost there?" he asked.

Murat nodded. She pointed down a side corridor and detailed off the three soldiers who had accompanied them.

"Take Dr. Crusher here to Infirmary Seven."

Crusher looked over at Picard, who nodded. The group departed, leaving Murat, Eardman, and Picard alone.

"I have another surprise for you, Captain," Murat said.

Picard looked at Eardman, who smiled.

"Sir, it's remarkable," she announced.

"I've had quite enough surprises today, Commander Eardman," he said pointedly. The smile quickly faded from the historian's face.

"Temper, temper, Captain," Murat said dryly. "You'd think that after two hundred years the menfolk would get a hold of themselves," she whispered confidentially to Eardman, who looked as if she would like nothing better than to hide under a rock. Picard ignored the interaction. It was becoming clear that he would have to overlook quite a bit to function effectively among these stubborn people.

"Madam, if you have any authority here I must inform you of our intent. As captain of the *Enter-*

prise and a representative of Starfleet, I am conveying to you that Starfleet desires all hostile actions
against the Tarn to cease immediately. If my away
team has not conveyed this to you, or if there was a
failure to understand my last communication to
Lysander Murat, then let me repeat myself: Starfleet Command is ordering an immediate cease-
fire."

"Lysander is my son, Captain, and no, we did
not fail to understand the order. We disregarded it.
We are waging a defensive war. Should I tell my
troops to open the barriers, bare their throats to the
Tarn, and open the filters to let the gas come in to
our children and elders?"

"No, of course not. But this fighting must stop.
There are implications far beyond the immediate
concerns here."

"Ah yes, other implications. Is that the standard
justification for abandoning one's troops and sell-
ing off worlds, to satisfy the immediate concerns of
those who don't actually do the dying?"

"Captain, could you please see something first
before we continue this conversation?" Eardman
interrupted.

Picard shot her a quick glance. At her age he
would never have questioned a superior this way—
or would he? *I would,* he thought. *I would and I did,
when enough was at stake.* The captain decided to
trust his instincts. And young Dr. Eardman's.

"Lead on then," Picard replied.

Murat led the way back through the maze of corridors and into a room filled with murals celebrating the glory of battles won. Picard made no comment as he gazed upon the icons and frescoes, but when he saw the doorway, the image of Lucian Murat, and the way in which Murat opened the door and beckoned for him to enter, the captain had a sudden sense of what was to come and his pulse quickened. . . .

The man lying on the bed in the middle of the tiny room was old, infinitely old. His hair had turned from white to an aged sickly yellow. At their approach, the old man moved his head restlessly. Though his eyes were open, there was no sight: the twin orbs were opaque, the face scarred by a fire from long ago. And yet, in spite of the age, the scars, the skeletal features, Picard knew . . . and in that knowing his heart froze. He felt a profound shock in that instant. It was as if he had come face-to-face with a dream, a legend again made flesh.

"Captain Lucian Murat?" Picard whispered.

A man, dressed in dirt-stained battle fatigues and standing by the foot of the bed, turned and looked at Picard. There was a small girl by the soldier's side. Still in shock, Picard noted that the man had the same Gallic nose, full lips, and high forehead.

"Captain Picard, my son Lysander," Julia announced, "second-in-command of this Federation base."

Lysander nodded an acknowledgment but Picard's attention was still focused on the frail body in the bed. For an instant, he wondered if he had been mistaken. Perhaps the old man was in fact dead; but then he saw the gentle rising and falling of the chest.

Julia stepped up to the bed and knelt down, whispering something. The old man nodded. Julia stood back up and came to Picard's side.

"He was resting," she whispered. "Give him a moment."

Picard nodded, still silenced by his own disbelief.

"Captain, there is much you do not know," Julia whispered. "When the survivors of *Verdun* landed on this planet, their captain was with them, but his vision and health were shattered by the fire on the ship's bridge. In spite of his injuries, it was Captain Murat who brought order out of chaos. It was he who had downloaded all the *Verdun*'s files into the last lifeboat that escaped, thereby giving his people the knowledge they needed to survive, rebuild, and prepare for the inevitable continuation of the conflict with the Tarn.

"As the years passed, his health faded. Our senior medical officer devised a plan. A stasis field was built, and our leader was thus saved. The illness devouring him is still there, but when needed, he could be awakened, for a day, or a week, to offer his guidance in times of crisis. When the

Tarn used the bomb on us we woke him for that, and thus he was with us when your ship announced its presence."

"Why didn't you tell me?" Picard asked.

"Because I was not ready for you to know," a voice, thin and reedy, whispered.

Picard looked over at the bed.

Julia went to the bedside and gently helped the ancient captain to sit up. His pale, ghostlike feet touched the stone floor, and then slowly he stood.

"Thank you, wife," he whispered.

Picard looked at Julia and then Lysander with open surprise.

"Yes, Captain," she announced, "I am the wife of Captain Lucian Murat, and Lysander is his only living son."

"Your husband? How?"

She smiled, and there was the flicker in her eyes of a young girl revealing a secret. Lysander was clenching his jaw, willing himself to be silent, and the effect it had on his mother's courage was evident. But apparently she had anticipated such a reaction. There was no purpose in going halfway.

"I am the commodore's third wife. I was chosen when I was sixteen to be the Honored Mother."

Picard hesitated. Lucian Murat was thirty-three when the *Verdun* was lost. That would make him nearly two hundred and forty years old. Granted, most of that time had been spent in statis, but the reality made Picard uncomfortable nonetheless.

He looked at the waxy, corpselike man. What kind of marriage was this? How many days did they have together; how many nights? She was married to a legend of the past.

"Perhaps you should address your questions to me," Lucian said quietly.

Embarrassed, Picard looked back at the sightless captain.

"Sir, no offense was intended."

"Nor was it taken."

"Lysander, status since this morning?" Lucian asked, abruptly shifting attention away from Picard as if he were simply another junior officer.

"Sir, we lost entry number seven less than an hour ago."

"I smell the scent of battle, son. You were there."

"Yes, Father."

"Good, that is where to lead from."

"Sir, we're being flanked through access ports seven and nine. Radial tunnel fifty-one is completely lost; by this evening they'll be within several hundred meters of the main perimeter to this city. We should be prepared for nuclear mines. It would be foolish of them if they chose not to use them at this point. Sir, I suggest evacuation from the upper levels begin immediately."

The elder Murat turned pale and tried to focus his useless eyes in the direction of Lysander, as if noting his presence.

"I will decide that, not you," the old man

replied. He cocked his head gently, assessing the atmosphere. "Ah, and I sense a youngster. How fares my granddaughter?"

"Your granddaughter prospers, as do your people," the child responded demurely.

"Good. You are teaching her well, my son. Take heed, she will become greater than you one day. She has been blessed with a smoother tongue than her father."

Lucian reached out with wavering hand and the child drew closer. He lightly brushed her cheek and smoothed back an errant wisp of hair, then withdrew his hand. Murat chuckled and then grew serious.

"So, now to our visitor."

Picard drew himself to attention with a slight clicking of heels. Lucian turned his head in the direction of the sound.

"Captain Jean-Luc Picard, sir. Captain of the *Enterprise* 1701-D. It is an honor to meet you."

The words were sincere and he struggled to keep the tone of hero worship out of them. Here was legend as flesh. What first-year cadet did not thrill to the stories of Lucian Murat as told in the Academy history classes? Who did not dream of sailing the seas and the stars as he once did?

Murat heard Picard's introduction with the ease of one who needs no introduction. He seemed neither surprised nor excited. Instead, he laughed with comical resignation. "I see."

Picard stepped forward. He nodded toward

Eardman, catching his mistake quickly before adding, "My ship's historian, Dr. Janice Eardman, has accompanied me."

"I know her, I told her to fetch you."

Picard stiffened slightly at the tone but said nothing.

"Well, I am sincerely glad that you have decided to join us. We shall have much to discuss, I imagine."

Picard was taken aback at Murat's reaction. If the roles had been reversed, if it had been he arising from the bed, his curiosity would be brimming with news of all that had transpired while he had languished at the twilight border of death. He sensed no such desire or tone from Murat. Picard had been expecting an onslaught of questions.

Instead, he felt a decided coolness from the man. Picard tried to shake the feeling, nearly convincing himself that it was in actuality his own sense of excitement at seeing the legend before him.

How long had it been since he began his study of the life of Murat? His endeavors, his failures, his philosophy toward exploration, toward survival. Every manual or novel he could find on the man he had read voraciously. The historian's perspective intrigued him, as did fictionalized accounts of his last days, but what kept him captivated were old copies of ship's logs and captain's records. Picard had spent hours unraveling the accounts these journals held, piecing together events and situations that revealed the character of the man.

Now he stood in front of him. Oddly enough, he could think of nothing to ask him. He had always thought that if he were ever given the chance to meet the man, he would stumble forth with a hundred questions.

"Yes, I am sure that there will be much to talk over," Picard replied, his tone neutral, not sure where to go next.

"You have seen my city by now." It was a statement intended to assess rather than to question.

"My first officer and Dr. Eardman have seen more than I. However, what I have observed has been quite impressive. You have done a great deal with what you had."

"Ah, the motivation has been formidable. I wonder if you understand how formidable."

Again, the coolness of before. Picard had the feeling that he was being measured, sized up. There was the tension of power, who held it and who wanted it.

"And are you equally impressed with the management of my city? Lysander is a wise leader."

Picard glanced at Lysander. His gaze was inscrutable; he was as unsure of the motive behind his father's line of questioning as was Picard.

Picard replied cautiously: "Your son's strategy is both inventive and skilled."

"Inventive and skilled. . . . Yes, he is both of these. . . . But you did not mention heroic and admirable?"

There was an expectant pause.

"I am afraid you took that as a slight, sir. I meant nothing of the kind."

"Of course not. You simply meant inventive and skilled rather than heroic and admirable." He spoke crisply, his words mechanically optimistic.

Lucian Murat stood up and slowly stretched. Picard remembered seeing an old holotape of Lucian on the bridge of the *Verdun* shortly after the ship was launched. The young vibrant man pacing back and forth, talking, issuing orders, all the time pacing, hands clasped behind his back. How different a picture Picard now had before him.

"Are you aware of just how intense this struggle has been, Captain?"

"Yes."

Lucian paused, sightless eyes fixed straight at Picard, who shifted uncomfortably at the pause, which signaled a desire for the old ritual.

"Yes, sir."

He caught a glimpse of Eardman standing by his side, still at attention, her eyes wide with wonder.

"Actually, I was awoken not for your arrival, but just before that to be given the information that the Tarn have achieved fission and have used an atomic weapon. Then you arrived. There is much for me to consider here."

He paused a moment and stepped closer to the voice of Picard. "A captain of the *Enterprise*," he murmured to himself with head lowered in thought, then sharply, raising his head so that his milky eyes were but inches from Picard's face: "What are your intentions, Captain?"

Here was the test; here was the reason behind the cool, almost abrasive front of hospitality. Picard noted the situation and chose to meet the attack with an equal measure of force.

"Sir, I think you already know that. By orders of Starfleet Command all Federation forces on this planet are to seek an immediate cease-fire with the Tarn."

"Starfleet Command. Why, thank you, Captain Picard. The war is over. . . ." He turned quickly in the direction of his son with apparent shock. "Lysander, are my people still topside and fighting the Tarn?"

"Yes, sir."

Picard watched Lysander. This was a soldier reporting to a superior, not a son to a father.

"Casualty report."

"At least nine hundred dead, wounded, or missing in this latest assault."

"Nearly a thousand lost today, Captain, and you say the war is over?" Murat replied, relief evident on his smiling face. "You see the absurdity of such a remark, Captain." Murat began his pacing once again, this time with the confidence of one who has much to orchestrate.

"Sir, the continued battle on this planet has no bearing on the status of the war between the Federation and the Tarn. That war has long since been resolved," Picard stated.

Murat smiled and without hesitation replied, "Well, then, you're just in time to help us finish up our fight. And then, from here we can sally forth to other systems. I understand there are Tarn ships in orbit above us as well."

"Yes, three ships," Picard replied, limiting his response to that one single point.

"I've faced worse odds. I remember the power of a starship captain."

For an instant, Picard felt as if the sightless eyes could see again, but what they saw was of another time.

"I remember it well," he whispered. "Engage warp-drive engines, set a course at warp three." His voice trailed off for a moment.

"Yes, the power. Do you have laser batteries, antimatter torpedoes, plasma bombs, and thermonuclear mines? Now, there was power. One spread of those torpedoes . . . what a sight it would be to see them launch, to acquire target and track down to impact. Preemptive strike, Picard, take them out now!"

Picard, looking over at Julia and Lysander, saw a look of awe in their eyes. Here was an old one speaking of the time before the fall, one who had transcended death itself. *"For I am Lazarus, come back to tell thee all,"* he thought.

"Finish them off up in orbit, then turn your batteries on the targets we'll designate down here and we will end this fight in a day. They are open for the killing blow."

"That, sir, I cannot do."

Murat halted his repetitive pacing. "I'm afraid I heard you incorrectly, Captain. What you meant to say was that you simply need time to coordinate a strike, correct?"

Picard hesitated. The coldness of Murat's words was deliberate.

Picard tried to imagine what Murat must be feeling. The entire universe was different in those early days of the Federation. The higher order of thinking was only just beginning to form. And then this war, this damnable, brutal war across the generations.

"Sir," he began patiently. "The situation as it currently stands . . . I think you need to be fully briefed."

"I am issuing an order, Captain," Murat snapped. "I expect it to be obeyed."

Picard looked over at Julia, but her face was a cipher, unreadable. Lysander, beside her, was looking at Picard in open surprise.

"Perhaps we should discuss this in private, Commodore," the captain suggested quietly.

"In private! Oh that's grand, Captain."

Murat paused a moment, his eyes squinting slightly in concentration, his head tilted to the right. "It's a pity the greatest ship in the universe is commanded by such a coward. I hope the crew doesn't fall in line with the captain's ideals. It could prove difficult when I remove you from command."

Picard clenched his jaw, his teeth bearing down upon each other.

"What has become of the legend of our history books?"

"He was never offered the luxury of dying." Murat turned, sightless eyes sweeping over the few gathered near him. "All of you, except for this captain, get out!" he shouted.

"Father, you have just awoken. Let me——"

"Leave me at once, boy," Murat raged.

Lysander flinched at the reprimand. He was a strong man unaccustomed to such slights. Picard nodded to Eardman, who reluctantly left the room. Only Julia remained.

"My husband, perhaps I should stay."

"Out. Now, dammit!"

She stiffened. There was a significant look in her eyes when she turned to walk past Picard, as if she wanted to convey that there was far more to this man than the rage. Picard shook his head, motioning for her to go.

As the door shut behind them, Lucian resumed his now familiar pacing across the width of the room. With wrists locked behind his back, one finger idly tapping the inside of his forearm, he appeared oblivious of the presence of Picard. His pacing grew more agitated as the silence continued. The idle tap of a finger became stabs of anger. Soon the whole hand was involved, pounding the arm as the man rhythmically mapped out a pattern on the floor. Still, he did not speak. His composition became rigid; he was the picture of a frail, futile man with nothing left but his anger.

"How dare you defy my orders," he whispered, still pacing, refusing to look in the direction of Picard. "You know nothing! You understand nothing!" He spat the words as if they were distasteful to the tongue.

Picard studied the shaky old man's broad shoulders, noting the concave bend, and struggled to find his hero in what had become a watercolor image of the past. The captain had known this man in earlier days, even if only through books. He understood Murat's proud nature, his dismissive arrogance, his precision and perfectionism. He was a man few would care to call their friend but any would serve under, fight for, and, if necessary, unflinchingly die for. Brilliant men such as the commodore were rare, and their rarity added to their alienation. Yet for all the complexities of the man, Picard felt that the intricate nature could be chiseled down to an unstinting need and drive toward honor. And it was this force that had molded the hero into the aged, stooped man before him. His honor had been scoffed at. The Federation that had sculpted that honor had abandoned their hero. And the degeneration of a great man was the result.

"Commodore, you have done your duty. You have been remembered for your diligence and your devotion to your crewmen. But the time has come to end this. Sir, return with me. Leave this madness behind and come back home to the honors you deserve."

"I did not create the madness, Captain." Murat's voice was quiet now, tired.

"No, sir, but it would be a breach of honor to perpetuate it."

"Fool!" Murat shouted, his softened demeanor rattled by another onslaught of rage. "Damn your pity! I am a sightless old man but I see what you are. You think you are better than I, that you would have ceased the fighting, become the mediator, spared the thousands, and created a peaceful world. Fool! You would have done as I did. Your duty to the Federation would have required that. You have taken an oath to fight, until death if necessary, and that is what you would have done. You want to talk about honor? Well, young man, a person with honor does their duty until the end . . . as have I. No one told us the war was over, Captain. We are simply following our orders."

Murat clenched his fist, the only act his limited strength afforded him. Then he seemed to uncoil, control returning. He drew closer.

"Picard," he whispered, "think on this. We are you without the luxury of peace. So save me your pity, Captain. You don't realize how depraved you would become if you were shoved into a pit of darkness and forced to live. Fate is the only thing that keeps you from stinking of me."

Picard felt as if he had been dealt a visceral blow. Murat's words cut into his very soul. *"As I am so you shall be,"* he thought, the realization frightening him as he gazed at the legend now consumed with rage.

Murat staggered slightly and moved to sit down. He waved his hand abstractly, saying, "Leave me now. If you have any of the respect for me that you claim, leave this old man to his frailties without the embarrassment of an audience."

Picard hesitated. There was one more question.

"And from the darkness of our souls, is redemption not possible?"

Murat groaned softly, head bent. "Redemption is the elaboration of a bored mind. Only those who are wise reject it."

Picard smiled gently and added, "Only those who understand that they are foolish embrace it."

When Murat lifted his head he found himself alone in his chapel.

Chapter Nine

THE RATTLE OF SMALL-ARMS FIRE caught Karish unawares. Ducking low, he looked to his left, watching as a platoon commander, standing silhouetted on a hill, was cut down. More gunfire erupted and Karish cursed as a reaction squad raced up the rocky slope, losing two more warriors before gaining the crest.

"I thought this area was secure!" Karish barked, looking over at Gadin, who stood dispassionate, arms folded.

"And as I said before, nothing is ever secured here," Gadin replied calmly.

The squad disappeared from view after tossing grenades, and went down into the spider hole that the sniper had fired from.

"Well, if it isn't secured, they'll know about this." As he spoke, Karish pointed to the heavy, four-engine plane that was lumbering in on final approach.

All those around him stood expectant, watching, holding their breath as the transport plane wove between two jagged peaks then nosed hard over, as if diving straight into the ground. At the last instant it pulled up sharply and flared, its rear wheels touching down hard. The plane bounced, floated, then settled back down again. A parachute popped out from the back, brakes squealed, plumes of dust swirled out as the props were feathered then thrown into reverse.

Karish watched the show with awe. Again, it was as if he were participating in a drama of the ancient days. All was coming to a climax. It was ironic that his participation in the raid underground had been the deciding factor, perhaps for the entire war. Initially, the raid had been terrifying, confusing, especially when they stormed into a lower level. It was there that he had seen Riker, wounded. For a moment he had stared at him from behind the sights of an assault gun. It had been a delicious, chilling moment. Here was the cherished first officer of Picard's, and all that was required to end his life was a flick of his finger. And yet he had not. Instead he whispered for the human to remain still and then tossed a discarded poncho over his wounded body. Strange—the thought troubled him now, this display of mercy.

But whether he had spared Riker or not no longer mattered. The information that his very presence offered was all that counted, for where the first officer of the *Enterprise* was, there also was the place sought by his comrades . . . the headquarters of the Federation forces. With that knowledge, the war was all but won. A secondary strike had actually brushed right into the edge of the underground city. They were finally on the target.

Nervously, he looked up to the heavens. They must know what this was, any sensor could pick it up. Why hadn't they reacted? In an instant, the realization came with a crystal clarity . . . they were impotent, they couldn't react. That knowledge alone gave him joy: the mighty Federation, before whom his people had once groveled, now stood by in helpless silence. So much for their strength, he thought as he barked in laughter.

The transport skidded to a stop and with engines still howling swung about, the clamshell doors beneath its tail opening up.

A ground team raced forward, running alongside a primitive, gasoline-powered tractor that backed up to the plane. And as the cables they attached to the back stretched taut and the tractor slowly inched away, a long cylinder emerged from the darkness of the plane.

Seconds after Worf materialized in the Tarn theater of operations, he fell from a height of nearly two meters, grunting as he hit the ground. Apparently Eddies still had a few bugs to contend with in the transporter room.

Unceremonious as his arrival was, Worf still did not feel his dignity had suffered much. The fact was, he had more honor in his little finger than these genocidal Tarn *p'taks* had in their whole army. As he rose from the ground and regarded the smooth, rounded side of the deadly bomb that stood before him, he reminded himself of his mission. He was to face these people and try to reason with them, warrior to warrior, though in his opinion none of the Tarn deserved that proud title. Nonetheless it was his duty to try, and though there were others on the *Enterprise* who could have beamed down instead, Worf had managed to talk Lieutenant Commander Data into sending him. This was, after all, really a job for a Klingon.

"Hold fire, don't shoot!" he heard a familiar, noxious voice cry out.

"It's a Klingon," Karish announced.

"Commander Karish," Worf announced.

"A surprise to see you, Klingon," Karish replied.

"I am not surprised to see you doing this," Worf said, motioning toward the bomb, which was inching away from them.

"This is a Klingon?" Gadin asked, coming up to join the two, gazing appraisingly at Worf.

Worf nodded.

"Legend says you are good warriors, worthy foes, almost as good as us," Gadin continued.

Worf suppressed an irritated growl. *"Almost" indeed!*

"Too bad I'm ordering you to be shot," Gadin announced as he gestured to several guards to carry out his orders.

"Wait!" Karish snapped.

Gadin turned to him with a bland look.

"This Klingon is from that Federation ship. He has been sent to interfere with our mission. Shoot him."

Worf drew himself up, a toothy grin creasing his features as he uttered something in Klingon.

Worf was looking straight at Karish. The Klingon felt no fear, only contempt.

He heard rifles being raised up, but still held his gaze.

Karish stepped forward, placing himself between the Klingon and the firing squad.

"I said, don't shoot him," Karish snarled.

Gadin, who was already walking away, turned and looked back.

"That's my order."

"Their ship is directly overhead. They're watching us. That's how this Klingon knew to beam down here."

"All the more reason to shoot him."

"All the more reason not to. They'll see his execution. It might arouse their captain to do something, to strike here, to destroy that," and he gestured toward the warhead.

Gadin hesitated.

"I know this for a fact, Gadin. Shoot him and your plan is destroyed. He came here for a reason. It was obviously not to stop us. They could just as easily have beamed an assault team down, or beamed the weapon away. I want to know why."

"You've got two minutes. Guards, keep an eye on them." Gadin turned and stalked away.

Karish looked back at Worf.

"Madness, Klingon. Why did you come?"

"It was my duty."

"To your Federation overlords?"

Worf stiffened. He was in no mood to play semantic games with this . . . lizard. He ignored the insult and got straight to the point.

"You were about to kill Captain Picard and the away team. I have come to stop you."

"Kill Picard?" Karish asked, and involuntarily looked up to the heavens.

"He is in the city below."

"How?"

Worf told him of Picard's beaming down, the assistance of the Tarn admiral, and the wounding of Riker. Karish shifted uncomfortably.

Worf looked at him closely. "You were there, were you not?"

"It was my duty. Yes, I saw him in the battle."

"If I could, I would rip your throat out," Worf growled darkly.

"You feel that much passion for a human?"

"A fellow officer," Worf snapped. "You almost

killed one, and now you will kill others with that bomb."

"It is war," Karish replied coldly.

"It is genocide! Bombing their city like that, murdering their old ones, the wounded, their children. There is no honor in this. It is not war, it is murder."

"Fight a two-hundred-year war, Klingon, and then see what you would do."

"They have, you have not," Worf snapped. "You have merely sunk to their level."

"Time is up," one of the guards announced, casually pointing his rifle at Worf.

Startled, Karish looked over at the guard.

"Go on," Worf growled. "Better yet, do it yourself, though know that my son will spit at the name of the murderer of his father. He will seek you with his blade and avenge me, as will my comrades from the *Enterprise.*"

"Your comrades," Karish repeated thoughtfully. Then he turned and gave an abrupt command to the guard.

"He's not to be shot," Karish announced.

The guards looked at him in surprise. "But Gadin's orders—" one of them began.

"And I am countermanding them for the moment. Guard this Klingon but don't shoot him."

The guard hesitated.

"Do you want the Federation ship above us to strike?" Karish argued. "If you kill this Klingon they will."

He hesitated for a moment. "That is what this Klingon just told me and I believe him. Shoot him and the bomb is vaporized by the ship above us. I'll go to speak to Gadin."

The guard finally nodded in agreement and Karish looked back at Worf.

"You'll live for the moment, Klingon."

Karish sprinted off to catch up to Gadin, who was escorting the bomb down into the tunnel.

"What in the name of all the ancestors are you doing?" Admiral Jord roared.

"Sir, the Klingon member of our crew beamed down to talk with Karish."

"I can see that on my screen," Jord snarled. "Why did you not inform me first?"

"Sir, there was no time," Data replied.

"They'll kill him."

"That is a possibility," Data stated.

"I don't understand this, it is futile."

"Apparently Commander Worf disagrees with your assessment, Admiral. He believes that he can reach an understanding with the Tarn."

The image of Admiral Jord flickered for a moment and Data realized that the Tarn commander had just shifted transmission frequencies and was scrambling the message.

"Listen carefully to me," Jord continued. "One of my ship's captains has his finger on the trigger and is all but looking for an excuse to shoot. This beam-down almost provoked that. We must keep this under control!"

Data could sense the tension in the admiral's voice.

"I apologize, sir. Please tell your captain that it appears he will soon have the pleasure of watching a bomb explode down there."

"Yes, I know," Jord replied, and again there was the moment of hesitation. "I observed, though, that a Federation team saw the bomb and most likely reported back. There should be time to evacuate the upper levels."

Surprised by the admiral's comment, Data nodded in reply.

"One can hope so, Admiral Jord."

A siren echoed through the corridors, startling Picard. The sound was ancient, a quavering, bone-chilling howl that rose, dropped, then rose again.

Kneeling by Riker's side, he looked up at Crusher, then over at one of the medics who jerked upright at the siren's cry.

"What is it?" Picard asked.

"The tone's not steady," the medic announced. "It's a bomb strike. Most likely one of their atomics."

She tried to sound professional, detached, but her voice was shaking.

"What do we do?"

"Brace yourself, hang on."

Out in the corridor Picard heard shouting, the stamping of boots. Crusher, who had been working to stabilize Riker's punctured lung, looked over at Picard.

"Can we beam him out of here?"

"It means we would have to move him. I don't think so."

"Well, Jean-Luc, find out what's happening," Crusher snapped. Picard could not help but smile. The relationship between them had always been close, but whenever she was practicing her profession something inside demanded that she take over.

He got up from the side of Riker's cot, weaving his way through the narrow room. Medics and orderlies rushed about, helping the wounded who could not move out of their cots, putting them under their beds to shelter them from falling debris.

Picard stepped out into the street. A column of troops moving at the double were racing past, weapons at the ready. He saw a young lieutenant at the end of the column and reached out to grab him as he passed.

"Where's access tunnel nine?"

The lieutenant pointed straight up the corridor. "That way, sir, just under a kilometer away . . . where we're heading."

"Thank you, Lieutenant."

The boy drew back and saluted.

Picard gazed into the boy's eyes. Throughout his

career he had ordered many to almost certain death, yet the anguish of giving that order was something that never really went away. As he gazed into the youngster's eyes he knew with a grim certainty that this lieutenant was about to die.

"Good luck, son," Picard whispered.

"We all got to die sometime, sir. I guess I'm at the head of the line, that's all."

The boy turned and sprinted into the darkness.

Picard stepped back into the aid station.

"We're moving!" he roared. "All walking wounded, try to help a comrade who can't. We've got to get out of here!"

A medic stood up. "Sir, we have no orders."

"You've got them now. Ensign, lead us in the opposite direction to access tunnel nine. Let's go!"

Picard pushed through the crowd and knelt down by Crusher and Eardman.

"Jean-Luc, I've barely got the bleeding under control," Crusher announced.

"I know, Doctor, but he's still safer if we keep moving," the captain said.

Picard struggled to pick Riker up, cradling him in his arms. Riker stirred and opened his eyes halfway.

"Captain? What's going on?"

"Going for a little walk, Will. You'll be all right."

"Feel like I just lost a boxing match with Worf." Riker grimaced as someone bumped into Picard. Apparently, word was spreading as to where the bomb was, and orders or not, hundreds were pouring into the narrow street, all fleeing downward, into the depths of the city.

Gasping for breath, Picard broke into a run.

Small-arms fire stuttered in the corridor ahead, a stray bullet ricocheting off the ceiling above Karish. Catching up to Gadin, he crouched down low as a wild melee of hand-to-hand fighting erupted directly ahead. His eyes were drawn to the ceiling: one second it appeared to be solid, and then the next a scattering of rocks caved in. A human jumped through, feet first, assault gun up and firing even as he landed. A guard next to Karish dropped the human, but not before he had cut down two technicians working to arm the bomb.

A grenade detonated behind him. It seemed as if the tunnel was coming alive with Federation warriors, all of them bent on the single goal of eliminating the crew and guards around the warhead.

Gadin stood up in the middle of the gunfire, raised a hand, and commanded the tractor crew to stop. Then he went up to the side of the bomb, Karish following. A hatch on the side was open, a technician working furiously to set the firing mechanism. A burst of rifle fire cut him down, and another stepped over the body to complete the process.

Gadin, crouched by the side of the bomb, cut down two Federation soldiers who appeared out of the gloom.

"Ten minutes!" Gadin roared. "Arm it for ten!"

"Barely time to get away," the technician shouted, trying to be heard above the roar of battle.

"We'll catch more of them that way."

The technician suddenly stood back and held his hands up.

"Its armed and running!"

"Back!" Gadin roared. "Get back!"

The units engaged ahead started to pull back, around the bomb.

"Can't the humans disarm it?" Karish asked.

Gadin barked a laugh. "Once armed, nothing will stop it. They can't open it and pull out the firing trigger or the uranium in time. It will be beautiful to see. It will . . ."

His words were cut off. He spun around, collapsing into Karish's arms.

"So close to victory," he gasped, shuddering once . . . and then was still.

Several guards gathered around Karish, looking down at the fallen soldier.

"Grab him!" Karish roared.

Crouching low, he fired a burst down the corridor, then started to run, ejecting the clip from his gun and slamming a new one in. In the shadows he could see the Federation fighters, moving ghostlike, flashes of light as they fired, bullets singing past.

Karish felt as if his lungs were about to burst and yet still he ran. He saw the guards herding Worf along and shouted for them to pick up the pace.

As he cleared the entrance of the tunnel, Karish scrambled up over the rocks and down into the trenches that had been cut to shield them.

The warriors carrying Gadin slid down by his side. All were panting for breath. One of them was counting down the final seconds.

Karish looked at Gadin and solemnly leaned over, dabbing fingertips into the entry wound over the fallen leader's heart and streaking the blood onto his forehead.

"For I am of your circle," Karish intoned. "I am of your blood, and you are of mine."

As he spoke he cut his arm and allowed his blood to drop onto Gadin's own.

Worf watched the ceremony and nodded.

"Very Klingon," he said, obviously moved.

"He was a good leader. A good warrior."

"And now who commands?"

Karish looked around at the warriors who were gazing at him expectantly.

"I do."

"Hail Admiral Jord," Data ordered, while moving to stand beside Captain Picard's chair. The screen flashed to life.

"It is difficult to determine, Admiral, but I believe a fission bomb is about to be detonated. If we are to act, now is the time."

"The Klingon, what happened to him? It was hard for us to track."

"He is with Karish."

"So, they didn't kill him?"

"Admiral, the bomb."

"Fate is fate," Jord replied. "My orders stand."

"Then, sir, it is upon your head."

It was evident that the Federation forces below had received warning. Perhaps they had evacuated. *If we had a full functioning transporter, we could lock on, and move the bomb out into space a second before detonation,* Data thought. But that was not an option.

He stood silent, waiting, thinking of Picard.

There was a strange instant of silence, so fleeting that Picard wondered if he had imagined it. It was a final instinctive moment of hushed quiet before the storm . . . and then the shock wave hit. Braced against the walls of a corridor, he knelt down, clutching Will, covering him.

The floor beneath him swayed as the shock wave from the bomb reverberated. After long seconds Picard raised his head, trying to sense the air. There was no heat. Good—the blast had vaporized walls, sealing passages with rubble. Hopefully, no radiation would reach this far.

But the air was thick with dust. Will was coughing. Picard laid him down on the floor, fumbled with the gas-mask pack someone had issued him, and struggled to get it on Will.

A light snapped on, someone holding a flashlight up, shouting for quiet. Discipline started to take hold. More lamps came on; then the dull red of emergency battle lamps set into the walls came back to life. Sections of the ceiling above had caved in on the street, dozens were hurt, but there was still air; they were still alive.

In the distance he heard a siren, still quavering out its warning. It snapped off, and a loudspeaker echoed, ordering calm. It was Julia's voice.

Strength, he could detect strength there, and it filled him with pride. She was still a Starfleet officer and she was taking control, her voice hollow but steady, detailing casualties to emergency clearing centers, ordering troops to repel any break-throughs.

"Captain?"

It was Crusher. She crawled up to his side, wiping blood from her eyes from a scalp wound, kneeling over Will.

"How's he doing?"

"Get me out of this," Will gasped, "and I swear, I'll always try and draw to an inside straight when I play poker with you."

She smiled and brushed him lightly on the cheek.

"Eardman?"

"Here, sir."

She staggered over to join him, wide-eyed.

Will looked up at her and she reached out, clutching his hand.

"So, how's my favorite historian?" Will sighed.

"Still with you, Will."

Picard stood up. "I'm going back to see Lucian

Murat," he announced. "Dr. Eardman, will you accompany me?"

She reluctantly let go of Will's hand, and then, as if on impulse, she leaned over, her lips lightly brushing against his.

"Almost worth getting wounded for," Will whispered.

"I'll be back," she announced, and then followed Picard into the gloom.

"Shall you take it to him, ma'am, or shall I?" The lieutenant facing Julia Murat phrased the question in a manner indicating his willingness to do the task himself, but his tone suggested otherwise.

"No, I shall take it to Lysander," she said quietly, her fingers trembling as she took the preliminary casualty report from the lieutenant's hands. "I shall take it to Lysander," she repeated dully.

Julia paused at the door, staring at the knob. She forced her hand to reach for the handle then paused again, fingers hovering above the latch. She glanced down at the papers she held in her hand and willed them to disappear. She put her hand on the latch.

"Who's there? Come in." Lysander had heard the latch move and called a greeting behind the closed door.

Julia opened her eyes and paused a final moment before entering. The room she moved into was in disarray, her son standing amid the scattering of papers and maps with arms folded behind him in thought.

"Mother, I was hoping you would come." He sounded pleased. "I've found the map of quadrant seventeen. It's been years since we sealed it off but I think we could use it now. I'd like to hear what you think about it. It's a long shot, of course, but—"

"Lysander." Julia interrupted softly.

Only now did Lysander raise his eyes from the map below him.

He stiffened. "What's wrong?"

"Preliminary casualty report, Lysander."

"How many?" he said quietly.

"Five hundred at least . . ." Her voice trailed off. Julia stood silent.

"Mother," and now there was fear in his voice.

"They found her in one of the old exit shafts—"

"No!" He spoke harshly in disbelief. He turned quickly, his head shaking back and forth. His breath was ragged. "It can't be her. I've told her not to play there. . . . It couldn't have been her."

"She was there, Lysander. Our Alissia."

"No!" The one word was a drawn-out whisper. "She promised me she wouldn't play up by those damned exit shafts."

She stood silent.

"It's a mistake. Mom, it's a mistake."

Mom. He had never called her that before; it was always "Mother." Julia lowered her head at the sound.

"God!" he suddenly shouted. "Not my daughter!"

He turned to his mother at the doorway, his face contorted with rage and confusion. "You are sure?" He trembled, every muscle in his face pleading for her to tell him that she had been mistaken, that his little girl would meet him at home later that night.

"They brought her to me, Lysander. It was her."

He stared blankly, struggling to comprehend what it was that she was saying, as if the enunciation had been foreign and he was in the midst of translating it to something more familiar. And then he shut his eyes to it all. Without opening his eyes, he said in a voice barely above a whisper, "Leave me. You have done your duty."

Julia hesitated. "I will not leave. Not yet."

He exhaled slowly. It seemed he had no strength to argue.

Julia watched as he turned and glanced at the maps scattered about, blueprints lying across chairs. His step was heavy as he moved about the room, picking up a map to place it neatly on a desk, rearranging a set of building plans into some semblance of order. His face was stony, composed, as he replied to her comment. "Stay or leave as you like."

He sat down with a blank gaze, no tears, just the blank stare.

"I need to plan the counterstrike," he finally whispered.

Julia wasn't sure if she had heard him correctly.

"Has your heart grown as cold as this? Have you no grief?"

"Hating takes less time."

"What have we become?" she whispered.

"Our father's children." He spat it out, his hands busy with cleaning.

Julia stood with disbelief etched on her face. "Don't you feel anything?"

He paused as if reflecting.

"What is the purpose of all this?" Julia asked, her voice awash in despair.

"An odd time to sprout a conscience, Mother," he offered dryly. She did not reply.

"Go to hell, Mother. There's nothing left now but to fight."

"I already am in hell," she snapped, struggling to hold back the tears of grief, not only for her granddaughter, but also for her only son, who had lost the ability to embrace grief.

Julia's face softened. "You stand a better chance than anyone of convincing your father to end this damned war."

Without even a moment of thought he said simply, "No.

"We still have the refined uranium. Sling it in a container beneath one of our Mustangs, spray it over where we think their processing factory is, that'll kill them by the thousands," he stated firmly, his confidence bolstered at the sound of his words.

Julia pulled to attention at his statement. She

whispered, "No, Lysander. No. We must listen to the captain who comes from the Federation. You must defy Lucian." She was insistent now, her voice raised in its urgency. He must hear her.

"Lysander, listen to me, Alissia is dead!" she screamed. "Now go to her!"

Her words struck like a physical blow. He felt it all; the shocked numbness was gone and he was filled with the horror of never holding the delicate hand again, never tucking the child in at night, never staring into gray luminous eyes and wishing for the stars to come a little closer so that she could brush one, just once, with eager little fingers. There was nothing left.

"We are all dead," he whispered.

"Not yet, Alissia yes, but not the rest of the children."

She stared at him. Lysander could see the hope in his mother's eyes. Finally he raised his head, went to the door, and opened it. An orderly waiting expectantly outside snapped to attention.

"Staff meeting in ten minutes," he announced hoarsely. "We must plan our counterstrike."

The orderly saluted and dashed off. Lysander looked back at his mother with hollow eyes.

"Lysander?" She started to raise her arms, as if to embrace him, but he stepped back, going rigid.

"I am my father's son," he whispered.

"Yes," and she nodded sadly, "I can see that you are."

Chapter Ten

MATERIALIZING ON THE TRANSPORTER pad, Picard
hurriedly accepted Data's updated report as he
angrily strode from the transporter room to the
turbolift. He looked over anxiously as Crusher
guided the heavily sedated Riker to sickbay. Dr.
Eardman was also alongside the stretcher. The
meeting with Murat had been fruitless. Its only
result was a colorfully issued order to journey to
the surface of the planet whereupon they reestab-
lished contact with the *Enterprise* and beamed
aboard with the help of Admiral Jord. The journey
had been harrowing. The party was nearly caught
in a Tarn raid. Picard let Crusher and Riker take
the lift first in order to have a moment alone with
Data, who crisply informed him that Worf was on

the planet's surface. The captain rubbed his eyes tiredly. It occurred to him that Lucian Murat probably never suffered the inconvenience of an officer interpreting his orders so . . . creatively. Of course, Murat had metastasized from hero to genocidal maniac. And if that was the price a captain had to pay for lockstep discipline, then Picard preferred his own somewhat less authoritarian style.

"Mr. Data, be ready to contact the Tarn again if we need to get Worf out of there and be certain to convey my thanks to Admiral Jord for beaming us up. Have Dr. Crusher contact me if there's any change in Commander Riker's condition."

With a curt nod of dismissal Picard indicated that he wanted to be alone, and stepping into his quarters, he collapsed in a chair. He was vaguely aware of his own stench, the dirt, filth, and blood streaking his uniform.

The stench of war, he thought grimly. *We've made it too clean up here in space. Usually it's a matter of a shield going down, a high-energy burst hulling a ship, the engulfing by a sterile vacuum, and then the long silence.*

Swinging his viewscreen around, he punched in a wide-angle scan of the battlefield below. Flames still licked out of the wound torn into the ground. Flashing red blips indicated Tarn troop movements. Another orange blip showed where the Tarn were loading their third nuclear device up at their main base three hundred kilometers away.

Failure, he thought bitterly. If only Lucian had cooperated, as he should have cooperated, this insanity would be over. But he had not, and Picard saw his mission as a failure.

"Captain?"

Annoyed, he looked back at the screen. It was Data.

"Sir, Dr. Crusher just reported that Commander Riker is doing well. She is putting him under for twelve hours so that he can get some rest. She also suggested, sir, that you consider standing down and getting some sleep."

Picard shook his head and switched the screen off.

Seconds later there was a knock at the door.

"Enter." There was a sharp edge to his tone, for he knew who it was.

Data came into the room and Picard wearily rose to his feet.

"Data, I don't need you."

"Sir, Dr. Crusher informed me you have gone over thirty hours without sleep. My circuitry allows such excesses but, sir, I must remind you that higher-level functioning in humans starts to suffer serious degradation at that point."

"Just get me a cup of tea, Data. I need to think. Go ahead and get something for yourself if you want."

Data went over to the food replicator and, seconds later, brought over a cup of tea and a drinking horn. Picard wrinkled his nose disdainfully.

242

"Don't tell me you've started drinking *Hammasi.*"

"Well, sir, I must confess that it does have a most curious taste. I find I rather like it."

"Data, at least in human company, you'll find very few companions with that stuff on your breath."

"Really, sir?"

Picard was silent, staring off while sipping his Earl Grey.

"A suggestion, sir."

"Yes, Mr. Data."

"Talk to Admiral Jord."

Picard awaited an explanation.

"Sir, I have observed that he appears to be carrying a similar emotional burden to your own."

Picard fell silent and nodded for Data to leave.

Collapsing back in his chair he looked off vacantly. For some reason he recalled the woods near his childhood home. What did that mean? He smiled grimly. In a way, there was something natural about his reflecting upon childhood at this point. After all, the people he had recently left on the planet, Federation and Tarn forces alike, were behaving like children playing a particularly vicious nasty little game.

He closed his eyes. "They are children . . ." Strange, snatches of poems came to mind: "I was a child and she was a child, in the kingdom by the sea."

Curious thought to now form, he thought. He had once enjoyed that poet . . . "Some sepulcher, remote, alone, Against whose portal she hath thrown, In childhood, many an idle stone."

He stirred uncomfortably. ". . . thrilling to think, poor child of sin; it was the dead who groaned within."

Why that poem? he wondered. And then he knew. Suppose the portal doors were opened. Suppose the child were given permission to gaze in full horror upon that which she had disturbed, and there was no escape.

He sat upright and reached over to activate his console.

"Mr. Data, get me Admiral Jord immediately."

Julia Murat advanced into her husband's chambers to find Lucian seated in the dark.

"Lysander?" Murat queried, the sound of the door stirring him from his thoughts.

"No, my husband, it is I."

"Julia." His voice was nearly tender. "Where is the boy?"

"Our son has been kept in a meeting with the staff officers," she replied without affect.

"The staff? Whatever for? He is to discuss strategy with me before going to them."

"Perhaps the time for strategy is past," Julia stated somberly.

"You too?" he snapped wearily. "I've had my

fill of this nonsense from Picard. Is he off the planet?"

"As you ordered, Lucian."

"And you disapprove."

"Yes."

There was a long drawn-out silence. Across all the years she had never dared to disagree for he was not just her husband, he was the Commodore, the legend.

"We lost our granddaughter today, you do know that, don't you?"

"I have lost dozens, hundreds."

"Damn you." The words were barely whispered, half in fear, but they were meant to be heard.

He turned his sightless gaze to her. She expected an explosion, but there was nothing, only silence, then a sigh.

"You will live to understand," he finally said, "live as long as me and you will understand."

"Lucian, I will stand with you no longer. I will fight for you no more."

The cloudy eyes flinched with pain. Murat tipped his head as if he did not understand. "If you do this, you will die a traitor."

"And what about all the others who wish to end the fighting?"

"You know that to defy me . . . to defy us," he added softly, "is to be named traitor. I would see any and all hanged for such a crime."

Julia faced him squarely. "Then it is a blessing

that you are blind. . . . Excuse me, I will bring Lysander to you."

As the transporter beam coalesced, Picard stiffened formally.

"Admiral Jord, thank you for coming over."

Jord grunted, looking around at the bridge.

"I still think you have too much room here, Captain. The living is too soft."

Picard smiled and said nothing. He felt a bit self-conscious, having no chance as of yet to change out of his uniform. Perhaps there was a note of stage playing to stay in it. Jord looked at him and sniffed.

"Even a Tarn might find your scent unpleasant."

"The smell of war, Admiral."

"I need a drink to mask that smell."

When his *Hammasi* was brought to him, Jord drained half the horn in a single gulp, nodding with approval as Data followed suit.

"Your plan, Captain, is outrageous beyond belief."

"That's why I think it will work."

"And you really expect me to go along with this?"

"Sir, you have seen the damage that the Tarn have inflicted. They are but hours away from completely destroying the Federation fighters."

"An unfortunate scenario," Jord replied, his intent unclear.

"But you are unaware of the Federation's plan for a counterattack."

Jord turned quickly to face Picard. He hesitated a moment and then replied slowly, "I did not believe they had a working nuclear bomb."

"They do not. But a few dozen kilograms of enriched uranium sprayed over the concentration of Tarn troops and their living areas will be similarly affected."

"And they would go that far?"

"To keep themselves from being annihilated? I have no doubt of it."

Jord paused in reflection. Clearly, he had not anticipated such news.

"This compounds the problem, Captain."

Picard struggled to keep a sarcastic reply from escaping. "Yes, the Tarn no longer have the sole advantage."

"But perhaps this is better?" Jord suggested. "It would result in a balance of power."

"It's hardly a balance, Admiral. There will be mass destruction, count on it. But neither side will have delivered a full killing blow," Picard added with emphasis. "They will be locked in a deadly embrace of slaughter that will spiral downward while you and I orbit above. Then our governments will send more ships to reinforce. Sooner or later there will be a mistake, Admiral, we both know that."

Picard allowed the weight of his words to sink in before continuing. "If you don't agree with my suggestion, we both know what will happen down there and finally up here as well. I believe, Admiral, that you see the madness in this as clearly as I do. Both of us want it to stop, both of us are constrained by our orders. And neither one of us can convince our side down there to stop fighting. So we stare at each other up here, just waiting for the provocation of the other side to give us the excuse to offer some form of aid. You know as well as I do that, given enough time, this incident down on Torgu-Va will escalate into a general war."

"And you really think this mad suggestion will stop it?"

Picard nodded. "Give a child too much of what they want, let them see what their desire leads to . . . sometimes that's the only way they can learn. Let them unleash the darkness and maybe they will learn."

Jord barked a short laugh. "I understand the point. 'I wanted a war, and for my sins the gods gave it to me.'"

"Admiral?"

"From a sacred text, never mind." Jord paced the deck for a moment sipping the rest of his drink, then finally nodded.

"I agree to your plan."

Picard sighed with visible relief and then smiled. He'd be willing to bet that the old admiral had made his decision before even coming over and had simply wanted to play out the drama.

"But Captain, if this doesn't work. If they go ahead?"

"Well then, Admiral, I think we'll both lose our commissions."

Jord laughed. "It might be a commission for you. For the Tarn, it involves a ceremony with one's own dagger."

Picard looked appraisingly at Jord. He knew he was asking a great deal. Jord knew the risks and was willing to play along. For this, Picard admired the Tarn commander.

"Mr. Eddies?" Picard asked, touching his comm-badge.

"Sir, it's inanimate, I think we can handle this, latest diagnostics indicate we're stable at least for the moment."

"Fine, then, beam the transmitter down to Commander Karish and make sure the second package is ready to go. It must arrive simultaneously with the Tarn's . . . gift."

"Yes, sir."

"Viewscreen, Mr. Data."

The forward viewscreen shifted to a split image. The better part of an hour had been spent intensively scanning the old-style frequencies in an attempt to get a lock on the command net of the Federation forces on the surface. Repeated calls for Lucian Murat had been sent in before a reply was indicated.

"Mr. Karish, please hold for a moment."

Karish looked at the screen and Picard sensed his discomfort at the sight of Admiral Jord standing by his side.

"Commander Karish, I believe you know Admiral Jord."

An unintelligible comment flickered between the two and Jord shook his head. Picard sensed his anger.

"Mr. Karish, I have only two questions. First, I expect that Commander Worf is safe?"

"Yes, the Klingon is safe."

Picard was silent.

"And the second question is, will the Tarn forces on the surface agree to order a cease-fire?"

"No, Captain Picard, that is impossible here. Further, I do not recognize Admiral Jord's right to order us to cease this fight as long as the Federation forces refuse to surrender. To follow such an order would be a dishonor after two hundred years of struggle. The honor of my circle demands victory."

"Fine then," Picard announced, and looked over at Data, who nodded. The second half of the screen activated. It contained Lucian Murat, his wife and son standing in the background.

"Commodore Murat, I have one more transmission, sir."

Murat wearily waved his hand in bored dismissal.

"I take it this message is your notice of departure from the system."

"Commodore, your screen is showing my image and that of the Tarn leader, Karish. Commander Karish, you can now see Lucian Murat, the commander of the Federation forces on the planet."

Both started to sputter their outrage but, with an angry gesture, Picard cut their protests off.

"Listen, both of you. I have tried persuasion and it has failed. The Federation has forbidden me to forcefully interfere. Admiral Jord here of the First Circle of the Tarn Empire has similar orders. We are both ordered as well to make sure that neither one of us attempts to aid our respective sides in your fight."

"Is that all, Captain Picard?" Murat snapped. "I have more important things to do than to listen to your weak pleadings."

"No, sir, that is not all," Picard snapped. Taking a deep breath, he stepped closer to the screen.

"Both of you can have your fight. I'm finished with it."

Murat, who had been reaching forward as if to switch his communicator off, hesitated.

Picard smiled. "Gentlemen, there is one technical point here that we have all overlooked." Picard looked over at Jord, who nodded, tapped his own communicator, and spoke something softly.

"You see, gentlemen, there is one order neither Admiral Jord nor I ever received from our superiors."

"And what is that?" Karish asked.

"We were never forbidden the right to provide aid to the other side," Picard announced smoothly.

Picard looked away from the screen. "Commander Data, is the transporter room ready?"

"Yes, sir."

"Then engage."

Picard looked back to the screen. Shouting erupted behind Karish and he turned away, then looked back at Picard.

"What are you doing?" Karish asked.

"Commander Karish, compliments of the *Enterprise*. The first batch of fifty photon torpedoes with short lift rocket stages attached, along with instructions on how to manually activate them, are being beamed down. You should be ready to launch within six hours. That's fifty torpedoes. We have also provided you with full targeting data on every Federation base that we've been able to locate while in orbit. Fuses on the rockets are set for deep penetration before detonation. Karish, there's more than enough to blow all Federation forces out of existence, though I'd suggest pulling your personnel back by at least five hundred kilometers if you decide to use them all at once. They're going to cause a firestorm.

"Traitor!" Lucian roared.

Jord stepped in front of Picard. "Commodore Murat," Jord began. "I am commander of the Tarn forces in orbit above your planet. Any second now you should be receiving a report from your security forces outside access tunnel number twenty-two. They will inform you that fifty photon torpedoes, similarly equipped and preloaded with targeting data, have just materialized. I send them to you, compliments of the Tarn. You should be ready to launch in six hours. I hope you enjoy them."

Picard chopped the air with an open hand and Data switched the screens off. He exhaled noisily and looked over at Jord.

The two retired to Picard's suite, and without bothering to ask, Picard drew another drink for Jord and a snifter of Napoleon brandy for himself.

"I've delayed relaying a report of this to my superiors," Jord said.

"Same here."

"Do you think it will work? I must say that the sight of a hundred photon warheads detonating down below will be quite a show."

"Mad," Picard whispered.

"Madness, is that what you mean?"

"No. MAD. An old acronym from long ago. Mutually Assured Destruction. We've given the children the chance to go all the way, but now they know the other side will do it as well."

"MAD. I like that. Perhaps they will see that darkness is not restricted to the enemy's heart alone. Let us hope that what they find is a desire to live rather than to perpetuate the madness. Because if it is the latter, Captain, you can come visit my ashes when you are a civilian and they let you out of jail."

Picard drank deeply and nodded. All they could do now was wait.

He leaned back and closed his eyes. . . .

"Captain Picard?"

Startled, Jean-Luc sat upright, momentarily befuddled. He looked at the console screen; over five hours had passed while he had been asleep. Data was on the screen.

"Sorry, sir. I thought it best for you to sleep."

"Fine, Data, any word?"

"Yes, sir, a hail from Karish."

Picard looked over at the couch in the corner of the room. The stench was appalling. Half a dozen empty drinking horns lay on the floor. Admiral Jord was snoring loudly.

"On my way, Data."

Picard shook Jord, the admiral waking, bleary-eyed.

"You make a good brew," he announced.

"We should be on the bridge, Admiral."

"Coming."

Rubbing the stubble on his chin, Picard wondered if he should change and shave but realized that there wasn't time. Stepping out onto the bridge, he walked down to his chair, Admiral Jord by his side.

"Report, Data."

"Sir. The Tarn forces have been pulling back rapidly. Air transports have been moving nonstop."

"Any action?"

"Nothing, sir."

"The missiles?"

"Both sides have activated the arming systems, the weapons are powering up and should be ready for launch on schedule."

"Put Karish on the screen."

"Captain Picard, why did you do this?" Karish asked.

"Why not?" he said with a smile.

"Captain," Data interrupted, "Commodore Murat."

"Put him on and downlink the signals to the opposing sides."

A grainy image filled the other half of the forward viewscreen.

"This is an outrage," Murat snapped. "We could have settled this on our own, Picard." He stood in the center of the screen, his son standing uncomfortably to his side.

"We wanted to help you out," Jord interjected.

"I'll not talk to a bloody Tarn admiral," Murat snarled.

"Sorry, Commodore, he's your ally now. You have to talk to him." Picard hesitated before adding, "So, if you're seeking technical advice, it's Admiral Jord who will provide it, not I."

Murat shifted uneasily.

"Well, gentlemen, you should both be ready for launch in exactly seven minutes and ten seconds."

Karish looked away from the screen. There was loud shouting behind him, arguing.

"Half of the staff here are screaming to launch immediately," Karish announced.

"And the others?"

"Some want to hold," Karish finally replied after a nervous pause.

"That's a lie. You'll launch," Murat snapped.

"Hear him out," Picard snapped back. "So, Commander Karish, why not?"

"If they launch first we all die and they win."

"Well, Commander, I'll tell you what we can do. The moment I detect a launch by the Federation I will warn you. That will give you time to get your missiles up in the air. I am certain that Admiral Jord will provide the same service to you, Commodore Murat, or will you not accept his friendly gesture?"

There was a long, awkward moment of silence.

"Five minutes, gentlemen," Picard announced. "Flight time should take under three minutes. So, eight minutes from now both of you will achieve your dream, the total annihilation of your enemies."

Picard held his breath, waiting. "Not to impose my values, but I'd suggest, in all fairness, that you tell the children and hatchlings what's about to happen so they have time to pray and say good-bye. They can be the final generation burned on the altar to avenge the deaths of their parents."

Murat covered his sightless eyes.

Lysander, silent to this point, stepped up quietly.

"Stand down," Lysander whispered.

"What was that?" Picard asked.

"Stand down, I said. We will not launch if the Tarn don't."

Lucian raised his head as if prepared to offer a final protest. Julia came up to his side.

"Husband, it is over," she whispered. "Lysander has ordered an end to it."

There was a drawn-out moment and finally the old man nodded and turned away.

Picard looked over at Karish.

"Did you hear that, Commander Karish?"

For the first time since he had met Karish, Picard felt that he could read an emotion. It was relief.

"We stand down," Karish replied.

"That means that a cease-fire is in place?"

Karish and Lysander both nodded.

"Fine, then. Admiral Jord, did you hear and witness their statements?"

"Yes, Captain."

"Admiral, I think you will agree with me that we can send down negotiating and observation teams to both sides."

"But of course."

"Admiral, your team will meet with Commodore Murat and his son, my team will meet with Commander Karish."

Protests started to sputter from both but Picard cut them short.

"Understand who is now allied to which side, gentlemen. We will contact you shortly."

Picard started to turn away as if the meeting was ended, and then paused and looked back.

"Oh, by the way. Neither my away team nor Admiral Jord's will disarm the photon warheads. If either side violates the cease-fire you can do what you want with them, though we will provide a remote sensing monitor to both of you so that there will be sufficient warning of a launch."

"Captain, I don't think that's necessary," Lucian Murat replied harshly. "I think your point has been sufficiently noted."

Picard stepped forward, wishing that Murat still had his vision so that he could see the anger and not just hear it.

"Commodore. You wanted a war, and you had it. All I did was offer you ultimate war, total victory and total defeat simultaneously. If you people want to figure out how to disarm the weapons, do it together. You'll get no help from me."

Murat lowered his head and Picard struggled not to show pity or remorse. Not now. Discipline, the path to truth, was more often than not a path of pain as well.

Murat started to say something, then fell silent. Finally he lifted his head.

"Long live the Federation," he whispered.

"This is Picard, transmission has ended."

Picard looked back over at Jord.

"Never thought I'd be sending my personnel to serve as negotiators for Federation forces."

"Travel offers all sorts of opportunities for new friendships," Picard replied, still trembling inside from the emotion of the moment and the dealings with Murat.

"Another drink, Captain?"

Picard wanted to say no but the look in the Tarn's eyes made him smile.

"Of course, my friend, of course."

Chapter Eleven

DR. JANICE EARDMAN, assigned to serve on Torgu-Va as part of the negotiation and disarmament team, slipped into the forward observation room, glad to see that Will was alone. Looking over his shoulder he saw her, smiled, and motioned for her to join him. Leaving her bag by the door, she came up to his side.

"Ready to go?"

"I think so. The conference between Lysander and Karish is wrapping up in the next room."

"How'd it go?"

"Tense, but it's a start. They're beaming back down shortly, along with the rest of the negotiation team."

"Where's the captain?"

"Down in sickbay at the moment, checking on our other guests. He said he'd be up shortly."

Riker nodded absently, his gaze wandering back to the planet below.

"You know, I was wondering," he began. "When you were first ordered to this assignment, what did you think?"

Janice looked up at him with a touch of surprise. "Actually," she began slowly, "I wasn't ordered. The choice to come was mine."

"Really?" Riker's curiosity was piqued.

Janice nodded.

"So . . . ?"

"Across the years there was always part of me that wondered," she said. "This was a chance to find out."

"And this was to be our chance to say good-bye," he said simply.

Her gaze was intent as she answered, "For now."

"So, you're off to dwell in the past," he stated quietly, watching as the strands of nostalgia slipped from her eyes.

She smirked knowingly before adding grandly, "And you to shape the future."

"Ah, Will, up and about, I see." Picard's voice broke into the room with the opening of the door. "And Doctor. Glad to see you once more before you ship off. Good job down there. You helped to open the path with Julia Murat. She speaks highly of you."

"It will be a pleasure to serve, sir."

Smiling, Picard shook her hand. "Will, you will see our delightful doctor to the transporter room?"

"Yes, sir."

The two made to leave but paused as the captain interrupted them.

"Dr. Eardman," he began. "Thank you. I believe we owe a good deal of the success of this proposed peace agenda to you. Your task now is hardly enviable, but I believe you to be capable of handling it."

"Thank you, sir."

"Godspeed." He smiled and the two left the room.

"You serve a good man, Will," Janice stated as the doors closed behind the captain.

"I've no doubt he will be the hero of many," Riker commented with pride.

As they stepped into the transporter room, the last of the negotiation team was just disappearing from view, beaming down to their respective posts.

Janice hesitated, looking toward the transporter deck, then turned, dropping her bag again, her arms intertwining around Will's neck. She held him fiercely, as if a lifetime of need could be expressed in the single, shared moment of an embrace.

"I know where to find you, right?" he said.

"That's assuming I don't find you first," she teased, her eyes glossy with tears. Then she stepped onto the transporter pad.

The beam of light faded and Riker stood in the

silence of loneliness. It rose about him, filling him, until he felt its emptiness threaten to steal the confidence he struggled to maintain. A moment he stood, noting, accepting, and finally smiling.

Captain Picard heard the door open behind him and waited for a brief instant, then turned, smiling.

The wonder was in their eyes, both of them. It was, after all, their first time. Two hundred years of exile was at an end.

"Julia, Lysander, welcome to the stars," Picard said softly.

They stood silent in awed wonder, hesitating for a long moment before clearing the door and slowly, reverently, walking to the windows.

"Dear God," Julia whispered, "the stars. I never dreamed . . . the stars."

"They're yours now. The exile is over. You can go to them any time you want."

She looked over at him, tears in her eyes. To his surprise, she leaned up as if to kiss him on the cheek. But her spontaneity was quickly checked by her notion of discipline. She hesitated, smiled, and stepped back.

"I never dreamed of actually seeing this. Thank you."

"Captain Murat, when things are secured on Torgu-Va I'll welcome you for a tour aboard the ship."

Lysander looked over at Picard, smiled wistfully, and shook his head.

"I think, Captain, that I have duties enough below." Yet even as he spoke his gaze returned to the heavens.

"How is he?" Picard asked, looking over at Julia.

"He'll be along in a second."

"I heard. I'm sorry."

She nodded, lowering her head.

The door behind them opened again. Picard left the two and stepped to the open door, where he formally drew himself to attention.

"Commodore Murat, welcome to the observation bridge."

Lucian Murat, dressed in the ancient uniform of Starfleet, nodded. Crusher had replaced the flame-scorched corneas and Picard looked into his eyes. He could see the power, the charisma, the legendary hawklike gaze. And for that instant the tragedy of what had been was forgotten. He was looking into the eyes of a legend. And within their reflection, he saw the lost dreams of a young ensign who had embraced the fantasy of serving with Murat.

Murat slowly stepped forward, shoulders braced. Picard moved aside, knowing that, for the moment, he was forgotten. Lucian approached the observation window like an ancient lover granted the wish of seeing, for one more time, the memory of a passion lost to shattered dreams.

He stood silent, unmoving, Picard respectfully waiting by his side. After several minutes of silence Lucian finally turned.

Tears streamed down his face. There was no

embarrassment, no need for either to explain to the other. They were captains, and both of them were, at that moment, sharing the masterful lover who had captured their hearts and would hold sway over them forever.

"Commodore," Picard said softly. "I wish you would reconsider your decision."

Murat smiled and shook his head.

"I've lived my life, Captain. What your good doctor is talking about is replacing most of what's inside me with machines. I'd rather die as I lived."

There was something more, Picard realized. Something unspoken. He had lived beyond the legend; the time was past. What more was there left to do?

Murat looked at him closely and shook his head.

"I heard you have a mechanical heart yourself."

"Yes. I was knifed in a bar fight when I was a senior cadet."

"Most dramatic. I didn't expect to hear such a story from you. A mechanical heart." Lucian chuckled.

Picard said nothing.

"Our Torgu-Va," he whispered, his eyes straining to take in the sight, to memorize it. "It's not as beautiful as I recall." He slowly began to pace, eyes still fixed on the heavens. Picard watched him, fascinated. Five paces, turn, five paces, turn. The distance must have been the width of his bridge so long ago, he realized.

As Murat walked past, Picard could see his lips

moving. He was whispering to himself. What distant commands were again being summoned? he wondered. Both hands were behind his back, fingers intertwined, clasping and unclasping.

"Fine, then," Murat suddenly snapped. "Time to depart."

The imperious tone was back, his gaze sweeping over son and wife. Both were silent. Picard could sense what was occurring in the son who had grown to manhood under the shadow of a legend. Lysander stiffened, his mother silent by his side.

Murat stared at them, then ever so slowly lowered his head.

"It's time for an old man to go home and die," he whispered. "Son, would you help me, please?"

Lysander's demeanor softened and, for the first time since meeting him, Picard saw the rigid need for control breaking away.

He stepped forward and offered a hand to his father. The old man sagged, the display of the last few minutes having sapped his strength. The legend was gone.

As they started for the door Lucian hesitated, turning back toward Picard and the field of stars behind him.

"It's yours now, Captain Picard." His eyes perused the captain, judging, speculating. "Do you know the story of the Roman generals?"

"Which one, Commodore?"

"When a general returned with victory he was offered a triumphal parade. The city would turn out to greet him and the multitudes would cry out his name. Standing behind the general, in his chariot, there would be an ancient man, bent with age. As the crowds hailed the general, the old man would stand behind the victor, whispering in his ear, 'Remember, all glory is fleeting.'

"All glory is fleeting," Lucian whispered to himself. "And you too, Captain Picard, shall one day become a legend. You too shall learn, as I have learned, that all glory is fleeting."

Picard stood to attention and saluted as Lucian Murat stepped through the doors and disappeared.

"He really was a legend," Julia said, stepping up to Jean-Luc's side.

Embarrassed, Picard did not know what to say.

"You destroyed that in a way."

"It had to be done."

"I know, and you were right. Tonight my son will bury his daughter. Hopefully, she'll be the last to be buried."

She looked back at the stars and smiled.

"We'll bury her above, on the surface, under the stars that should have been hers."

She fought back the tears, then looked once again at Picard.

"Lucian maybe has a month, that's what the doctor told me. She gave me medicine so he'll be comfortable. He told me that he wants to spend his last days on the surface, to gaze up at the battlefield that was once his. He'll rest then by his granddaughter."

"And you? What then?"

"There's a nation to build. My son will do that, but I'll be there to help. Maybe when things have settled down I'll take you up on your offer to visit."

"I'd be delighted to have you aboard."

She paused, her eyes serious. "Maybe another ship, Captain. There are so many memories here."

"I'm sorry."

She nodded.

"What will you say about him in your official report?" she asked.

"The truth. That is my duty."

"And what is the truth, Captain?"

Picard smiled. "There was once a legend and his name was Commodore Lucian Murat. There were things he did that were glorious, things he did that evidenced bravery beyond all expectations of bravery."

He hesitated for a moment. "And there were mistakes that showed just how human he truly was. For within every legend there cowers a man."

She forced a smile.

"Thank you, Captain."

Coming to attention, she saluted in the old, traditional military style and, turning, walked out the door.

Picard stood alone. He heard the door open and felt annoyed to be disturbed. There was so much to think about, to sort out now. But then a most unpleasant smell wafted about him and he smiled.

"Admiral Jord." Picard grinned as the Tarn

admiral approached, drinking horn in one hand, a snifter of brandy in the other.

Jord held the snifter out and Picard gratefully took it.

"Just how much do you drink?" Picard asked.

"Enough to not quite remember." Jord chuckled.

"You won't hold command long doing that."

"Been doing it for years, Captain."

"So, what was the reaction back home to our little maneuver?"

"Ah, explosive to say the least. It neatly kept the First Circle in power even though I should add that they felt that a war, at this moment, was the one way to ensure their remaining in power. Must say it caught them by surprise. They were getting ready to send an entire flotilla out here in anticipation of a full-scale fight."

"I must say my own command was a bit surprised by the beam-down of weapons. But, as they say, nothing succeeds like success. I guess we'll be forgiven."

"Well, even as we share a drink up here I understand that Karish and Worf have gotten, how should I say it, slightly intoxicated in your Ten-Forward. Your Worf has made quite an impression on Karish and his followers regarding the military prowess of your Federation and their Klingon friends. I guess they think if the Klingons would deem to be your friends you just might be bloodthirsty enough to win Tarn approval."

"Worf does have a way about him."

"Karish now has his own world. And I couldn't be happier for him. Or myself." Picard cocked his head quizzically in response. Admiral Jord leaned in and whispered confidentially, "Surely you don't think you're the only one who found him troublesome. The rest of the First Circle will hail me as a hero for tucking him away on Torgu-Va. Do you suppose I'll get a parade?"

Picard chuckled and proposed a toast to all manner of heroism. The Tarn admiral returned it. Then both commanders grew quiet and somber.

"Strange, we could have had a new war here, as vicious as the one we fought two hundred years ago, as vicious the one down there. And if we had, my friend, what would you and I have thought of each other? If we had wound up stranded below, as they were, what would we have done to survive, to ensure victory?" Jord asked.

"Maybe what they did," Jean-Luc replied softly. "What is the line? What keeps us from that?"

"Ourselves, the memory of what we saw."

"But is that enough?"

"It's a start, my friend."

Jean-Luc smiled and raised his glass.

"To glory," Admiral Jord said as he raised his horn and drained it.

"Yes, to glory," Captain Picard whispered, "to glory."

OUR FIRST SERIAL NOVEL!

Presenting one chapter per month . . .

**The very beginning of the Starfleet
Adventure . . .**

**STAR TREK
STARFLEET: YEAR ONE**

A Novel in Twelve Parts

by

Michael Jan Friedman

Chapter Two

Captain Daniel Hagedorn studied the stars streaming by on his forward viewscreen, wondering how many Romulan warships he was bypassing in his passage through subspace.

Thanks to the people at research and development, this was the longest faster-than-light jump he had ever made. In fact, it was the longest faster-than-light jump *any* Earthman had ever made.

And it couldn't have come at a better time. They had finally pushed the Romulans back far enough to get some sense of their military infrastructure, some idea of how to cripple their war effort.

Hence, this mission to take out the enemy's number one command center—the nexus for all strategic communications between the Romulan fleet and the Romulan homeworlds. Without it, the Romulans would quickly find their forces in disarray. They would have no rational choice but to withdraw instantly from Terran space.

Hagedorn frowned ever so slightly at his own eagerness. After all, he didn't like to let himself think too far ahead. Captains got into trouble that way. It was better to focus on the objective at hand and let the results take care of themselves.

He turned to his navigator, positioned at a freestanding console to his right. "How much longer, Mr. Tavarez?"

The man checked the monitors on his shiny black control panel. "A little more than a minute, sir."

"Thank you," Hagedorn told Tavarez. Then he looked to his helmsman, who was situated at the same kind of console to his left. "Ready to drop out of warp, Mr. St. Claire?"

The helmsman tapped a couple of studs to fine-tune their course. "Ready when you are, sir."

Finally, the captain addressed his weapons officer, a petite Asian woman who was seated directly ahead of him, between helm and navigation. "Power to all batteries, Lt. Hosokawa."

Hosokawa's fingers crawled deftly over her instruments. "Power to lasers and launchers," she confirmed.

Hagedorn took a breath and sat back in his padded leather center seat. Since his Christopher 2000 was still tearing through subspace, there was no point in trying to contact the captains of the half-dozen other starships who had been assigned this mission under his command. Still, like any good wing commander preparing for an engagement, he reeled off their names and his impressions of them in the privacy of his mind.

Andre Beschta. A rock, a tough, relentless warrior—willing to put his life on the line for any one of his friends. Seeing him in combat, one would never suspect what a clown the man could be when he was off-duty . . . or how well-loved he was by his crew and colleagues alike.

Uri Reulbach, quiet and studious by nature but utterly ruthless in battle. Reulbach was their point man, their risk-taker, the one who took the heat off all the rest of them.

The Stiles brothers, Jake and Aaron, both of them fiery and determined. No Earthmen had demonstrated as much courage against the Romulans as the Stiles family—or gotten themselves killed quite as often. All in all, three cousins and an uncle had perished at the hands of the invader. It had gotten to be a grim joke between Jake and Aaron as to who was going to die next.

Amanda McTigue, thoughtful and compassionate, who by her own admission felt every blow she struck against the enemy. Fortunately, it didn't stop her from demonstrating a predatorlike ferocity that none of her wingmates could ever hope to match.

Finally, there was Hiro Matsura—the newcomer in their ranks. The youngster had joined them only a couple of months earlier, but he had earned the respect of his wingmates right from the start. Matsura seemed to do best when paired with Beschta, who had taken the tyro under his wing.

And how did Hagedorn see *himself*? As the glue that held them all together, of course. He wasn't the toughest of them or the fiercest or even the most effective—nor did he have to be. His job was a simple one—to make his wingmates work as a single unit—tight, efficient, and economical in achieving their goal.

If they succeeded, it was because they had been strong and deft and courageous. If they failed, it was because *he* had failed *them*. It might not have been fair, but that was the way Hagedorn's superiors looked at it—and as a result, the way he had come to look at it, too.

"Permission to leave subspace, sir," said St. Claire.

The captain nodded. "Permission granted, Lieutenant."

As they dropped out of warp, Hagedorn saw the starry streaks on the viewscreen shorten abruptly into points of light. Of course, he observed silently, a few of those points were actually nearby planets reflecting their sun's illumination.

And unless they had badly miscalculated, one of those planets was Cheron, the barren world deep in Romulan territory that was their objective. But not for long, if Hagedorn and the others had anything to say about it.

"Confirm our position," he told his navigator.

"Confirmed," said Tavarez. "We're on the outskirts of the target system. Cheron is dead ahead."

Before the man could finish his advisory, Hagedorn saw one of the other Christophers become visible off his port bow. A second later, one of her wingmates joined her.

Then the subspace radio checks began coming in. As Hagedorn knew, they were more of a ritual than a necessity—like a pregame cheer before an ancient football game—but that didn't make them any less important.

"Beschta here. You can't get rid of me so easily."

"Stiles, Jake . . . present and accounted for."

"Stiles, Aaron . . . right behind you, sir."

"McTigue, on your starboard flank."

"Matsura here."

Hagedorn waited a moment. "Captain Reulbach?"

No answer.

He bit his lip. "Uri?"

Suddenly, the last of the Christophers rippled into sight above and slightly forward of Hagedorn's vessel. He breathed a sigh of relief.

"This is the *Achilles*," said Reulbach. "Sorry about the delay. We had a little trouble with our port nacelle. Fortunately, it won't be an issue until we re-enter subspace."

Hagedorn frowned. He didn't like the idea that his comrade might be hobbling home. After all, they didn't know how many enemy ships might be guarding the command center. Even if they were successful in their mission, they might wind up with half the Romulan fleet on their tails.

But he couldn't call off the mission because of one crotchety nacelle. "Acknowledged," he told Reulbach.

Then he set his sights on the viewscreen again, and in particular on the pale blue star in the center of it—which wasn't really a star at all. He didn't have to consult Tavarez to know that it would take them nearly eight hours to reach it at impulse speeds.

Eight hours, Hagedorn thought. For the first seven and three quarters of them, he and his wing would likely not be detected by the Romulans. After all, the enemy didn't have any reason to expect them there. But once they came in scan range of the command center . . .

That, he knew, would be a different story entirely.

As he sped toward the blue world fixed at maximum magnification on his viewscreen, Jake Stiles used the controls embedded in his armrest to establish a comm link with his brother.

"Stiles here," said Aaron, his voice clear and free of static.

"Stiles here too," Jake responded.

His brother chuckled over the link. "I was wondering when I'd hear from you, *Anaconda*. Feeling lonely?"

"Only for the moment," said Jake. "Before long, I bet, we'll have a few Romulans for company."

"I know what you're going to ask," Aaron told him. "And don't worry. I'll take down twice my share of birdies. That way they won't have to dig a hole for you back home."

"Funny," Jake responded. "I was just going to tell *you* the same thing. I guess they're right about great minds thinking alike."

"I guess so," said his brother. "Except no one ever told me I had a great mind. And now that I think about it, I doubt they ever told you that either."

"All right," Jake conceded. "So maybe mediocre minds think alike too. And this one is thinking what a shame it'd be to go home alone."

Aaron grunted. "I hear you. Especially with the war effectively over, if this little gambit works the way it's supposed to. So I guess we'll just have to keep on bucking the family curse."

"I guess so," Jake agreed.

Silence for a moment. "Stiles out," said his brother.

"That makes two of us," Jake told him.

"Captain Stiles," said his navigator, a sturdy blond woman named Rasmussen. "Scanners are picking up an enemy squadron." She pressed a series of buttons to extract more data. "Looks like eleven ships. Heading three-one-four mark six."

Eleven of them, Stiles reflected. They had hoped not to encounter so many, especially this far out. And there were likely to be a lot more of them hanging back closer to the command center.

But this was Earth Command's best wing. One way or another, the captain told himself, they would get the job done.

He looked back over his shoulder at Lavagetto, his communications officer. "Transmit our readings to the other ships, Lieutenant. Then request orders from Captain Hagedorn."

"Aye, sir," said the comm officer.

Stiles eyed the viewscreen. "When can we get a visual?"

"In about thirty seconds, sir," Rasmussen replied.

"This is Hagedorn," their wing commander broke in, his voice ringing from one end of the Christopher's bridge to the other. "Assume bull's-eye formation and go to full impulse."

Stiles pressed his comm stud. "Acknowledged," he told Hagedorn. He turned to Myerson, his helmsman. "You heard the man, Lieutenant."

"Full impulse, sir," said Myerson.

"The Romulans have picked us up," Rasmussen reported crisply. "They're heading right for us, sir."

The captain's teeth ground together. He always felt much better when he could actually *see* the enemy. "How about that visual?" he asked his navigator, trying to mask his discomfort.

Rasmussen worked at her controls. "Coming right up, sir."

A moment later, the ghostly blue disc of Cheron gave way to a squadron of eleven Romulan warships. They were traveling in a honeycomb formation, a typical birdie approach.

But they wouldn't be flying that formation for long, Jake Stiles mused. Not after he and his pals had blown a hole through it.

"Laser range in three minutes and twenty seconds," reported Chang, the *Anaconda*'s veteran weapons officer.

Stiles eyed the enemy warships. "Raise shields."

"Aye, sir," came Chang's reply.

The Romulans seemed to loom larger with each passing moment. The captain felt his mouth go dry as dust. But then, he thought, it always seemed to do that before a battle.

"Two minutes," the weapons officer announced.

Stiles nodded. "Target lasers."

"Targeting," said Chang.

In his brother's ship, the captain told himself, Darren would be doing the same things—receiving the same information and giving the same orders to his crew. And in a dark, secluded part of his mind, he would be thinking about the family curse.

It was hard not to.

"One minute," the weapons officer reported.

Hagedorn's voice came crackling over their comm link. "Maintain formation," he told them, so there wouldn't be any mistake.

"We're with you," Jake Stiles assured him.

"Forty-five seconds," Chang announced. "All systems operating at maximum efficiency, sir."

The captain considered the viewscreen again. There was no break in the Romulans' formation. Obviously, they still didn't believe the Earthmen were planning to barrel right through them.

"Thirty seconds," said the weapons officer.

The captain felt a bead of perspiration tracing a trail down the side of his face. "Fire on my mark," he told Chang.

"Aye, sir," came the reply. "Twenty seconds . . ."

"Good luck," he told his brother.

"Fifteen," said the weapons officer. "Ten. Five . . ."

On the viewscreen, the Romulans' weapons ports belched beams of cold blue flame. Stiles's ship shuddered and bucked under the impact of the assault. But her shields held.

Then it was the Earthman's turn. Glaring at the swiftly approaching enemy, he yelled "Fire!"

The Romulans were rocked by a dozen direct laser hits. However, none of them was forced out of line.

A second time, Stiles's vessel took the brunt of the enemy's barrage. And a second time, he returned it with equal fury. Then they were on top of the Romulans. It looked as if they would have to rotate to find a gap in the birdies' wall, if they were to survive.

But at the last possible second, the Romulans lost their nerve. Breaking formation, they peeled off in half a dozen different directions. Inwardly, Stiles cheered Hagedorn's nerve. A less confident commander would have blinked and made easy targets of them.

As it was, he had made easy targets of the enemy.

"Target and fire!" the captain called out.

With Chang working his controls, the *Anaconda* stabbed a Romulan's bird-bedecked belly with a pair of sizzling, blue laser beams. And before the enemy could come out of her loop, the Earth vessel skewered her again.

"Their shields are buckling, sir!" Rasmussen called out.

"Stay with her!" Stiles barked.

Myerson clung fiercely to the Romulan's tail; Chang ripped at her hindquarters with blue bursts of laser fire. Before long, one of the birdie's nacelles fizzled and went dark, and a moment later the other nacelle lost power as well.

The Romulan was dead in space, unable to move. But the captain knew she could still be dangerous. Once before, he had seen a crippled birdie reach out with her lasers and rake an unsuspecting Christopher.

But not this time. Stiles leaned forward in his seat. "Target and launch!" he snapped.

The weapons officer bent to his work again with grim efficiency. But instead of another laser barrage, he unleashed a black-and-gold missile at the enemy ship.

As the Earth captain looked on, the projectile penetrated one of the Romulan's empty nacelles. For a heartbeat, nothing happened. Then the enemy vessel shook itself to pieces in a blaze of atomic fire.

"Romulan off the starboard bow!" Rasmussen called out.

"Get it on the screen!" Stiles ordered.

The navigator had barely accomplished her task when the Romulan rolled under a spectacular laser volley. A moment later, Stiles saw the source of it, as McTigue's Christopher came twisting into view.

The captain made a mental note to thank the woman when he got the chance. But in the meantime, he could best express his gratitude by adding some firepower to McTigue's attack.

"Mr. Chang!" he cried out. "Target and fire!"

Stiles's lasers sent the Romulan rolling even harder, creating a web of destructive energy that spread outward from the point of impact. Then McTigue hit the enemy again, showing no mercy.

The Romulan tried to get off some shots of her own, but she was too beleaguered to target properly. Finally, with her shields torn up, she was easy prey for Stiles.

"Mr. Chang," he said, "target and launch!"

The *Christopher*'s missile sped through space like a well-thrown dart. When it reached its objective, the enemy spasmed and came apart in a blinding, white rush of energy.

But Stiles and his crew weren't done yet. There were still as many as nine Romulans carving up the void, their laser sights trained on the *Anaconda* or one of her wingmates.

"Romulan to port!" Rasmussen shouted suddenly.

"Evade!" the captain told his helmsman.

Under the navigator's expert guidance, the enemy vessel slid into sight on their forward viewscreen. Stiles almost wished it hadn't. The Romulan was right on top of them, ready to release a close-range laser barrage—and he knew there wasn't anything they could do about it.

"Brace yourselves!" he roared.

The viewscreen blanched suddenly, causing him to blink and turn away. Then came the impact—a bone-rattling blow that tore Stiles halfway out of his seat and made a geyser of sparks out of an unoccupied aft console. But when it was over, the *Anaconda* was still in one piece.

Someone moved to the damaged console with a fire extinguisher while the captain glowered at the forward screen. Fortunately, it still afforded him a good view of their adversary.

"Shields down seventy-five percent!" Rasmussen told him.

"Mr. Myerson," Stiles growled, "get that birdie off our tail! Mr. Chang—target and fire at will!"

But before they could obey either of those orders, the Romulan veered to starboard and began to put distance between herself and the Earth ship. For the merest fraction of a second, the captain was caught off-balance. Then he turned to his officers.

"Belay that last set of orders!" he told them. "Effect pursuit, Mr. Myerson! Don't let that Romulan get away!"

"Aye, sir!" the helmsman responded, moving to tax the ship's impulse engines to their fullest.

Suddenly, the enemy tacked sharply to port—and a moment later, Stiles saw why. Two of the other Christophers were approaching from the opposite direction, one of them less than a kilometer ahead of the other.

He recognized the vessels by their markings. Reulbach's ship was the one in front, of course. And the one behind it, looking as good as it had ever looked in its life, was his brother Aaron's.

The captain didn't know how the rest of the battle was going, but he liked the signs he was getting. After all, he had seen a Romulan turn tail in the middle of an engagement. And though her retreat had become a three-on-one, none of the other birdies were coming to her rescue.

Best of all, his brother was still alive and well. Good portents indeed, Jake Stiles told himself.

But he had barely completed the thought when he saw

something that wasn't good at all. As Reulbach and Aaron homed in on the enemy, Reulbach's ship began to rotate for no apparent reason.

What the devil's going on? Stiles wondered, a chill cooling the small of his back.

Then Reulbach's port nacelle exploded in a flare of white-hot plasma. And before the captain knew it, before he could even contemplate a rescue, the rest of the ship blew up as well.

"My god," Stiles muttered. And it wasn't just Uri Reulbach whose death had emblazoned itself on his eyes.

Because Aaron's vessel was right behind Reulbach's—so close to it that the younger Stiles couldn't avoid the Christopher's explosion. So close that Darren couldn't help running into the expanding plasma cloud, which could do to deflectors and titanium hulls what acid did to tissue paper.

Unable to take his eyes from the viewscreen, Jake Stiles shook his head. No, he thought numbly, it can't be. Not my brother. Not this way, caught in the blast from a lousy nacelle.

Then he saw something emerge from the burgeoning plasma cloud—something that looked a lot like the nose of Aaron's ship. As Stiles leaned forward in his seat, spellbound, he saw the rest of his brother's vessel slide out of the cloud as well.

He scrutinized the Christopher with eyes that didn't dare believe. But as hard as he looked, as intensely as he scrutinized her, he couldn't find anything wrong with her. Against all odds, Aaron's ship had come through hell, unscathed.

"Sir!" Rasmussen called out. "Romulan behind us!"

Stiles stiffened at the news. When no one came to the other birdie's rescue, he had allowed himself to relax—to imagine the enemy was falling back. Obviously, he had jumped to the wrong conclusion.

The Romulan in question slid onto his viewscreen. It was close—even closer than the other birdie had been. So close, in fact, that Stiles could barely see anything else.

"Helm," he thundered, "evasive maneuvers! Weapons—target and fire!"

The enemy fell off his screen again as Myerson pulled

them into a gut-wrenching loop. The captain felt his jaw clench as he waited for information from his navigator.

"They're hanging with us!" Rasmussen exclaimed. "Range—half a kilometer! Bearing two-four-two—"

But before she could finish her report, Stiles felt his head snap back like a whip. As he fell forward again, he realized that something had slammed them from behind—and slammed them *hard*.

Chang turned in his seat. He didn't look happy. "Sir," he said, "the shields are gone."

There was a silence afterward that seemed to drag on for hours, but couldn't really have lasted even a second, absorbing all hope, all possibility of survival.

Then the Romulans bludgeoned them again.

Stiles felt the deck jerk savagely beneath his feet—once, twice, and a third time, touching off explosion after explosion all around him. Somehow, he managed to hold on to his seat. But his bridge gradually became the substance of nightmare—a field of fire and sparkling consoles and thick, black plumes of smoke.

As they cleared for a moment, he saw Myerson. The man was slumped in his chair, his control panel aflame.

The captain started forward, imagining he could help the man—until the crewman slithered to the deck and his head lolled in Stiles' direction. Then he saw Myerson's blackened husk of a face and the sickeningly liquid eyes that stared out of it and he knew his helmsman was beyond help.

The captain looked around with smoke-stung eyes. He couldn't find any sign of Chang or Rasmussen . . . or Lavagetto either, for that matter. He didn't know where they had gone or if they were dead or alive.

But he knew *one* thing. He had to get them out of this mess—at least until the other Christophers could free themselves and come to his aid. And if Myerson's controls were slagged, he would have to reroute helm control to Rasmussen's navigation console.

Making his way through the smoky miasma, Stiles found the right console and slid in behind it. Fortunately, it hadn't suffered any serious damage—only a few scorchmarks on its left side. He pulled on the switches that would establish a link to the *Anaconda*'s helm.

Nothing happened.

The captain cursed, his voice cutting through the sputter and sizzle of his dying ship. The console was all right, it seemed, but the ship's helm function had been thrown off-line. He wouldn't be able to take control of it from the bridge or anywhere else until repairs were made.

And there was no time for that. No time at all, he thought.

As if to confirm his conclusion, something exploded in his face and sent him flying. He had a vague impression of coming down again, but he wasn't sure how or where or even why. He only knew that he was in the grip of a terrible, searing pain.

Fighting it, Stiles managed to lift his head and open his eyes. He couldn't see anything except thick, dark waves of smoke. They were moving slowly but certainly, reaching out to claim him like some infernal surf.

And there was nothing he could do about it.

Nothing.

As the pain throbbed deeper within him, his head fell back to the deck. And unexpectedly, despite his torment, he began to laugh.

All this time, he had been worried that the family curse would strike his brother. And in the end, whom had it claimed? Which Stiles had it added to the funeral pyre?

Him.

Hiro Matsura eyed his forward viewscreen, where a Romulan vessel was pounding the daylights out of one of his disabled wingmates.

"Target and fire!" he told his weapons officer—for what seemed like the hundredth time that day.

Twin laser beams shot through space and sent the Romulan reeling. But still she maintained her attack on the *Christopher*.

"Their shields are down fifty-five percent!" his navigator announced.

"Fire again!" the captain ordered.

His lasers dealt the Romulan another blow—but it didn't stop her from blasting away at the Earth ship, burning away even her serial number. Matsura felt his teeth grind together.

"Their shields are down *eighty* percent!" his navigator amended.

Matsura knew his atomics would get the enemy's attention faster than another laser barrage. However, he had only half the eight missiles with which he had started out from Earth—and with even a portion of the Romulan's deflectors up, an explosion wouldn't destroy her, anyway.

As a result, he picked the only other option left to him—the one Captain Beschta had chosen a month earlier when it was Matsura's vessel hanging in space, waiting for a grisly end. "Lieutenant Barker," he said, "put us in front of that Christopher."

"Aye, sir," came the helmsman's reply.

A moment later, the Romulan seemed to swing around on the captain's viewscreen. But in reality, it was an Earth ship that was moving, interposing herself between the enemy and her battered wingmate.

It was a maneuver that came with a price—and Matsura paid it. His vessel shuddered violently as she absorbed a close-quarters barrage. Still, he was in a better position to weather the storm than the other Earth vessel.

And then it was *his* turn.

"Fire!" Matsura told his weapons officer.

As before, twin laser beams speared the Romulan. But this time, without its shields to protect it, it didn't just lurch under the impact.

It crumpled like a metal can under an especially heavy boot. And it kept on crumpling.

Finally, the enemy vanished in a rage of pure, white light. And when the light was gone, there was nothing left but debris.

But Matsura didn't have time to celebrate the Romulan's destruction. Turning to his navigator, a woman named Williams, he called for a scan report on the damaged Christopher.

When she had gathered the required data, the navigator's face told the story even before she spoke. "No sign of survivors, sir—and her warp core is approaching critical. In fact, it's a wonder the damned thing didn't blow some time ago."

No sooner had the woman spoken than the Christopher went up in a blaze of plasma. Captain Matsura swallowed and accepted the loss as best he could—though at this point, he still had no idea whose ship it was.

Not Beschta's, he thought. It had better *not* be Beschta's. The big man had been his mentor, his friend.

"Bring us about," Matsura told his helmsman, "and find me a Romulan with whom I can work out my anger."

"Aye, sir," came the response.

But as the image on the viewscreen expanded to a wider view, Matsura began to wonder if there were any Romulans left. As far as he could tell, the only vessels around him were Christophers.

His navigator confirmed his observation. "There's no trace of the enemy, sir. Either they've fled or they've been destroyed."

The captain breathed a sigh of relief. "And the good guys?" he asked, steeling himself for the verdict.

The bridge was silent for a moment. Then his navigator said, "Two down, sir. I make them out to be Captain Reulbach and Captain Stiles. That is . . . Captain *Jake* Stiles."

Matsura winced. They had both been brave men. He wished he had gotten the chance to know them better.

"May they rest in peace," he said awkwardly, never good with such things.

Suddenly, Captain Hagedorn's voice surrounded him. "You can stand down—the battle's over. Transmit reports."

Matsura did as he was told. After a minute or so, he heard the wing commander's voice again.

"It could have been worse," Hagedorn told them, his voice slow and heavy despite his appraisal. "On the minus side, we lost two of our wingmates. On the plus side, all enemy ships have been accounted for—and the vessels we've got left are viable enough to press ahead."

Matsura took a deep breath and let it out. He knew what the commander would say next.

"Let's go," Hagedorn told them, never one to disappoint.

Seeing one of the Christophers come about and head for Cheron, Matsura turned to his helmsman. "Follow that ship," he said.

"Aye, Captain," responded Barker.

And they resumed their progress toward the command center.

* * *

Aaron Stiles knew he had two choices.

He could die by degrees, wasting away inside under the crushing weight of his sorrow. Or he could try to put his brother's death behind him and make the Romulans pay for what they had done.

In the end, he chose the latter.

Aaron Stiles followed his wing commander eighty million kilometers deeper into enemy territory, to the very brink of the command center orbiting serenely around the blue planet Cheron. And there, he did what he had set out to do. He made the Romulans pay with every ship they threw against him.

Not just for his brother, he told himself. But for all the members of the Stiles family who had died to keep their homeworld free. For Uri Reulbach and a dozen others who had perished serving alongside him. For all the Earthborn heroes whose names he had never known.

After all, he had enough hate and anger inside him to go around.

It didn't matter to him that he and his comrades were outnumbered two to one. Aaron Stiles plunged through the enemy's ranks like an angel of death, absorbing hit after hit, wishing he could see the Romulans' faces as they painted the void with the brilliance of their destruction.

And when he looked around and saw that the enemy's vessels had all been annihilated, he went after the command center itself. Of course, it wasn't without its defenses—but none of them fazed Aaron Stiles. He hammered at the center with his lasers and his warheads and his rage, and eventually it yielded because he wouldn't accept any other outcome.

And when it was all over, when the Romulan command center was cracked and broken and spiraling down to the planet's surface, when all his fury was spent and his adversaries smashed to atoms, Aaron Stiles did one thing more.

He wept.

Continued Next Month . . .

Look for STAR TREK Fiction from Pocket Books

Star Trek®: The Original Series

Star Trek: The Next Generation®

Encounter at Farpoint • David Gerrold
Unification • Jeri Taylor
Relics • Michael Jan Friedman
Descent • Diane Carey
All Good Things • Michael Jan Friedman
Star Trek: Klingon • Dean W. Smith & Kristine K. Rusch
Star Trek VII: Generations • J. M. Dillard
Metamorphosis • Jean Lorrah
Vendetta • Peter David
Reunion • Michael Jan Friedman
Imzadi • Peter David
The Devil's Heart • Carmen Carter
Dark Mirror • Diane Duane
Q-Squared • Peter David
Crossover • Michael Jan Friedman
Kahless • Michael Jan Friedman
Star Trek: First Contact • J. M. Dillard
The Best and the Brightest • Susan Wright
Planet X • Michael Jan Friedman
Ship of the Line • Diane Carey

#1 *Ghost Ship* • Diane Carey
#2 *The Peacekeepers* • Gene DeWeese
#3 *The Children of Hamlin* • Carmen Carter
#4 *Survivors* • Jean Lorrah
#5 *Strike Zone* • Peter David
#6 *Power Hungry* • Howard Weinstein
#7 *Masks* • John Vornholt
#8 *The Captains' Honor* • David and Daniel Dvorkin
#9 *A Call to Darkness* • Michael Jan Friedman
#10 *A Rock and a Hard Place* • Peter David
#11 *Gulliver's Fugitives* • Keith Sharee
#12 *Doomsday World* • David, Carter, Friedman & Greenberg
#13 *The Eyes of the Beholders* • A. C. Crispin
#14 *Exiles* • Howard Weinstein
#15 *Fortune's Light* • Michael Jan Friedman
#16 *Contamination* • John Vornholt
#17 *Boogeymen* • Mel Gilden

Star Trek: Deep Space Nine®

The Search • Diane Carey
Warped • K. W. Jeter
The Way of the Warrior • Diane Carey
Star Trek: Klingon • Dean W. Smith & Kristine K. Rusch
Trials and Tribble-ations • Diane Carey
Far Beyond the Stars • Steve Barnes
The 34th Rule • Armin Shimerman & David George

Star Trek®: Voyager™

Flashback • Diane Carey
The Black Shore • Greg Cox
Mosaic • Jeri Taylor
Pathways • Jeri Taylor

#1 *Caretaker* • L. A. Graf
#2 *The Escape* • Dean W. Smith & Kristine K. Rusch
#3 *Ragnarok* • Nathan Archer
#4 *Violations* • Susan Wright
#5 *Incident at Arbuk* • John Gregory Betancourt
#6 *The Murdered Sun* • Christie Golden
#7 *Ghost of a Chance* • Mark A. Garland & Charles G. McGraw
#8 *Cybersong* • S. N. Lewitt
#9 *Invasion #4: The Final Fury* • Dafydd ab Hugh
#10 *Bless the Beasts* • Karen Haber
#11 *The Garden* • Melissa Scott
#12 *Chrysalis* • David Niall Wilson
#13 *The Black Shore* • Greg Cox
#14 *Marooned* • Christie Golden
#15 *Echoes* • Dean W. Smith & Kristine K. Rusch
#16 *Seven of Nine* • Christie Golden
#17 *Death of a Neutron Star* • Eric Kotani
#18 *Battle Lines* • Dave Galanter & Greg Brodeur

Star Trek®: New Frontier

#1 *House of Cards* • Peter David
#2 *Into the Void* • Peter David
#3 *The Two-Front War* • Peter David
#4 *End Game* • Peter David
#5 *Martyr* • Peter David
#6 *Fire on High* • Peter David

Star Trek®: Day of Honor

Book One: *Ancient Blood* • Diane Carey
Book Two: *Armageddon Sky* • L. A. Graf
Book Three: *Her Klingon Soul* • Michael Jan Friedman
Book Four: *Treaty's Law* • Dean W. Smith & Kristine K. Rusch

Star Trek®: The Captain's Table

Star Trek®: The Dominion War

Star Trek®: My Brother's Keeper